When it [...] **the colors,** [...] **kiss—her head was spinning.**

Reaching for something to hold on to, her hands found Richard's. The moment his fingers grasped hers the spinning stopped, but the light inside her didn't fade.

"Marina?"

She shook her head, trying to remember where she was, who she was. As that all became clear, she asked, "Why did you do that? Why did you kiss me?"

"I don't know," he said, dropping her hands. "I shouldn't have. Forgive me."

Marina closed her eyes briefly, still trying to make sense of what had happened—not the kiss or his apology, but the change inside her. Everything about her was warm and bright.

"It's you," he said roughly. "You've put some sort of spell on me."

Author Note

There are many myths behind the Salem Witch Trials—including stories shared within my own family.

I'd heard for years that there were 'witches' on my paternal grandmother's side of the family, but it wasn't until my son was digging deep into an online ancestry programme that I actually researched any of those stories. It turns out that my eighth great-grandmother was accused and imprisoned for being a witch. However, she never stood trial because her son-in-law petitioned for her release and paid her bail. He also promised to return her to the courts for trial within a few months, but that didn't happen because the trials ended almost as swiftly as they started. I say 'swiftly' only in reference to a period of time, because I can only imagine that for the people who lived through this horrific event their lives were changed for ever.

Upon researching and reading many different viewpoints of the cause and effects of the trials, I was so captivated I decided to write a story set in that era. I used bits and pieces from my research, but *Saving Marina* is purely a fictional story. A tale of a sea captain and a woman who has been led to believe she's a witch. I hope you enjoy Richard and Marina's story as much as I enjoyed creating their journey to happily-ever-after.

SAVING MARINA

Lauri Robinson

Published in Great Britain 2016
By Mills & Boon, an imprint of HarperCollins*Publishers*
1 London Bridge Street, London, SE1 9GF

© 2016 Lauri Robinson

ISBN: 978-0-263-91680-5

Printed and bound in Spain
by CPI, Barcelona

A lover of fairy tales and cowboy boots, **Lauri Robinson** can't imagine a better profession than penning happily-ever-after stories about men (and women) who pull on a pair of boots before riding off into the sunset—or kick them off for other reasons. Lauri and her husband raised three sons in their rural Minnesota home, and are now getting their just rewards by spoiling their grandchildren.

Visit: laurirobinson.blogspot.com, facebook.com/lauri.robinson1, twitter.com/laurir.

Visit the Author Profile page
at millsandboon.co.uk for more titles.

To my Johnson aunts:
Mable, Violet, Pat, Linda and Faye.

Chapter One

Massachusetts, 1692

"Thou shalt not suffer a witch to live."
Exodus 22:18, King James Version

The beast of burden beneath Richard Tarr was aptly labeled. With a broad, short back and powerful hindquarters, the horse was more suited for labor than riding. No amount of prodding could urge the massive brown steed into a pace faster than the jarring trot that had threatened to rattle the teeth right out of his mouth. Appreciating the teeth that had never given him any trouble, Richard resigned himself to letting the animal trod along. Unused to such travel, Richard found the saddle awkward, and the hot summer sun had sweat trickling down his back. All of it, the horse, the heat, the very mission, spurred his frustration.

His own two feet would have been faster. Or a

rowboat. That would have been his choice. Water travel was in his blood, even when his feet were on solid ground.

A boat hadn't been an option, not unless he'd wanted to portage across several miles of swamp. Therefore, he was atop the dull brown beast, plodding along as if time made no difference.

He'd traveled this land route before, the road of less than twenty miles that led from the Boston Harbor to the village of Salem. It was a long and lonely trek, and he was accompanied only by a dark dread that sat in his gut like a sleeping giant awaiting an opportunity to wake. Stretching and yawning, the giant seemed to take great pleasure in rising from an eternal sleep to trouble Richard's mind and soul. Sometimes it was for no more than a flickering second; other times it would fully wake and haunt him for hours, never remembering its presence did not need to be verified.

That sleeping giant had taken root years ago, and though Richard chose to believe it rested comfortably while he was at sea, his soul knew differently. It knew he'd made a choice based on carnal and selfish needs and that the outcome of it had left a heavy grudge inside him. Therefore, the inner part of him that housed the sleeping giant relentlessly assured Richard he'd never know complete peace again.

This, he thought as the horse clip-clopped over

a crusted trail sprouting barely a blade of grass, *is my punishment. My sentence, and I have no choice but to abide by it as if it were decreed upon me by the king of England.*

The child wasn't to blame. No child ever was. He'd come to accept that years ago. Born a seaside waif, he'd never known his parentage. Never knew how he came to be living on the streets of London, stealing scraps of bread and drinking from rain barrels. Those were his earliest memories. Whether he actually remembered those incidents or whether they'd been placed in his memory by Captain Earl Burrows, Richard wasn't sure. Earl claimed Richard had been about five when Earl found him scavenging along the docks. Although not known for deeds of charity, Captain Burrows had taken Richard aboard his ship. Perhaps Earl had figured that was the only act of benevolence he needed to provide. Either way, some twenty-odd years ago, Richard had begun his life of sailing. He rose up the ranks from cabin boy, and five years ago, when Earl knew his days were numbered, the captain turned over the love of his life, the *Concord*, to Richard.

All his years at sea had played well in Earl's favor, and that too had been bequeathed upon Richard. The *Concord* was but one sea vessel—albeit his favorite—in his fleet, which sailed from England to the colonies, then on to the West Indies and Spain before returning to England. The fleet served Richard well and would continue to for years to come.

The trail upon which the horse trod widened, suggesting they would soon arrive at their destination. Bracing himself, for he knew the inner giant would soon stir, Richard scanned the horizon. Blocked by trees, it was nothing like the image he was used to seeing, where if a man didn't know better, he might believe he'd sail right over the edge of the world. From the deck of the *Concord*, the horizon was always a glorious sight. Water as far as one could see—an image that always stirred the part of his soul he did know. The part of him that relished his life at sea. The life he was born to live.

That wasn't so today. Around the bend would be a village. The one after that was where he would collect his daughter. A child spawn from his loins and born on land after he'd taken to sea again.

His breath tightened in his chest, and he transferred the reins to his other hand in order to dig into his shirt pocket for the crisp slip of paper. It was a brief note, simply stating the death of his wife and where his daughter was awaiting his imminent arrival. A daughter he had no idea what he would do with other than collect. That much he understood as his duty.

Without guidance from him, the horse rounded the corner. Then the heavy hooves stopped, and everything about Richard went still as he lifted his gaze.

The horse stomped and tossed its broad head, sensing the death Richard's eyes had locked onto. A single large and gnarly tree stood upon a hill on the edge of town, next to a rocky cliff that bespoke an ominous aura even as the summer sun shone above. Off the lowest branches hung several ropes and at the end of those ropes was the most catastrophic sight his eyes had ever gazed upon.

Eight—he counted them twice—bodies dangled eerily. Although he was a distance away, it was apparent the poor souls, whoever they may have been, had their hands tied behind their backs and their legs bound.

Closing his eyes, questioning the sight, Richard drew a breath before lifting his lids again. The image hadn't changed. If anything, it appeared darker, more sinister. A curse rumbled deep in his throat. The majority of the bodies were clothed in dresses.

A shiver crawled up his spine at the evil gloom that seemed to penetrate the entire hilltop and block the otherwise bright sunlight from shining down upon that singular tree.

It was then he noticed the crowd gathered lower

on the hill. Not on the rocky side, but the grassy side that gently sloped downward and eventually opened up into the village green of the community. A plethora of sounds reached him, or perhaps they had always been there and he'd been deaf to them, too stunned by the sight to take in more.

The horse tossed his head again and took a step backward, as if unwilling to go any closer. Richard didn't blame the animal. There wasn't crying or protests. Instead, an almost joyous chant echoed through the air. As if the bodies swinging from the tree were a glorious sight to behold.

Richard reined in the horse to keep it from twisting about. In doing so, the note crinkled in his hand. Once the horse was settled, he flattened the paper on his thigh before holding it up to read where his daughter would be located. Urgency arose inside him. The sooner he completed his business, the better. He'd entered corrupt ports during his voyages and instinctively knew this place hosted a sinister core.

Staying near the outskirts of Salem, as far from the hill as possible, he steered the steed onward. With little more than a tap of his heel, the horse's speed increased, putting distance between them and the hill. Like him, the animal was leery of entering the town.

The note described a large home between

Salem Towne and Salem Village. The two were no more than five miles apart and, as he'd learned before, very separate communities. One more welcoming than the other. However, the spectacle he'd just witnessed had him wondering if his recollection was correct.

Not that it mattered. He'd leave both villages before nightfall and never return.

A short distance later, he crossed a bridge. On the other side farms scattered the road, some close by, some set back. Locating the one he was looking for among the smaller, more crudely constructed homes became an easy task. It stood out, if only because of its size.

Richard rode to the back side of the house, where a water trough would quench the animal's thirst and hopefully keep it occupied while he gathered his daughter. He was thankful the tree upon that rocky hill was miles behind him and far from sight, yet he couldn't help but turn in the direction from which he'd traveled, wondering again if he'd truly witnessed what his mind continued to recall. The roadway had been empty, the yards and houses along the way quiet, which added to the growing foreboding inside him.

With the horse secure and drinking, Richard made his way around the house to the wooden stoop of the front door. It was indeed a large home. Whitewashed and rectangular in shape and shaded by tall trees. The steeply pitched roof framed two tall and wide gables, and the sunlight glistened against the four symmetrical windows on both floors.

A long, narrow awning shadowed the stoop, blocking the sunlight from shining on the windowless door. Richard raised a hand to knock, but the door opened inward before his knuckles touched the wood.

"State your business."

The woman's tone didn't match her structure. She was tiny, with a mass of curls as golden as the sun rays on his shoulders. The straps of her stiff cap were tied beneath her chin, leaving the curls to burst out from beneath the cloth like a bundle of wool tied in the middle. He'd expected an old woman, not one with skin as milky white as her linen cap.

"I'm looking for—" His mind went momentarily blank. Lifting the note still clutched in one hand, he scanned it for the name at the bottom.

"Step inside, Captain," she said briskly.

Richard made no attempt to move. Having noted the signature on the paper, he stated, "I'm looking for Mrs. Lindqvist. Mrs. Marina Lindqvist."

"I'm Marina Lindqvist," she answered, stepping aside while moving her arm in a graceful wave to indicate he should cross the threshold. "Your daughter is here. Please enter."

An unusual chill rippled his spine. His daughter. Richard had acknowledged he had a daughter. A small infant the one and only time he'd laid eyes on her. Yet having this woman say it aloud made the child more real than his own thoughts ever had. "I'm here to collect her," he said, not taking a step forward. "To take her back to Boston. If you'd be so kind as to call to her, we'll be on our way."

"That's impossible. Do come in."

Richard refused to take a step. "How can that be impossible? Your note said I was to collect her posthaste."

"I'd prefer not to stand on the stoop and discuss this matter, sir. It requires more privacy than that."

The sharpness of her tone couldn't cover how her voice shook; nor did it hide the apprehension shimmering in her blue eyes. When she shot a nervous glance around his frame, he instantly recalled the sinister hillside and revolting tree. Anger rose, burning his throat as he growled, "What kind of trap have you set here? Where is my daughter?"

"There's no trap," she insisted. "Your daughter is here. Just, please, enter before you are seen."

An uneven clip echoed inside the house, drawing his attention beyond the woman.

A short man with a wooden leg crossed the room. "She speaks the truth, Captain. Enter swiftly. I swear on my sailor's oath there is no trap set in this house. However, I give no promise for what lies beyond my yard."

The blood in his veins turned so cold Richard tightened his shoulders to ward off a shiver. He held no doubt the man was a sailor. His aged face was leathered from the sun and sea, and the lower part of his left leg, now a wooden stick, had been carved from a ship's rail. Only a man of the ocean might recognize that, and only another would know the severity of swearing upon his sailor's oath.

The woman moved farther to the side, giving him a wider entrance path. "Please, for your daughter's sake, I beg you to enter."

Her whisper sounded as if it could shatter as easily as glass at any moment. Richard crossed the threshold, and since the woman was no longer next to the door, he closed it behind him. "Where's my daughter?" he demanded. Once he had the child in his arms, he'd mount up and whip that beast of a horse into a gallop the likes of which his kind had never known.

The old sailor stepped forward, his hand held out, not in courtesy but something that went deeper considering the sincerity of his gaze. "My name is William Birmingham, once the captain of the *Golden Eagle*. This is my niece, Miss Marina Lindqvist."

"I've heard of you," Richard acknowledged and shook the man's hand. There was barely a ship or a captain that had sailed the oceans that he hadn't heard of.

"As I have of you and your predecessor," William said. "Captain Burrows and I sailed together years ago, on a Queen's ship."

Earl Burrows wasn't remembered for his friendships or deeds of goodwill. However, Richard owed the man for everything he had, including his very life, and would forever remain devoted. At this point in time, he moved beyond whatever William might think of Earl and repeated, "Where is my daughter?"

William nodded toward the woman. "Marina, take the good captain up to see Gracie."

Without a word, the woman turned about and headed toward the staircase on the far side of the room. Richard followed but eyed his surroundings. The furniture was sparse considering the size of the room. A long wooden bench and a couple of chairs with high backs and tapestry seat cushions, a desk with another chair. Several small tables were positioned throughout the area holding vases of wildflowers or candles. A

Bible sat upon the table near the fireplace, pages
open. The intricate carvings on the bulky furniture said it wasn't homemade. Most likely the
pieces had been hauled to the colonies on one of
the ships William used to captain. If recollection
served right, Birmingham had sailed passenger
ships, people bound for the New World, but the
holds would have been full of cargo, all the items
those same passengers would need to start their
new lives.

Richard glanced down a hallway as he started
up the steps. A table surrounded by chairs suggested the kitchen was at the end of the hall.
Again, the furniture wasn't built of square
wooden planks like that in the home he'd once
visited in Salem Village. Briefly, for he really
didn't care, he wondered about all the furniture
he'd had delivered to his wife's family's home.
Expensive, solid pieces, for he'd never shied away
from providing for his daughter.

The open-beam ceiling supporting the floor
above grew near as he climbed the steps. The
stairs turned a corner then, blocking the ground
floor. Richard's gaze landed on the skirt trailing
each step ahead of him. The dull gray of home-
spun cloth went all the way up to her waist, where
it was gathered and disappeared beneath the black
formfitting sleeveless waistcoat over her white
peasant shirt. The fashionable gowns worn else-

where, including parts of America, were not welcome in this community. He'd discovered that on his last trip here. Just as he'd discovered he wasn't welcome.

"I beg you to keep your voice soft," the woman stated after they'd climbed the stairs and traversed a narrow hall with windows at both ends. She paused near a door, her hand on the knob. "Gracie frightens easily."

He'd known the child had been given the name Grace upon birth but, until this moment, hadn't thought of her as anything other than his daughter. Growing impatient with himself—and everything else, for that matter—Richard gestured for the door to be opened.

A beam of sunlight shone directly upon a bed of such a large size that the tiny child lying upon it was almost invisible. Her body was so small the blankets looked merely wrinkled. If not for the dark hair on the pillow, he'd have thought the bed empty.

The woman walked to the side of the bed. Richard followed, choosing the opposite side.

"Gracie," the woman whispered, leaning down and brushing tendrils of hair off the child's face. "Your papa's here."

There was a shift beneath the bedcovers as the child rolled onto her back. Her eyelids, which were edged by long, dark lashes, lifted, exposing big brown eyes. Other than her eyes and her hair, the child was as white as the pillow she rested upon. A tiny smile tugged at her lips as her sleepy gaze settled on him.

The twinge that crossed his chest momentarily stole his breath. This was his child. The life of his loins. A miniature person as real as he himself.

"I prayed you were real."

Richard knelt down, questioning if he'd heard her weak whisper or if it had been his own thoughts repeating themselves. "What?"

The girl pulled an arm from beneath the cover and lifted it so her tiny fingertips brushed his cheek. "I prayed you were real," she repeated.

Her fingertips were cool, her hand shaking. As he curled his much larger fingers around hers, something happened inside him. An opening, a warmth as unique and precious as a sunrise the morning after a hurricane. "Of course I'm real," he answered, wanting to offer some sort of assurance to this tiny being. His throat burned, an unusual occurrence, and grew thick. Almost too thick for him to whisper, "I'm your papa."

Her tiny smile disappeared as she closed her eyes again and the thin arm connected to the hand he held went limp. His heart thudded and he shot his attention toward the woman on the other side of the bed.

Chapter Two

Marina Lindqvist closed her eyes and willed her heart to slide back down into her chest before it strangled her. Gracie was so tiny, so fragile. Turning the little girl's welfare, her very life, over to a stranger tore at Marina's very soul. It was what had to be done. She understood that, as unsettling as it was, as badly as it hurt. Soon she'd be unable to care for the child, to offer her protection.

The sigh that built in her lungs burned. She'd fought, she'd prayed, she'd begged for things to be different, to be like they used to be, but that wasn't about to happen. There'd been no choice but to accept, so that was what she'd done and would have to again.

Perhaps it would be easier if Captain Tarr wasn't so frightening to look upon. The moment she'd opened the front door, the terror she'd known once before filled her. If not for the innocent little child lying upon the bed, she'd never have led this black-haired man upstairs. Never have let him into the house. She had, though, let him in. She'd been the one to summon him to Salem Village. Therefore, for Gracie's sake, she'd willed her mind to understand the difference between the past and present and did so again.

"Sleep is what Gracie needs," Marina whispered, holding her gaze on the angelic little girl. The horror of what could happen to unprotected children was something else she'd never forget. At times it was hard to differentiate between memories and the visions that appeared in her mind, the very ones that left her with no choice but to accept they would become realities. Too many had already come true for doubt to linger.

It was a curse of who she was. Of what she'd become.

A loud sigh penetrated her musing, and for a moment, she wondered if the captain had feared Gracie had perished rather than fallen back asleep. Unable to look upon him, for he so closely resembled the heathens who'd shattered her life it made her tremble, Marina brushed aside yet another strand of Gracie's dark hair. "I'm sorry you traveled so far, but as you can see, Gracie is in no condition for the ride to Boston."

"Why is she so—so tired?"

"She's been gravely ill," Marina pointed out. "Hopefully, she can travel in a few days." Upon sending the note to Boston, she'd assumed it would be a length of time before the message reached him. Not a great length, but longer than a single day. Uncle William hadn't known when one of Captain Tarr's ships would port, and they'd agreed sending a personal note to the captain was better than sending for an agent on his behalf at the seaport.

She should be glad he'd responded so quickly, but she wasn't. Strangers were not welcome in the village, and the presence of this man wouldn't go unnoticed.

"The pox?"

"No," she answered. "She was spared the outbreak that took so many." Her note had briefly mentioned his wife had died of smallpox last winter. Those were terrible messages to pen, ones of death and dying, things that had become too commonplace.

"Then what's wrong with her?"

Gracie stirred slightly. Marina stepped back and gestured toward the door as she started in that direction.

"What's wrong with her?" he repeated once they were in the hallway with the door closed behind them.

"I'm not a physician," Marina said, "but I believe Gracie was close to dying from starvation."

"Starvation?"

"Shh," she said as his voice echoed off the walls.

"Why was my daughter starving to death?" he asked more quietly but just as harshly.

Marina started down the hallway so Gracie's nap wouldn't be further interrupted. The child was on the mend, but just days ago she had barely been able to hold up her head and Marina had feared it was already too late. An unexplainable instinct had told her where to find the child, but she'd been shocked by Gracie's condition—and infuriated. Her refusal to turn Gracie over to the authorities angered many, but that was also when she'd completely understood why she'd been chosen. The ability to save this child had been bestowed upon her, and at that moment, while defying Hickman, it truly had felt like a gift rather than the curse she'd believed it to be since awakening in Maine.

"And why is she here?" the captain continued. "Where are her grandparents?"

Marina was still trying to understand why she'd been *chosen*. Gracie, too. Why had this child had to suffer so? Answers weren't easy to find, and right now, the captain's massive bulk and looming presence had the walls of the narrow passageway closing in around her, making it difficult to breathe. Haunting memories started flashing in her mind, and she hurried toward the stairs. "My uncle will provide answers to your questions."

A solid hand grasped her arm. "I want answers now."

Her heart stalled and her throat tightened while the images flashing behind her eyes grew stronger. Indians with blood-covered tomahawks. Shoving her back and forth between them, pulling at her hair and clothes. She could almost feel how they'd torn little Gunther from her arms before—

"Captain Tarr!"

The shout echoing up the stairway shattered the dark memories, but fear still had her trembling.

"I am the man of the house," Uncle William shouted, "and will answer all of your questions."

Her uncle's voice penetrated the pounding in Marina's ears and gave her enough sense to know this wasn't Maine. It wasn't the dark of the night. It wasn't cold or raining. However, the panic clawing at her insides remained, and she rushed forward, barely slowing her speed to maneuver the steep steps.

Uncle William stood near the bottom step. "Are you all right, child?" he asked softly.

"He must leave until Gracie is well enough to travel," she whispered while hurrying off the steps.

Marina didn't stop until she was in the kitchen.

Standing there, trembling and clutching the edge of the table with both hands, she silently recited the Lord's Prayer.

Asking for salvation from the very God who'd forsaken her had become the only thing that took away the pain.

In case God's grace didn't come soon enough, Marina silently told herself, *Richard Tarr is not an Indian. He is Gracie's father, and she needs him. Needs him as strongly as I needed Papa when small and scared.*

The solid wood, the sunshine filling the room, the smell of the chicken soup she'd set to simmer and repeating the statement several times gradually eased her torment. As things settled deep within her, for her fears never truly completely disappeared, she drew in a breath and then another.

When her body stopped trembling, she released her hold on the table. Although she'd never forget the savages who'd attacked her home, the scriptures told her to forgive. Forgiving something so heinous was rather impossible, but she'd discovered the Indians weren't to blame as much as the evilness that had possessed them. The same evilness that now had the inhabitants of Salem Village massacring one another as unjustly as the Indians had her family. Which was why she was here, witnessing people betraying one another, sentencing neighbors to death, just as it was written in the Bible.

If she'd been given mystical powers when the hand of God had touched her, she'd have already stopped it. But no one had that kind of power. Not even witches. Yet no one but her seemed to understand that. Nor did they understand that the evil upon them wasn't witches. It was a false prophet. A wolf in sheep's clothing.

Being a chosen one was far from a blessing, but she'd never shied away from work and wouldn't this time, either. Her father had told her she must save others, and she would. After finding Gracie, she no longer questioned why she'd been sent back to earth, why she'd been turned into a witch, and understood there was far more to do than just save the child. Despite what the reverend thought, the bargain she'd made with him included her. Only her. Not Gracie. He'd granted her the time she needed to make Gracie well, but she knew he'd done that instead of imprisoning her because he was afraid. Afraid of her and the powers he believed she possessed. She wished she did have mystical powers, but even without them, she would make sure Gracie was far from Salem when she turned herself over to the council as she'd promised.

With her spirit once again intact, Marina lifted a wooden spoon off the table and carried it to the large hearth, where she stirred the soup. Every two hours since bringing the child home, she'd fed Gracie tiny spoonfuls of broth. She'd feared the girl's little stomach had been empty for so long it had forgotten its purpose, but each day Gracie ate a bit more than the previous and that gave Marina hope.

She turned away from the hearth. She should have suspected Richard Tarr would have black hair. Gracie must have inherited it from somewhere. It hadn't been her mother. Sarah's hair, from what Marina could remember, had been red. She'd seen the woman only a couple of times in the market square and truly only noticed her because of the child at her side. Gracie had been healthy then, with plump cheeks and chubby fingers, and, despite all her painful memories, Marina had somewhat fallen in love with the adorable little girl. Gracie's big brown eyes, wide with wonder, reminded her so much of Gunther.

To recall that it had been only seven months ago when Gracie had been healthy, a happy child toddling behind her mother at the market square, seemed a bit unreal. So much had happened since then.

Uncle William apologized regularly for how unfriendly the village had become, but Marina had seen that before. How quickly people changed. How hatred arose. Yet it hadn't been until she came face-to-face with the reverend that she saw the root of the calamities overtaking the community.

"Marina?"

She set the spoon back on the table and slowly made her way down the hall to the front room. With each step, she reminded herself there was no need to fear Richard Tarr. His long black hair, skin browned from the sun and chiseled features just made him look like an Indian. And his lack of facial hair. All men other than Indians had beards and mustaches.

Uncle William didn't approve of what she'd done in order to save Gracie, but he did agree with saving the child. He claimed Captain Tarr was a fair man and would take responsibility for his child. Marina sincerely hoped so, for she questioned why Captain Tarr hadn't taken responsibility of his daughter before now. Uncle William suggested he had, from the sea. That it was no different for a sea captain to go to sea than for a farmer to go to his field. Father or not. Husband or not.

"There you are, child," Uncle William said from where he and Richard sat beside the window. "Captain Tarr..." With a nod her uncle corrected himself. "*Richard*, as he's asked to be addressed, has several questions. Could you join us? I'm not able to answer those about Gracie's health."

She'd gladly voice her opinion that the captain could return in a few days. Grace would be able to travel then, could get away without the reverend or anyone else knowing. Uncle William, too.

Appreciative that her uncle's home was not like most others, where women were expected to remain silent, never subjecting others to their opinions, Marina crossed the room. Her own home, that of her parents, had been full of bountiful conversations that included everyone. And laughter. Oh, how her brothers had laughed. Of all the things she missed, that might be the one she missed the most. Laughter. It was good for a person's soul. Made life easier, lighter, even in the darkest of times.

Just as she was about to sit upon the squat stool Uncle William put his good leg upon while resting, the captain stood.

"Allow me," he said.

Hesitant, Marina remained standing, eyeing him cautiously. He was very tall and muscular, and his stride was distinct, purposeful and sent a shiver up her spine. Confused as to what his purpose was at this moment, she watched him walk to the desk. There, he picked up the chair and turned, carrying it back to where she stood.

"Thank you, Captain," Uncle William said.

Marina chose to remain quiet and sat down as Captain Tarr returned to his chair. She had to wonder, given the act he'd just performed, if he was like her uncle or more like the other men in the community. Very few in the village would permit Uncle William to request that she or any other woman participate in a conversation. That had been hard for her to accept when she'd first arrived, and questioning it had been enough to make her an outsider long before her true identity had been revealed.

"You'll find our home a bit unorthodox compared to others in the area," Uncle William stated as the other man sat back down. "Marina and I converse regularly. I like it that way and value what she has to say. Perhaps because I was always surrounded by mates. After the *Golden Eagle* ran ashore on a reef near the Bahamas, I found myself too old to repair her and traded her for this place. Of course, I kept my cargo," he added with his gravelly laugh. "Wiggins Adams is who I got this place from." He lifted a gray brow. "You heard of him?"

"Yes, I have," Captain Tarr answered. "Captain Adams and I have crossed paths several times."

"He promised it was a solid plot of land with a big house outside of Boston."

"He didn't lie," Richard pointed out.

Uncle William chuckled. "No, he didn't, but he didn't tell me it was surrounded by Puritans until after he hauled me and all my belongings here. That was two years ago. If Marina hadn't come to live with me a short time later, I may have given up on the place and gone back to the sea. Still might someday."

Marina remained silent. As much as Uncle William spoke of returning to the sea, she knew it wouldn't happen. Not without assistance. He'd never accept charity or pity, but his mind was outliving his body on land. He often repeated stories or rambled, and climbing the stairs to the second floor winded him. She'd taken apart his bed and carried it downstairs to the room off the hall leading to the kitchen to save him from climbing the stairs last winter. Convincing Captain Tarr her uncle wasn't a washed-up old seaman, and to take him, along with Gracie, might not be an easy chore, but there wasn't anything easy about her lot in life anymore.

A smile almost tugged at her lips because, for a brief second, she could hear her father's voice proclaiming there wasn't a task a Lindqvist couldn't complete.

"Marina's family had a bit of a mishap up in Maine," Uncle William said. "She came to live with me winter before last. It was a cold snowy day when you arrived, wasn't it, child?"

Marina agreed with a nod. Although she considered her home being attacked and her entire family killed more than a mishap, that was how

Uncle William referred to it. As if calling it less than the calamity it had been would lessen it in her mind. Nothing could ever do that, but she never made mention of that to Uncle William, either. Perhaps because she wanted him to think she wasn't trapped in the past. That she didn't regularly recall the savage attack that caused her to be persecuted by neighbors until she had no choice but to flee. She told him she'd dreamed about him the night before his friend had arrived in Maine, but he hadn't thought it significant. She did. It was the first time one of her dreams had come true.

If Captain Farleigh hadn't arrived that snowy night, she'd have died again. Not by Indians or the wolves terrorizing the few chickens left in the barn, but at the hands of those who used to be friends.

Uncle William refused to speak about that, about what she'd told him, and she could understand why. It was hard for nonbelievers to accept. She'd struggled with it, too.

"Marina's always been special. Always had a glow about her," Uncle William said. "From the day she was born, she lit up the world."

She'd heard that tale before, from her parents and brothers. If her family had known how different she was, what her destiny would be, she wished they'd mentioned it to her. A little preparation would have been helpful.

"Her grandpappy was my brother, and after having so many grandsons, he was beside himself to have a little girl to bounce upon his knee. I don't know how I got along until she came to live here. Of course, things were different before. When Puritans weren't set on killing one another."

"Killing one another?" Richard shook his head. "The Puritans may have strong beliefs, but I don't believe killing is one of them."

Marina held her breath, curious about whether she would now learn why he'd deserted his family. An act she couldn't fathom.

"Tell me, Richard," her uncle said. "What do you believe?"

"About the Puritans?"

"Yes," Uncle William replied.

Marina refrained from looking at the captain, even while her curiosity made it difficult. Her family, upon arriving in the New World from Sweden eighteen years ago, had settled along the costal shores of Maine. Communities there were far apart and needed every member's participation in order to survive. Therefore, religious tolerance, of how or when their neighbors worshipped, was more accepted. Even though, in her case, religion hadn't been the cause of her banishment, she couldn't help wondering if it had been the reason behind him leaving his family.

"They are attempting to repopulate the world," the captain said with more than a hint of disdain. "Will do anything to increase the population of every Puritan village up and down the coastline."

"Indeed," Uncle William said. "Are you one of them?"

"No."

The response was so fast and stern, Marina couldn't stop her gaze from snapping in his direction. She'd never questioned how her uncle had known who Gracie's father was or how he knew where to find him. She, like most of the villagers, had believed he'd perished at sea.

As if he realized how harsh he'd sounded, the captain added proudly, "I'm of the Christian faith."

"But your wife was a Puritan," Uncle William stated.

Richard's eyes were on her and boring in so deep Marina looked down at the floor and swallowed hard to ward off the shiver rippling over her shoulders. In the far recesses of his eyes, she'd seen pain and recognized it as something he didn't want revealed. She didn't like when that happened, when it was as if she could see into another person's soul. No one should be able to do that.

"Yes, she was," the captain said. "I refused to convert. Therefore, Sarah chose to remain with her family. I agreed to provide for them financially."

"I know the life of a sea captain well," Uncle William said. "Wives and families in ports all around the world."

"Sarah was my only wife," Richard replied coldly. "Grace is my only family."

Marina could no longer remain silent. He'd opened the opportunity for her to ask a question that took precedence over all others. "Will you return to the sea when you and Gracie leave here?"

"Of course I will."

"What about Gracie?" she persisted. Her heart had almost broken upon finding the little girl so ill and dirty. From that moment on, determination filled her to see Gracie healthy, safe and well. Perhaps because it was her only chance to do so. It was a known fact witches—real witches— couldn't conceive children. "She needs a family," Marina stated with all the fortitude filling her. "A father, not just a provider."

For a woman who'd stared at the floor, not mumbling a word, Miss Marina Lindqvist certainly wasn't afraid to let her contempt be known when the moment arose. Richard, on the other hand, was skilled at keeping things inside, where no one but that sleeping giant judged him. Unwilling to explain his plan for his daughter, he asked, "How did Grace come to be here? With you?" Although dressed like one, this woman was not a Puritan, nor was she married, as he'd assumed from her note stating his daughter could be found at "our" house. However, knowing those two things only increased the number of questions rolling around in his head.

William was the one who responded while his niece remained silent. "Because of Marina, your daughter is alive, Richard. Despite those intolerant fools."

Anger set Richard's jaw tight. The tiny child upstairs had been neglected. Neglected until she was little more than skin and bones. He may have visited his wife and family only once, but he'd sent money regularly and other things. Goods and materials, furniture, seeds. Anytime he'd heard someone mention an item the colonials needed, he'd sent a good supply to Salem Village in Sarah's name. When he discovered who'd withheld food from his daughter, he'd throttle them with his bare hands. "What intolerant fools?"

"Practically everyone in the village," William said. "That new *preacher* has blinded the lot of them. The poor fools were so hungry for a leader they don't recognize they've been duped."

Richard didn't miss the emphasis the man used. Sea captains weren't known for their religious affiliations. He'd never known one who'd held regular church services upon their ship—other than him. He'd captained the passenger ship that had carried Sarah and her family to America. It had taken less than two months to sail from shore to shore, and during that time he'd wedded Sarah, who was pregnant with Grace before he lowered the sails for the final time. He couldn't say he'd been coerced into marriage—that had been Earl's explanation when he'd told the man what had happened. A part of him may have fallen in love with Sarah, longed for a communion with her, or at least the young, supple body she'd so readily offered. He hadn't told Earl that but had mentioned he wasn't the only one to become wedded on that trip. A total of six mates had joined him at the makeshift altar aboard his ship. All but two had been at his side when he'd set sail for England a week after landing in Boston. Earl had chided the lot of them. Claimed that was what the new order of Puritans did—sought out strong, healthy males to impregnate their women in order to gain new bloodlines in their communities. In his berating, Earl had described them as nothing but studs needed for service. Richard had been demoted to first mate for the next six months. The punishment may have lasted longer if a fierce winter storm hadn't set pneumonia into Earl's lungs. Unable to captain the ship, the illness getting the best of him, Earl had called Richard to the helm.

"That man is as corrupt as his papa was," William was saying. "He made a mess of things in

Barbados and again in Boston. Guess preaching was the only thing he hadn't tried."

Richard hadn't heard who William was talking about. If the other man had said a name, it had been while he'd been recalling other things. Setting his mind on listening, Richard asked, "What's he doing?"

"Filling their heads with lies and misinterpretations," William said. "Ideas have changed since the first Puritans came to America. The original founders have died off and the next generation isn't satisfied with their lots. They seek power and wealth, just like the rest of the world. Some have become merchants and businessmen, and those set in the old ways have grown resentful of any who won't give the church all of their income or spend hours worshipping each day."

If for no other reason than the things William was saying aligned with Richard's own beliefs, he nodded. Changes were happening all around the world, and those not willing to accept that would never flourish. He'd used that fact, how sailing was his means to provide for his family, as an argument when Sarah's father had insisted he needed to choose between the sea and his life as a married man. The two, his father-in-law had insisted, could not be one. Blasphemy. This very country had been settled by those escaping religious persecution and he hadn't been about to become a victim of such unjust piety. Nor had he been willing to become a farmer.

"Salem Village was once the farming parish of Salem Towne," William said, "but when those in Salem Towne began to prosper, the poorer farmers in the village grew resentful. They petitioned separation and the right to form their own community. They wanted their own church, too, and to hire their own minister, not one chosen by the Salem business owners. I figured things would settle down once that happened. It didn't."

"The new preacher you spoke of…" Richard said. His attention was spiked by the way Marina had started to fidget in her chair. She didn't seem bored with the tale her uncle was unraveling. In fact, the way she wrung her hands together told him she was nervous about something her uncle might say. That was what Richard wanted to hear. Instincts said it included his daughter. Whoever had almost let his daughter starve would pay dearly.

"Yes," William said. "I can't say why they hired him. Samuel didn't know. Samuel Godfrey, that is. He owns a store in town and only ventures out this way occasionally to deliver the things Marina orders from him. She and I don't get out much."

That too spiked Richard's interest. William was old. Traveling even the short distance to town would be exhausting, but Marina was young. He saw no reason she couldn't venture to town. "Why don't the two of you get out much?"

William lifted both bushy brows. "Because we don't want to lose everything, including our lives."

Marina's swallow was visible, as was the way she shook her head, trying to stop her uncle.

Richard quickly asked, "How would that happen?"

"They'd stretch our necks," William said flatly.

The tree he'd seen earlier flashed before his eyes. "What for?"

"For being witches," William said.

Chapter Three

Marina's stomach fell and she closed her eyes. That was Uncle William, going on and on about differences that truly didn't concern them and then bluntly cutting to the quick of the story. He didn't believe she was a witch, despite the proof she offered. Holding her breath, she maintained her silence. For as unorthodox as her uncle's home may be, there were still boundaries. He was the man of the household and she had to respect that, but if he started to share her story, she'd interrupt. There was no telling what the captain might do if he learned she was a witch.

When the two men refrained from speaking, and their gazes settled upon her, she stood. "Excuse me." Perhaps if she reminded them as to why Richard was here, her uncle would get to the true heart of the matter. "I must see to the soup and check on Gracie. The sooner she gets well, the sooner she can travel to Boston."

Marina left the room without a backward glance. Perhaps now Uncle William would tell the captain to return to Boston until Gracie was able to travel. That amount of time—until the child was well—had been granted, but she wouldn't put it past Hickman to pay a visit to the house. He'd claim it was on behalf of the church, but she knew better.

After ladling broth into a bowl, Marina went out the back door to collect water from the well. The huge horse Richard had ridden stood next to the water trough she filled daily for the chickens. Back home, tending to the animals had been her chore, one her father prided her on, and seeing a creature uncomfortable didn't settle well.

Nellie, their single cow in the paddock, bellowed a low welcome as Marina led the horse into the shade of the barn and reminded her she'd need to find a home for the cow, too. She also pondered removing the saddle from the horse's back but, considering Richard would soon leave, chose against it. Her dream last night had shown Gracie healthy and was the most enjoyable one she'd had in months. Tending to the child the past few days had been extremely pleasurable. Something she'd always treasure.

Marina stopped that thought from going further—to babies that could never be—by focusing on settling the animal. The horse was frightfully large but gentle, and she patted its long neck and side while walking out of the stall wall. As she dropped the board in place to keep the animal stabled, a shadow cast upon the barn floor.

"So, you're a witch."

For the first time in ages, Marina wanted to smile. The image of this man, who was indeed as beastly in size as his horse, fleeing when she said yes was the cause. She'd seen that happen in Maine, grown men flee at the thought of encountering a witch.

The bright sun cast a haze of light around the frame standing in the doorway, from the toes of his knee-high boots to the top of his midnight-colored hair hanging past his shoulder. It made a remarkable sight, for his size and stature made him a formidable being. That told her something else. This man wouldn't flee from a witch. Real or imaginable. He'd stand his ground.

Needing to know if that was true, she asked, "Do you believe in witches, Captain Tarr?"

"I've given you permission to call me Richard," he said, bracing one hand against the door frame. "I'm only a captain while at sea."

She gave a single nod, just to prove she'd heard him. "Do you believe in witches, Richard?"

He stood silent, making her wonder if he would answer or not. The breeze made the sleeves of his white shirt billow slightly, and for a moment she didn't want to know his answer. The strength of the arms beneath that shirt had to be as solid as the rest of him. If he believed as the other villagers did, and chose to use his strength to capture her, she'd end up in Salem's jail before assuring Grace and Uncle William's escape.

"Witches," he said, "are akin to angels. In some religions, that is. Some claim you can't believe in one and not the other."

Such a compromising answer was not what she'd expected. Discussing religious beliefs other than Puritan ones was illegal in the village and highly punishable. She considered telling him as much, but that in itself was punishable, as well. A man married to a Puritan woman would know such things and would not tempt punishment. As much as she'd relish the opportunity to debate her beliefs, to defend the holistic religion she'd participated in from birth, it would be a waste of breath. She doubted this man had ever read the Bible. She'd read it daily for as long as she could remember and sincerely missed having others to help her comprehend the parables. Uncle William was very little help with that. He did not see the connection between the Indians destroying her family and what was happening in the village.

She did.

She was a witch. There was no denying it. And no changing it. There was no comparing it to an angel, either. The two were as different as day and night. Alive and dead. Pure and evil.

Swallowing the bitterness that coated her tongue, for there were still things she had to accept, she nodded. "I didn't unsaddle your animal. My hope is that Gracie will be able to travel by the end of the week."

He stepped forward. "I'll unsaddle him."

Sidestepping in order to keep a fair amount of distance between them because his nearness made her insides tremble, she said, "I didn't unsaddle him, so you could return to Boston. There is no need for you to remain here. You must realize Gracie can't travel right now."

He looked at her pointedly. "I do, but I'm not leaving. Not without Gracie. When she's well enough, we'll travel to Boston."

Marina's heart leaped into her throat. "But you can't stay here."

"Why?"

"Because…" She closed her eyes as dread filled her soul. "It's too dangerous." Drawing strength from within, she lifted her lids. "Far too dangerous. Please, you must leave."

"Not without my daughter."

"It's for her sake that you must leave."

He shook his head. "It's for her sake that I must stay."

Desperation flared. She couldn't save those

locked in jail while taking care of William and Gracie. If that was the case, she'd already have done it. "You'd barely laid eyes on her before today."

"That is true. A fact you knew when you summoned me to collect her." He lifted the brace bar to step into the stable. "And that is exactly what I'm here to do."

Marina couldn't argue the fact she'd summoned him, but she couldn't chance another child harmed. Another child murdered, the tiny corpse maimed. "It's not safe for you to be here."

"Safe?" He was on the other side of the large horse, already loosening the saddle cinch. Tall enough to see over the animal, his dark eyes watched her intently. "Why isn't it safe for me to be here? I've done nothing to anyone."

"It's just not safe for you to be here," Marina repeated. "The reverend—"

"I'm not afraid of a Puritan minister, Marina."

"There are things you don't understand," she said, attempting to keep her composure, but her head had started to pound. Flashes, images of Hickman's men storming the house caused sweat to form on her brows.

"Like what?"

"Witches?" Her breathing was uneven and burning. "Are you afraid of them?"

Hoisting the saddle off the horse's back, he

draped it over the side board of the stall and then turned around to pull off the blanket. "Don't try to frighten me away with such foolery. I'm not leaving until—"

"Until they kill your daughter?"

The giant that arose inside Richard wasn't the one he expected. Instead of the old, guilt-driven ogre, an angry one emerged. One that was as driven to protect his daughter as it was to protect his own life. Tossing the blanket over the saddle, he marched out of the stall, slamming down the end board. "Nobody will harm my daughter ever again. Nobody."

"Others have boasted as much, but they couldn't stop their loved ones from being imprisoned or worse. Sometimes evil can't be stopped."

Richard paused, both in his steps and his thoughts. The last bits of color had slipped from her already white face, leaving even her cheeks ashen. "Yes, it can," he replied, although he knew she spoke of more than Grace. A touch of compassion for this woman arose inside him, for she clearly was afraid of something, but he'd been here for the better part of an hour, and other than discovering his daughter was ill, he knew no more than when he'd read her note back in Boston last evening. "With the right information, and that's what I want. I want to know who almost let my daughter starve to death. I want to know where her grandparents are and how she came to be living with you and your uncle. And I want to know who those poor souls were hanging off that tree back in Salem." That last bit slipped out before he realized it. Mostly likely because of the terror in Marina's eyes. Did she truly believe in witches, fear for her own life? He'd suspected that was a ploy, but her fear appeared real. Very real.

A single tear slipped out of the corner of one eye, which she quickly swiped aside before she bowed her head. "I'd prayed that wouldn't happen."

He had a great desire to reach out and lay a hand on her arm, offer a touch of comfort. That was as unusual for him as most everything else he'd encountered this day. Therefore, he remained still, his hands at his sides.

After a moment of silence, she snapped her head up and started for the door. "I must see to Gracie."

The change of her demeanor, from tears to stoic determination, confused him as much as it surprised him. Women, though—all women— were not something he needed to ponder or understand. "Where are her grandparents?"

Barely pausing as she crossed the threshold, she answered, "They died along with your wife.

During the smallpox epidemic last winter. A great number of lives were taken."

There was urgency in her steps as she left the barn, and Richard had to hurry to follow her. "Has Grace been here since then? Since last winter?"

"No, she's only been here a few days. I just sent the note to you yesterday."

"A few days?" That too was confusing. "Where had she been all this time? Since her mother died?"

Marina entered the house. "In the village."

"With who?" He followed her through the door. The way she headed directly toward the hearth caused a final nerve to flare. He was a man of action—found the problem and took care of it. When he asked a question, people answered. Tired of attempting to be polite, he slapped a hand on the table. "Damn it! Why are you making me fight for every morsel of information? Why can't you just tell me what I want to know?"

She spun around and the fire that shot from her eyes startled him slightly. When her burning gaze landed on his hand, he practically felt the heat and lifted his hand off the table.

"A smart man does not meddle in things that don't concern him," she said icily.

"A smart—" Letting out a growl, he planted his hand back on the table. "This does concern me. Anything that concerns my daughter concerns me."

"Very well." She picked a bowl and spoon off the table. "Once I've seen to Gracie, I'll join you and my uncle and answer any questions you have on that matter."

Steam hissed inside his head. "On that matter?" Richard blocked her way around the table. "I'm tired of this cat-and-mouse game. I have questions on several matters I want answered now." Once again slapping the table, he added, "Right now!"

He'd expected to startle some sense into her, but the only things that jumped about Marina were her eyes, moments before they turned as bitter as a nor'easter.

"And I want you to leave," she said as frosty as her blue eyes. "Which you will do."

Richard kept his gaze locked on hers, letting her know he wasn't moving until he was ready.

Her eyes never left his as she lifted her chin. "However, *right now*, I must see to Gracie."

She could easily have turned and made her way around the other side of the table, but she didn't. Instead, she walked directly toward him. A spark of respect flared for this uncommon golden-haired woman. He'd made note of how she carried herself, earlier. Head up and purposeful, unlike most women, who rarely met a man eye to eye.

"If you were any kind of a father," she said without a footstep faltering. "A real father. That is where your concern would lie—in her health and that of her recovery."

Richard had been chastised by men far more powerful than she'd ever be. On a bad day, Earl could send sharks swimming in the opposite direction with little more than a shout and a fist waving in the air. This woman, however, possessed a different kind of power, one he couldn't explain. "I am her father," he answered out of defiance. "And I am concerned about her health and well-being. That is why I'm here."

Her glare remained ice-cold. "Then you'd be interested in knowing I've been giving her broth every two hours, not enough to upset her stomach but enough to get it working again."

It flustered him that a rebuttal wouldn't form in his mind, but what could he say to that? He'd stood his ground with opponents around the world, yet, right now, he stepped aside so she could leave the room.

Which she did.

His gaze followed her. Marina Lindqvist was not what she appeared to be. A matter of fact, if he'd ever believed in witches, he might wonder about her. Not in the evil, brewing-up-potions kind, but in the kind who could cast spells upon men without them knowing it. There was no other explanation. With little more than those blue eyes, she'd knocked the wind right out of his sails.

Flustered with himself, he entered the hall. William was still in the front room, and the snore that shook the old man's body confirmed what Richard already knew. William wasn't just old; he was tired, worn-out from his life at sea. For a brief moment, Richard was reminded of Earl and the fight the man had fought against aging, against giving up the life he'd known. Earl had died at sea, doing what he loved. William wouldn't, and for that, Richard experienced a pang of sympathy.

Switching his thoughts, he started up the steps. When the time came, he wanted to be like Earl, sailing into the sunset as his days ended. Until then, he had things to do. A legacy to maintain so his daughter would never again know the pains or consequences of hunger.

The door to the bedroom was open. He'd been only a few steps behind Marina, yet she was already sitting on the edge of the bed, spooning soup into Gracie's mouth. His daughter was sitting in the middle of the bed and her eyes widened when she saw him in the doorway. A slight and wobbly smile turned up the corners of her lips.

Richard's heart fluttered inside his chest. The sensation was as remarkable as it was foreign. He hadn't expected this immediate connection to his daughter, for it hadn't been there the first time he'd seen her, when she'd been a tiny infant. Then again, at that time, he'd already been told he'd never see her again, that he wasn't welcome in Salem Village, nor would he ever be. That had been shortly after Earl's death, and on that very day, Richard had fully accepted the advice his mentor had shared before dying. "Let them go," Earl had said. "Forget you ever had a wife or child. The sea is all you'll ever need."

"Your arrival seems to have worked wonders," Marina said. "Grace was awake and ready to eat."

Snapped out of his musings, Richard crossed the room. "That's good news. To see her well is my greatest wish." He chose not to delve too deeply into the things happening inside him. Grace was his daughter, and every father wanted his children to be healthy and well. However, he was aware now that Earl's advice was no longer relevant. He'd accepted the loss of his wife long before her death, but he had a second chance with his daughter and didn't need anyone's advice on what to do.

"Goodness," Marina said. "You've eaten the entire bowl." She brushed a clump of black hair off Grace's cheek. "Would you like more?"

"Yes, please."

"Very well. I shall get you some." Marina stood and bestowed a sun-kissed smile upon the child. "I'll be back in little more than a moment."

Richard didn't know much about ill children but knew shipmates got well faster once they were up and about, and despite refusing to leave, every instinct he had was still telling him to get his daughter and depart this place as soon as possible. "Perhaps Gracie would like to go downstairs to eat."

Gracie's eyes lit up. For a moment, he saw himself in her and knew that must be how his eyes glowed when they settled upon the great span of water surrounding his ship. Smiling brightly, she pushed aside the covers and scooted toward the edge of the bed.

"The stairs may be a bit much for her yet," Marina said gently.

"Not if I carry her," Richard supplied. Without waiting for Marina's answer, he asked his daughter, "Would that be all right with you, Grace? If I carried you?"

She nodded enthusiastically.

Marina, on the other hand, seemed torn. "I don't want her to lose the ground she's gained."

"She won't," Richard assured her. "I'll carry her back upstairs, too." Without further ado, he plucked the child off the bed. She wasn't any heavier than one of his ledger books and felt far more fragile. Far too fragile. Once again something inside him fluttered. The life of a sailor had always fulfilled him, never left him wondering or wanting more, yet holding his tiny daughter in his arms made him question if he'd made the right choice years ago. If he'd remained in Salem Village rather than returning to the sea, Gracie wouldn't be in this condition and Sarah might still be alive. They could even have had more children.

"We all have regrets."

He lifted his head and caught Marina's thoughtful expression.

"It doesn't pay to dwell on them," she added with a smile as gentle as the one she'd given his daughter. "Forgiveness, including ourselves, is the pathway to salvation."

She was right. No one could change the past; nor should they allow it to possess them. He owed Marina his gratitude, too. If not for her, Grace may have died. He would never have known his daughter then. That thought hit solemnly in his mind and gut.

Not ready to react to that or to let her know she'd read his mind, he gathered the length of material dangling beyond Grace's feet. "What is all this?"

"Gracie is wearing one of my nightdresses." Marina had walked around the bed and brushed his hand aside in order to twist up the extra material and tuck it between Grace's thin frame and his chest. "I needed to wash hers this morning."

Richard heard what she said but chose to interpret the statement to mean Grace didn't have ample nightclothes. That should not be. He'd sent material to his dead wife regularly. Yards upon yards of sturdy cotton, knowing the finer silks and other materials he'd once shipped would not be welcome. The last shipment should have arrived this spring, after Sarah's death. Of course, he hadn't known she'd died then.

He pondered on that as he carried Grace down the narrow hall. His wife had died. Should he be in mourning? It wasn't as if he'd held any ill will toward Sarah. It wasn't as if he'd held any great love for her, either. The affection that had sparked between them had never been given the chance to grow. Not as it should have. Which was just as well. Sailors had no right taking a wife. They were already married to the sea. He'd known that even back then but had let his physical needs overshadow his good sense. Earl had pointed that out to him, and he'd come to accept it over the years.

Richard shifted Grace in his arms, not because of her slight weight—he could have been carrying a sparrow for all she weighed—but because he didn't want her to bump the wall of the narrow stairway. She lifted her head and gazed upon his face deeply and perhaps a bit critically.

"Are you really my papa?"

"Yes, I am."

"Marina told me if I prayed hard enough, you'd come."

Richard glanced briefly toward the woman moving down the stairs ahead of them. He still had more questions than answers. "She was right."

"Where's your boat?" Grace asked.

He grinned. "In the Boston Harbor."

A tiny frown formed before she nodded.

"Would you like to see it?" he asked.

The smile returned tenfold. "Yes."

"Well, then," he said, "as soon as you're better, I'll take you to see the *Concord*."

"You will?"

"Yes, I will. It's a mighty ship," he said. "But you have to eat and get strong. It's a long way to Boston."

Her little head bobbed up and down. "I will."

It had been years since he'd seen Sarah, and he wondered if Grace looked like her. He should remember, but an image of his wife no longer formed in his mind. There was no explanation as to why, other than that she'd become nothing more than another payment, akin to taxes or merchant fees. That was no way for a man to think of his family or something he was proud of, even if it wasn't out of the ordinary. Plenty of captains had wives and families, sometimes numerous ones, just as William had said, in ports all around the world. One of the things he'd carried pride in was the fact he wasn't like all other sea captains. Not in that sense or in others. He treated his shipmates fairly, along with the merchants and countries whose cargo he hauled. His reputation was well established, and now it would also become known that he took care of his family. He didn't need to vow it; he knew it.

"What do we have here?" William had awakened from his nap and was precariously rising to his feet as they entered the front room. "Is that Gracie?"

The girl nodded while Marina answered, "Yes. She wants to eat at the table. Would you care to join her?"

"I've been smelling that chicken you've been boiling all morning," William said, using both hands to get his stump leg solid on the floor. "It'll be good to eat some."

Marina waited for her uncle to cross the room. Richard did, too, while noting how the young woman stood ready to aid William if the need arose. It didn't. Once the old man got the wooden leg in rhythm with his other one, he scurried past them with the speed of a sailor with two good legs.

"You will be joining us, Richard," William stated.

It had been hours since he'd partaken in a brief

repast before leaving Boston, and all sailors were known for one thing—that of never bypassing the offer of a meal. "Thank you," he answered and waited for Marina to enter the hall.

In the kitchen that, indeed, did host a very appetizing scent, Richard paused before setting Grace on one of the chairs. Her chin would barely come up to the tabletop if he set her down. Noting a pine box on the shelf near the brick oven built into the side of the fireplace, he crossed the room. "May I use that?" he asked, pointing at the box.

"The salt box?" Marina asked. "Whatever for?"

"Yes, the salt box," he assured her. "For Grace to sit upon so she can see over the table."

"That's a splendid idea."

The expression on her face was a mixture of surprise and delight, a sight that intrigued Richard. He pulled his eyes away and gathered the box. After he set it on the chair, he lowered Grace upon it and took a seat himself. The table was soon set with plates and silverware and a host of foodstuffs in plated dishware. It made sense that William would have such luxuries while many colonials still used wooden spoons and trenchers. Ships hauled crates of dishware and utensils to America regularly, had for years.

"Marina insists on feeding us more than two times a day," William said. "She claims her family ate morning, noon and evening, even on Sundays. I've told her on a ship, a man eats when a meal's prepared, whether it's the middle of the day or the middle of the night." He chuckled before adding, "I've grown accustomed to her ways, those of my family from the old country that I'd forgotten about until she arrived, although that too we keep private."

Having traveled the world, Richard had eaten meals at all times of the days, but he knew a custom of the Puritans was two meals a day, morning and midafternoon, after church services. He also knew their penchant for allowing no work of any kind on Sundays, including preparing meals. If there were no leftovers, they ate bread and water or fasted. He'd witnessed it on the ship that had carried Sarah and her family to America. From what he'd seen so far, Marina did not fit into the Puritan world in any way. So why was his daughter here rather than with one of the families in the village?

"We're not trying to pull the wool over anyone's eyes," William continued. "We just don't need any more fingers pointed at us."

Although he could assume, Richard asked, "Why would fingers be pointed at you?" Following William's gesture, he began to ladle food onto his plate. The bowl Marina had set before Grace contained clear broth, while the soup he spooned onto his plate had been thickened and contained chunks of chicken, carrots and potatoes, as well as dumplings. There was also bread and a thick pudding that smelled of maple syrup, and cider for their earthen mugs.

"I told you." Sighing heavily, William looked at Marina, who'd just sat down, before he said, "They believe Marina's a witch."

Tension returned to Richard's neck—his entire spine, actually. This witch business was more than frustrating. It had become an assault against his good sense. Over the years, he'd spent time with many types of people and cultures. In some countries people worshipped witches; in others, they feared them. Went so far as to hire witch hunters to eradicate them from the countryside far and wide. He'd never believed one way or the other, but had met a few witch hunters and would be hard-pressed to come up with a more evil profession comprised of more wicked men.

His gaze crossed the table to land on Marina. Her chin was up and her gaze solid as it met his, eye for eye. He might admire her grit, but others wouldn't. A witch hunter he'd met in Scotland a few years ago, John Kintor, claimed that was how he recognized a witch, by the way she stared into a man's soul. Kintor's father had been a witch hunter, too. Several years ago father and son had captured more than two hundred witches in less than a year—or so they claimed.

A cold knot formed in Richard's stomach at the thought of Marina encountering the likes of Kintor. "Why would they believe that?"

Her gaze drifted toward Gracie for a fraction of a second before she stated, "Because I agreed to stand trial for being one."

"Only be—"

"Uncle William," she interrupted before her uncle could say more. "The food is getting cold."

"Oh," the old man said as if he'd just noticed the food on the table. "Eat up, Richard."

Richard opened his mouth but closed his lips when Marina bowed her head and recited a prayer quietly. He'd never encountered a witch and doubted he ever would, but either way, he highly doubted they prayed before eating.

When she lifted her head, her attention immediately went to Gracie. "Go ahead," she said softly. "You can eat all you want."

Gracie glanced his way and Richard responded with an affirmative nod, quite amazed that his daughter would expect his approval. He had very little experience around children. None, actually, other than the few who'd been on the passenger ship he'd captained years ago, the same one that Sarah had been on. He had a child now and held no regrets on it. Last night had been a sleepless one, full of worries about what he'd do with a daughter. Today, it didn't seem so bad. Hiring a family to take care of her wouldn't be hard. He just needed to figure out where he wanted that to be. There were plenty of choices in numerous ports around the world. Perhaps he'd let her decide.

With that thought, Richard lifted his spoon and began to eat.

As far as meals went, it was tasteful and filling, but far quieter than he was used to. Sailors were a hearty bunch. Given food, ale and others to talk with, they became even more boisterous. The only noise at this table was the clink of silverware and thud of ale cups. That was strange for him. Certainly out of the ordinary. The men he sailed with were first-rate and energetic, and mealtime was a noisy affair.

Richard glanced across the table. Not even a witch would be able to keep them in line. The idea almost brought a grin to his lips. Marina was no more a witch than he was, but if she chose to believe otherwise, so be it. Once Grace was well enough, he'd leave this place and never return.

A question of how Grace would fare on his ship formed, but it was not something he needed to worry about. As his daughter, she'd be more protected than gold. Setting down his spoon, he reached over to roll up the sleeve that had fallen to almost cover her hand. "You like the soup?" he asked.

She nodded, but her eyes went toward the plate of bread in the center of the table.

Richard retrieved a slice and pulled away the crust. Breaking up the soft center, he dropped the chunks into her broth. Grace smiled and he patted her head, half expecting a chiding from Marina. Prepared, he lifted his gaze to the woman.

A gentle smile graced her lips, and she made no attempt to pull her gaze from his. She was patting her lips with her napkin, and Richard held his breath, wondering what she was preparing to say.

Instead of her voice, a knock on the back door interrupted the silence.

Chapter Four

"Marina, I wouldn't believe it if I hadn't seen it with my own two eyes," Anna Pullman said with tears streaming down her cheeks. "They killed her. Just like that. They put a rope around her…"

"Hush now, Anna," Marina whispered while stepping out on the stoop. Her friend had used the back door, which was fortunate if anyone was on the road but unfortunate considering those sitting at the table could hear. "Come to the garden with me," she said, pulling the door closed behind her with one hand and the other on Anna's shoulder.

"The garden?" Anna stammered. "They just killed Elizabeth. I can't think of carrots and onions. People cheered and clapped. Oh, Marina, what are we going to do?"

"We are going to walk to the garden," Marina said gently. "We don't want anyone to see us being idle." If anyone on the road saw Anna talking to her, the young girl would be arrested, but Anna needed comfort right now and Marina couldn't overlook that. There were a few families who'd befriended her and Uncle William, and she'd come to care for each of them.

"Of course we don't," Anna said bitterly as they walked toward the garden beside the barn. "Lord knows what Reverend Hickman will do if he learns of two idle women. Oh, Marina, it was so awful." Anna sniffled as new tears began to fall. "Elizabeth cried and pleaded, swore on the heavens she wasn't a witch, even while they were putting the rope around her neck."

"Hush now," Marina said again, this time because she didn't need a description. Her mind had already shown her the scene of Elizabeth Pullman being hanged, along with several other community members. In truth, it made her neck tingle. A fate that was sure to be hers before long. It was written in the scriptures. She'd be handed over to councils and flogged, brought before witness, and persecuted. A sacrifice. The only thing she'd had to offer in exchange for Grace had been her own life.

"I can't hush," Anna insisted. "With Mama in jail, Father is beside himself. He's insisting upon going to the tree tonight, before they cut down the bodies and push them over the ravine. He's going to collect Elizabeth and bury her on our farm beside little Daniel and baby Christine."

"That would be extremely dangerous," Marina whispered. "It's foolish to venture out at night. Sentries are posted everywhere."

"I know," Anna said, "but Papa can't stand the idea of Elizabeth not having a proper burial. It's just…" Unable to carry on, her friend clutched Marina, sobbing.

Thankful the barn hid them from prying eyes, Marina hugged Anna and let her cry. No words of comfort formed and she figured that was just as well—they wouldn't do Anna much good. Elizabeth had been Anna's older sister, and Marina knew too well the pain of losing those you loved. Tears still came some nights when she thought of her family.

Time had helped, but it also left her tired. She was so very tired of death.

The creak of wagon wheels and thud of hooves forced Marina to release Anna and grasp her friend by the shoulders. "Others are returning home, Anna. You can't be seen here. It's far too dangerous." The reverend had vowed he'd arrest anyone he saw her talking to. Without waiting for Anna to respond or catch her bearings, Marina pulled her to the back of the barn. "Quick now—take the path through the woods and return to your house."

Anna was shaking her head, but Marina pushed her toward the small trail hidden by first brush and then taller trees. "Hurry, and talk to your father. Do not let him return to that tree tonight."

When Anna acted as if she wasn't going to leave, Marina said, "Hurry. Reverend Hickman could be in any one of those wagons. Go. And don't stop until you're home."

Anna shook her head. "I didn't want to believe it was true, but it is. Isn't it? You've changed, Marina. You used to be my friend."

"I'm still your friend—"

"No, you aren't. You're—you're a witch. That's why you wanted that old crone's familiar so badly."

"Go home, Anna."

Anna shook her head as she said accusingly, "You brought her here so you could fill her with your blood, fashion her after the likes of you so—"

"Anna!" Fury ignited in Marina's stomach, and withholding it from spewing forth burned. Anna was too full of grief to know what she was saying. In a more normal state of mind, she'd know Gracie wasn't a familiar. She was just an innocent child. Too innocent to be surrounded by such evil. "Go home, Anna. Go home where you're safe."

"No one's safe," Anna said. "Even you." She spun around then and hurried into the woods.

Marina watched, making sure her friend had left before she let out a sigh. Her heart was so heavy her stomach ached. She had changed, because she'd had to. Being a witch wasn't easy.

"What old crone?"

She spun around. The storm of reproach on Richard's face made her legs wobble.

"Who," he barked, "is accusing my daughter of such vile things?"

Marina's entire being quivered, but she held her head up. "I must go see to—"

"No." He stepped forward, blocking her path. "You aren't going anywhere, not going to see to anything." Taking a hold of her arm, he added, "Not until you answer my questions."

Marina wasn't afraid of his touch, but she was afraid. Rightfully so. He threatened everything. "My uncle—"

"Is looking after Grace," he said. "So start talking."

Any mingling hope dissolved. As much as she wished it, he wasn't going to leave, not without answers. It was only right. She had summoned him here and should tell him the truth, or at least as much as she could. The problem was she had no idea where to start, how to explain things that were unexplainable.

"I can stand here all day," he said stoically.

She shook her head at how she couldn't stop a wayward grin, one that had wanted out because of the memories his statement had revived. "My brothers used to say that." Sighing, she admitted, "That seems so long ago."

Other than a slight frown, Richard didn't reply, and she didn't expect him to. She waved toward the house. "It's a rather long story. Perhaps we should go inside."

"Where you'll find another task to see to," he said. "No, we'll stay right here. There's no need for me to repeat my numerous questions. I'll let you decide where to start."

That was just as well. People were still on the road. What about this man had made her overlook that? Perhaps it hadn't been him, but rather the weight hanging heavy around her neck. "I'm not sure where to start," she answered honestly. "Uncle William believes it all started with the new reverend, but…"

"You don't?"

Marina studied his expression for a moment. Here too she was reminded of her brothers. Tough, stern men and, just like Richard, they'd had wrinkles near the corners of their eyes from laughing on a regular basis. Then again, maybe his came from squinting at the sun while sailing the seas. Though he showed a gentleness around his daughter, it didn't appear to be commonplace.

"I haven't lived here long," she finally said. The Puritans' beliefs didn't align with her own. From what she'd witnessed, no one was inter-

ested in performing God's will by loving one another. What had happened to her hadn't aligned
with her beliefs, either, not until she'd sought a
deeper understanding of the scriptures. Seeing
the evilness in Reverend Hickman's eyes had
confirmed her path, even though fighting him
filled her with fear. "But Reverend Hickman is
a powerful man."

"Hickman?" Richard's frown grew. "*Reverend*
Hickman?" he repeated. "What's his first name?"

"George."

"George Hickman," he said, drawing the name
out as if settling it into his brain. "That's who
your uncle was talking about when he mentioned
Barbados and Boston?"

"Yes." A queer tickling in her stomach had her
asking, "You know him, don't you?"

"If it's the same George Hickman I'm thinking of, then, yes, I know him."

Her hands shook. "Are you friends with him?"

His eyes grew stormier. "Friends? No. When
did he become a reverend?"

Marina twisted her hands together, hoping to
hide the shiver rippling her insides. "I don't know,
but I do recall hearing this is his first parish."

"When did he arrive here?"

"A year ago this spring," she answered.
"Shortly after I'd arrived." Marina had no idea
why she chose to add that. Maybe because she

wanted to appear innocent, which she wasn't. In truth, there didn't appear to be any innocence left in the world. Other than in the smallest of children. That she did still believe in.

There were other things she believed in, too, and she glanced toward the woods where Anna had disappeared. Just as the scriptures described, brothers were accusing brothers, children were rebelling against adults, accusing them of outlandish acts until they were arrested. "Hickman's arrival was greatly welcomed," she said. "People acted as if he was the answers to their prayers. A savior."

"But not you?"

"No." Prayers were often answered differently than expected, and George Hickman was closer to the devil than God.

"Why not?" Richard asked.

The pages she read every night told her not to fear those who could kill the body, for they could not kill the soul. That was a fact she'd witnessed, and the conviction that rose up inside her was stronger than ever. She couldn't help but wonder what Richard would think if she told him everything.

She spun about. The resentment in his eyes couldn't be denied, and her shoulders slumped. He'd never believe her. She hadn't believed it herself, not at first. "For one," she said, "I'm not of the Puritan faith. I'm a Protestant."

"You've been accused of being a witch because of that?"

"No."

He lifted a brow, clearly waiting for more of a reason.

Stories of witchcraft had plagued the Old World and still did, for all she knew. There had been a time when she'd been convinced they'd been nothing more than tales that had no basis in being real. That had changed. "Have you read the Bible?" she asked.

"The entire thing?"

Once again, for the briefest of moments, a grin tugged at her lips. He truly reminded her of her brothers. Perhaps referring to the Bible wasn't the right route. Her brothers had never taken to its readings without serious prodding from their mother.

"I've read enough to know what it's about," Richard said.

Accepting his answer with a nod, she changed her tack. "From my witness, the Puritans are quick to judge. They believe only a few are selected for salvation, predestined before birth, and although they claim no one knows who the chosen ones are, they instantly condemn others to eternal damnation for the simplest acts. Blame one another for every misfortune that occurs, from a cow dying to a child questioning something they are too young to understand." She'd seen all these things and couldn't understand the irrationality the people of the village maintained in such simple maladies. She took a couple of steps, to where a weed grew next to the barn. "Something as simple as this weed could lead to an entire family being exiled."

"That's preposterous."

"I know," she said. "To us, but to the Puritans in the village, it's not. It's a sign of the devil— at least that's what Reverend Hickman preaches. He's full of hellfire and brimstone, and the elders quickly followed him, leaving no room for common sense to prevail. His sermons are full of paradoxes that are as confusing as they are frightening. Everything is based on the Old Testament. There are no lessons on the coming of Christ or the forgiveness of sins."

"You attend his church?"

"No, we've never been invited to, but we don't mind. Uncle William and I have our Bible and our faith." Not wanting the conversation to revert to her, she quickly added, "I've heard about his sermons from others and heard him shouting in the marketplace. It's frightening to the women and children, especially the young ones, like Gracie, who are so gentle and innocent."

"How did she come to be with you instead of a Puritan family?" he asked.

"The smallpox epidemic was widespread. Reverend Hickman declared that all of the families affected were agents of the Ould Deluder."

"Satan."

She nodded. "Members who'd survived the outbreak were no longer welcome in the village." The injustice of it had Marina placing a hand over her heart. "Even the tiniest of children. The other men agreed with him, believing when he insisted it was the only way to prevent the disease from spreading, but—"

"But that's no excuse for allowing children to starve to death." Richard finished her thought precisely.

"I agree, but few others do. His sermons filled them with fear of the entire village dying from the disease."

He was pacing back and forth, as if dwelling on what he'd just learned, but he stopped and leveled a stare on her. "If all this happened last winter, where was my daughter before she came here?"

Guilt bubbled inside her. Things might be different now if she'd understood her father's message earlier. She hadn't, though, not until seeing the evil in Reverend Hickman's eyes. That was when she'd pleaded for him to allow her to take the child's place. To be arrested as a witch, if he let her heal the child.

"Where was she?"

Lifting her shoulders, Marina said, "Everyone believed she'd died along with her mother and her grandparents."

"Where did you find her?" he demanded.

Marina closed her eyes and pinched her lips together. Reverend Hickman had finally agreed to her request, but she'd seen beyond his words. For some unexplainable reason, he wanted Gracie, and that was when the witch inside her rose up as it never had before. Out of nowhere she'd vowed to reveal the truth behind all his evil actions.

"Where did you find her, Marina?"

Her insides burned, but she couldn't reveal the truth. There was too much danger in that. "Please just be content with knowing I did and that soon she'll be able to travel to Boston."

"Not soon enough," he growled. "Sitting at the table tuckered her out. I laid her down on William's bed before coming to find you."

Concerned, Marina glanced toward the house. "But she is getting better. Yesterday she barely had the strength to sit up long enough to eat."

When she turned to face him, her heart stalled. The storm in his eyes demanded answers. More answers than she could give. Marina had no choice but to harden her stare in return, refusing to provide any more information. There was too much at stake. If she told him all that had happened, he'd never leave. Not without confronting Hickman. In that sense, too, he reminded her of her brothers. One man couldn't battle an entire community.

The breath in her lungs rattled as the standoff continued. A duel that consisted of nothing but their eyes, their mental strengths. She brought forth such events in her past. Arguments with her brothers where she'd never backed down from their steely stares and mental challenges. Momentum grew within her as she vowed to not yield until the bitter end. Until she'd won.

Her chin began to tremble, her legs wobble, but by sheer will alone, she kept her stare steady, her mind focused. In truth, it was for him she fought. And Gracie. And Uncle William.

Her win, if she could call Richard's gaze being the first to drop, held no victory. Nearly exhausted, she let out a sigh as Richard, looking stormier than ever, swung around and marched away. Her reprieve, that of drawing in enough air to fill her lungs, ended abruptly when the barn door thudded.

Hitching her skirt out of the way of her feet, she scurried around the barn. Richard was inside, throwing the saddle over the blanket he'd already laid across the massive horse's back. Real relief filled her then. Keeping him hidden until Gracie was well enough to travel would have been impossible.

"I'll send a message to your ship," she said. "As soon as Gracie is well enough. You can expect it by the end of the week, I'm sure."

While threading the leather strap through the cinch ring, he said, "There will be no need to send a message."

"Very well. If you want to return on Saturday—"

His glare stopped her from continuing. Accepting there was nothing more to be said, she stepped outside the barn door and took several long glances up and down the road. There were no wagons, no lingering travelers from the groups who'd made the trek into Salem Towne to watch the hangings, and for that she was thankful. If he hurried, his departure would go as unnoticed as his arrival had been.

Upon hearing the thud of a horse's hooves, she turned back to the barn, where Richard led the animal out into the sunlight. She waited until he mounted before saying, "Safe travels to Boston, Captain."

His glower was chilling. "I'm not going to Boston, Marina. I'm going to the village. Where I'm sure to find someone who'll answer my questions."

"No." Despite the size of the beast, she grabbed

the leather chin strap of the horse's bridle. "You can't go to the village. No one can know you're here."

His laugh was close to sinister. "It's too late for that. The girl that was here…the one you called Anna. She saw me. Why do you think she scurried into the woods so fast?"

Marina slapped her free hand over her mouth to contain her gasp, and Richard's tug on the reins freed the animal from the hold of her other hand.

"Please." It was all she could think to say. "Don't."

"I have no idea what you are trying to hide but, rest assured, before the sun sets, I will know. I will have answers to all my questions."

"They'll arrest you—"

"For witchcraft?" He laughed. "Let them try."

His words lingered in the air, echoing in her ears as he kneed the animal.

"Stop! Please!" Hitching her skirt, she started to run but made it only a few steps when a solid grasp caught her arm. She'd have fought it but realized her momentum was already making Uncle William teeter on his good leg.

"I have to stop him," she said.

"No, child," Uncle William said. "You don't have to stop him. She's his daughter, not yours."

Her legs threatened to collapse beneath her as the captain disappeared up the road.

"Come inside, Marina," her uncle said. "We'll know soon enough what the captain's fate will be."

Chapter Five

The horse seemed to know what was good for it and didn't test him this time. Lucky for it. Richard had been taxed enough. Miss Marina Lindqvist would do good to take a lesson or two from the horse. All her talk of witchcraft. The woman must be light in the head. People had been frightened of witches for years. Foolish people, that was. Rational ones realized it was all superstitious. The smarter ones looked for the real cause behind the accusations. There was always something, and he had a good idea of what it was this time.

Richard entered the village, which was little more than a marketplace with a long overhead shelter where members brought goods to share or trade, a tavern and a small church off to one side. The home behind that structure was what caught his attention. Not just because of the crowd gathered there but because the home was twice the size of the church. Neither building, the church or the parsonage, had been here when he'd been in the village years before. With that thought, his gaze went to the west, toward where the home of Sarah and her family had stood. Now there was nothing but an open field planted with a poor crop of rye. He glanced in all directions, trying to verify that he was recalling correctly.

"You there, on the horse. What do you want in our village?"

That voice answered one of his other questions. This was the George Hickman he knew. The man who'd swindled more people than the devil ever hoped to. The same one who was now the reverend of Salem Village. Anger twisted a tight knot in Richard's gut. Rather than fight it, he chose to use it in his favor.

Upon dismounting, he led the horse to the front of the tavern and tied the animal to a pole before he took his time walking the rest of the way around the building to where he'd get his first good look at George Hickman. It would be George's first time to get a good look at him, too. The man would remember him. They'd sparred over merchandise in both Barbados and Boston. He hadn't given in either time, and Hickman hadn't found another ship captain to shortchange, either, not after the word had spread. However, Hickman's false charges had forced the *Con-*

cord to stay harbored for a month, which had cost Richard not only time but money.

"You there, I say!"

"You say what?" Richard asked, stepping around the corner and coming face-to-face with Hickman. He let his never-forgotten disdain fill his tone, along with the anger now rolling in his stomach.

Shock, then spite flashed in Hickman's eyes. "Tarr," he snarled. "What are you doing here?"

"I was thinking the same thing," Richard answered, giving a long look at the man's black doublet and breeches, as well as the white ruff around his thick neck and his black hat. "What are *you* doing here?"

George Hickman was a squat man in structure, with a barrel chest and stomach and bowed legs. He tried to make up for his meager height by his attitude, which, as far as Richard knew, hadn't worked, up until now perhaps. Hickman had inherited a sugar plantation from his father in Barbados and in little more than a few years had lost everything. Demanding top dollar for an inferior product had left him without a way to ship his sugar to markets off the islands, and cruel treatment had forced his slaves into desertion—something few ever did. Their punishment was usually death, but that was also what they'd faced working for Hickman.

After a few years Hickman had landed in Boston, where he'd conveniently inherited a merchandising business from the father of a woman he'd married in that area. There again, his demands had left him without ships to fulfill his orders. That had been the last Richard had heard of him. Then again, he hadn't cared enough to listen if someone had spoken Hickman's name.

"The likes of you aren't welcome here, Tarr," Hickman hissed.

"I can't believe the likes of you are welcome here," Richard replied. A rotten egg never lost its stench, and right now the odor was strong enough to make a grown man gag.

Louder, in order for the other men standing several yards away to hear, Hickman spouted, "Be gone. We have no need for sailors in Salem Village."

"Good," Richard answered, just as loud. "Because I'm not here as a sailor. I'm here as a father."

The alarm that flashed in Hickman's narrow eyes told Richard all he needed to know. The man had known Grace was his daughter and was behind her condition. Renewed anger mixed with full-blown loathing boiled in Richard's veins. As much as he'd like to unleash his fury, letting it control his actions wouldn't get the results he now wanted. Exposing Hickman for the impostor he was would be something to relish. He'd make sure it was done correctly. He owed it to his daughter.

Hickman's nostrils were flared and his face turned redder with each silent moment that passed. Other than allowing his hands to ball into fists, Richard refrained from permitting his internal rage to show. This act was unlike him, but he had his daughter to consider. Righting the wrong that had been thrust upon her wouldn't be solved by beating Hickman to a pulp. Even though it would provide immense satisfaction.

With a great deal of emphasis, Hickman waved a hand and shouted, "Be off with you, stranger, before the wrath of God strikes you for attempting to foil our blessed community!"

Richard pulled his lips into a tight grin and took a step closer to hiss, "Shout all you want. A pulpit won't protect you from me."

The man's thick jowls shook as he stepped back. His beady eyes glanced toward the onlookers before he hoisted both arms into the air. "I am an ordained messenger of the Almighty God!"

"Ordained by whom?" Richard asked. "Yourself?"

"Our good reverend attended Harvard University," a tall man replied as he approached. "You'll do as requested, sir, and exit our village."

Several others of the group were moving forward, and the conceited grin growing on Hickman's face said the man thought he'd won. Richard considered telling him no army of cronies would frighten him or change what he was set on doing; however, he had time and would relish watching the other man squirm a bit. If these men were supporting Hickman, he needed to know why. Still, he wasn't going to let anyone think they worried him—because they didn't.

Eyeing each man, including Hickman, individually and intently, Richard finally moved his attention to the one who'd spoken. "I will leave your community when I've concluded my business."

With that, he turned and made his way back around the building. Ignoring the mumblings for what they were, he didn't retrieve his horse but instead entered the tavern. Puritans didn't abide drunkenness, but they drank ale from sunrise to sunset. As with almost every community ever established, a tavern was the first building erected, even before homes or a church.

Hosting only two windows and a few short candles, the interior was dark and dank, but that hadn't stopped men from gathering around tables and emptying tankards a barkeep kept full using a pitcher he refilled from the line of barrels resting upon a rack on the far wall. Richard walked across the room, which was unusually quiet compared to most taverns he entered, to where a man stood behind a long board stretched between two barrels.

Without a word, Richard laid down a coin. Using one hand to slide the coin across the wood, the barkeep grabbed a wooden tankard with his other hand. The coin dropped into a hole at the end of the bar, clanking against others when it hit the bottom. After pouring ale into the cup, the barkeep set it before Richard.

Giving the droopy-eyed man a nod, Richard lifted the cup to his lips. The ale was strong and bitter, stealing his breath as he swallowed. He turned then to survey the men at the tables. A few were returning his gaze. Curious, no doubt. He didn't let his sights rest on them. Answers were what he needed, not questions.

A single man, thin, with his head hung low, sat alone in the farthest, darkest corner. The flame of the short candle on his table flickered as if burning up its last bits of tallow. Richard walked to that table and asked, "Care if I join you?"

The man shrugged. "I make sorry company."

"It's not company I seek," Richard replied. "Merely a chair to sit upon while drinking my ale."

With a hand, the man gestured to the opposite chair. His expression hadn't changed, nor his posture. The man was clearly downtrodden, browbeaten to the edge of his being. Richard had seen that before.

He took a seat and another swallow of the pungent ale. "Your community holds the air of hostility." There was no sense denying the surliness filling the room.

"The evilness is everywhere." His companion's voice was a whisper. "Ye'd be better off to keep traveling. There's no rest for the weary here. No escape, either. Except perhaps death."

"You sound like a man with no hope," Richard acknowledged.

The man closed his eyes but not before Richard saw moisture, as well as a tear that escaped and trickled down the man's sunken cheek.

Richard waited a moment, wasting that time by lifting the tankard to his lips again. His mouth refused to accept another drop of the vinegary brew, and he set the cup down. "Why?"

Lifting his chin slightly, as if it was all he could manage, the man shook his head. "My mother was hanged today." His gaze slowly turned to the other occupants in the dim room. "Along with some of their family members." Turning back, he croaked, "There was nothing we could do. Nothing any of us could do."

"What were their crimes?"

"Witchcraft." The man wheezed in a breath of air. "Those who denied the accusations were hanged in Salem Towne this morning." His fingers shook as he wrapped them around the handle of his tankard. "I begged her to confess, but she insisted upon taking her chances of being one of God's chosen few rather than rotting away in jail, awaiting the devil's arrival."

Marina's image instantly appeared inside Richard's head. "What had she done?"

The man's lips pulled tight and a spark of anger glistened briefly in his eyes. "Took a switch after the reverend's daughter for snitching out of our garden. She was accused of putting a spell on the children to make them behave so and then for scorning them instead of leading them toward salvation. The girls were at her trial, claimed she was pinching them from across the room and that they'd seen her in their dreams, with a familiar suckling her blood." Another tear escaped the corner of his eye. "The court ordered the removal of her clothing to reveal her extra teat. When one wasn't discovered, the girls fell upon the floor on all fours and started barking like dogs. That was ruled evidence enough."

"By whom?"

"The court of Oyer and Terminer."

"What is your name?" Richard asked in hopes of gaining alliance as well as more information. Calling his companion a man was deceiving. The lack of facial hair said this was a lad, less than twenty years for sure. Richard scraped away the whiskers from his face regularly by choice. The itching was far too irritating.

"John Griggs."

"Tell me, John," Richard continued, using the man's first name on purpose. "Does the pious Reverend Hickman sit upon that court bench?"

"Yes, as well as several of those who brought him here."

"And why did they do that?" Richard asked. "Brought in a reverend unknown to your people? Surely you had ministers already in residence."

The man shoved his cup aside and flattened his hands upon the table. "Because those who had been here couldn't abide with the opposition between Salem Village and Salem Towne and left." Slumping lower in his chair, John whispered, "Perhaps I should follow Marina's advice. There is nothing here for me."

Richard's stomach churned. It could have been the ale, but he doubted it. "What advice was that?"

"Relinquish my property and leave."

"Relinquish your property to whom?"

"The church," John said. "It'll save them the trouble of confiscating it and keep my neck from getting stretched."

No church he'd ever heard of confiscated property. Then again, it sounded like just the kind

Hickman would oversee. "And Marina," Richard said. "Will she leave with you?"

Another bout of sadness crossed the man's face. "No, she won't leave. Just like Mother, she believes she has to stand trial."

"For witchcraft?" Richard asked. He'd believed all Marina and William's talk had been fabrications, but a chill overtook his senses at the young man's seriousness.

John nodded and then leaned across the table to whisper, "She threatened to put a hex on Reverend Hickman."

The chill inside him sent a quiver up his spine. "Marina?"

John nodded again.

"What sort of hex?"

John shrugged. "I don't know for sure."

"Why?" Although he could think of several reasons, Richard couldn't imagine Marina threatening anyone in such a way. She was stubborn but not malicious. "Why would she put a hex on the reverend?"

"Because he was going to throw that little girl in jail."

Instantly knowing, Richard still asked, "What little girl?"

"The one who'd been living in the woods since her family died last winter. We all thought she'd died, until the old woman who'd been taking care of her was arrested. The widow begged for someone to go get the child, but the courts ignored her. Marina was the only one who went to look. Then they tried taking the girl away from her. Claimed the child was a witch because she couldn't recite the Lord's Prayer."

Richard grew so furious the handle of his tankard cracked inside his clenched fist. When the tavern door flew open, he bounded to his feet, ready to unleash his wrath. A hint of satisfaction arose when the first man through the door was Hickman.

"There he is," Hickman shouted. "Arrest that man and the one conversing with him."

Richard slammed his tankard upon the table, not caring how the wood split and ale sloshed across the table. "Arrest me for what?"

Hickman didn't answer; instead, he shouted at the others. "That man is the devil! The devil, I say! Arrest him!"

Bounding across the room in little more than a single step, Richard grabbed Hickman by the white ruff around his neck. He twisted the material until it was tight enough to block the man's airway. "I'm not the devil," he seethed. "But you will soon wish I was. The devil would take your life swiftly, but I shall see you suffer."

With eyes bulging and his face bloodred, Hickman clawed at his ruff with both hands. Richard rendered another twist before he shoved the man backward while releasing his hold. Hickman fell to the floor, gasping for air. The men who'd so gallantly rushed through the door moments ago were now cautiously backing out over the threshold.

Narrowing his gaze upon those men, Richard stepped forward. "There will be no arrests made here today," he announced. "I don't believe in your Puritan blasphemes, but I do believe in an eye for an eye. A tooth for a tooth. That is what you shall soon see."

The men scattered. Sensing someone at his back, Richard spun, expecting to see Hickman. The reverend was still on the floor. It was his table companion standing behind him.

John Griggs quivered like a mouse in a corner before he swallowed so hard his Adam's apple got hung up on his shirt collar. "I'll follow ye out," he squeaked, "if ye don't mind."

Richard gave him a nod before casting a glare of loathing toward Hickman, who was being assisted to his feet by the barkeep and another man. Hickman didn't have a single redeeming quality, and the fact he'd befuddled the people of Salem Village soured Richard's throat worse than the stale ale.

"We best be leaving," Griggs whispered near his shoulder.

Stepping over the threshold into the bright sunlight did nothing to wash away the darkness that had settled upon him while inside the tavern. Richard wanted to twist his shoulders and shake like a horse might upon being assaulted by flies but withheld the desire. It wouldn't do any good. The evilness of this place filled the air heavier than a storm.

"Which direction are ye headed?" Griggs asked as Richard walked to his horse.

"Why?"

"I thought I might tag along." Glancing over his shoulder, the young man added, "I'm sure to be arrested if I stay here."

The air that built in his lungs had to be released. Richard did so, letting the sigh linger as he untied the reins of his horse. John Griggs was right. He would be arrested for associating with him as soon as Hickman caught his bearings. "I'll be going to Boston in a few days," Richard answered, quiet enough for only John to hear.

"They'll have ye convicted and hanged in a few days," John said solemnly. "Ye best head that way now."

"I have things to see to first," Richard answered, stepping up to mount his beast.

Griggs hung his head and shook it sadly. "It's all over for me."

From the saddle, Richard pulled a foot out

of the stirrup and held out an arm. John looked younger in the light of day than he had in the darkness of the tavern. A lost soul if there ever had been one. "Climb up," Richard said. "I put your life in danger. I'll now protect it."

"I—"

"Grab my arm, John."

After a moment of hesitation, John grabbed his arm and swung onto the horse behind him. "Where are we going?"

Richard steered the animal onto the road leading out of the village. "To Marina Lindqvist's home."

"You know Marina?" John sounded astonished.

"The child she saved is my daughter," Richard said.

He couldn't be sure but thought the mumbling he now heard was John praying.

Chapter Six

Marina stood at the table in the front room, holding the large Bible and flipping through the pages. She'd tried to read the passages but found no reassurance in the words. Richard Tarr was to blame. His arrival had put her at his mercy. She hadn't been prepared for that. Nor could she get his image out of her mind. Why did he have to be so stubborn? Why couldn't he have been an amicable, agreeable man?

A new thought had her closing the Bible. If he wasn't who he was, she wouldn't have needed to rescue Gracie and therefore would never have discovered why she'd been transformed into a witch.

"Sounds like your captain is back," Uncle William said from his chair.

"He's not my captain," Marina said. Twisting in order to peer out the window over William's balding head, her heart fluttered upon seeing two people riding the beast.

"Who's that with him?"

"It looks like John Griggs," she whispered. "His mother was scheduled to hang today, along with the others."

Uncle William shook his head. "Poor lad."

Marina nodded—the burning of her throat wouldn't allow more. John was sure to be distraught, and the anger she'd felt moments ago at Richard Tarr transferred back to Reverend Hickman. He'd destroyed so many lives, torn apart so many families.

The Puritan religion had once been based upon her very own Protestant beliefs, but instead of hope and love, fear and hatred had become the basis of their daily living. Hickman's sermons decreed the devil roamed the earth and sought entrance into every home. Rather than seeking salvation in the presence of God, he preached of procuring life based on the absence of Satan, who he claimed was behind every misdeed or calamity. Even something as irrelevant as a toothache. Not even the smallest of children were given a margin of error, and every infraction, no matter how slight, was publicly disapproved.

She'd witnessed all this with her own eyes and found it so difficult to believe. So hard to accept. It saddened her and was far harder to understand than even her own circumstance. Anger mounted inside her. She'd been returned to the living and brought to this place in order to put an end to all this debauchery and, by God, she would, despite Richard Tarr's interference. Spinning about, she marched across the room.

"Invite that young Griggs lad to eat with us," Uncle William said. "He'll need a friend or two about now."

"I will," Marina assured him, already heading up the hallway and toward the back door. The mumble of voices could be heard as she crossed the yard, but the tones were too subtle to make out actual words. That made her increase her speed. Although close to her age of twenty years, John seemed much younger. He'd been a devoted and dedicated son to his mother and must be mourning her loss immensely.

Both men turned as she entered the barn. She purposefully kept from looking toward Richard but noted when he stepped away, leading the horse into a stall.

John shifted his feet as if unsure what to do. The way his bottom lip trembled brought Marina closer. There were repercussions for displaying emotions in front of others, but she truly didn't care what Richard thought and knew full well the pain filling John. Wrapping her arms around his slender shoulders, she hugged him close. "Your mother was a chosen one," she whispered in his ear. "I'm sure of it. God called her home to heaven so she would no longer need to suffer here on earth."

His body shook against hers. No one—no man, woman or child—was immune to bereavement and she sent up a silent prayer, asking the God she knew to be good and kind, to offer his comfort to John. To settle his weary and confused mind.

A moment later, with a sniffle, John lifted his head and took a step back. Without a word to her, he turned to Richard. "I'll see to the horse, Captain. Unsaddle and brush him down. I'll feed him, too."

Richard glanced at her, and for a moment her breath stalled. There was profound understanding in his eyes, as if he too felt compassion for John and his loss. A completely different kind of softness formed in her chest—one she couldn't quite explain but also couldn't ignore.

"Thank you, John," Richard said, walking out of the stall. "I appreciate that." His long legs had him at her side within a few steps. "Marina and I will be inside the house."

A tremble rippled up her arm as Richard's hand folded around her elbow, and her anger returned. Once they'd exited the barn and were out of earshot, she demanded, "Why did you bring him here?"

"I had no choice."

"Why? What happened?" She wanted to believe John hadn't been accused of being a witch but knew that was a very real possibility. So was the fact that if he hadn't been already accused, he would be now.

"I'll answer your questions as soon as you answer mine," Richard said, pushing open the back door of the house.

He hadn't shrunk in his absence, yet his size no longer concerned her, nor did his dark complexion and long black hair. When she looked at him now, she was reminded of how he'd rolled up Gracie's sleeve at the table and broken a piece of bread into pieces for the little girl to eat. None of that said she could trust him, not completely, and she almost wished it did. That fact twisted the anger inside her a bit tighter. "I thought you left in order to get your questions answered."

"I did. And that produced more questions." He let go of her arm in order to close the door before he scanned the room.

"Uncle William is in the front room, and Gracie is still asleep." Marina crossed the room, needing to put space between them as badly as she needed time to settle the turmoil rising inside her.

Requiring something to keep her busy during his absence, she'd melted down a supply of beeswax and poured it into candle molds after she'd cleaned the kitchen and set a pot of beans to soften for the evening meal. There was always so much to do, and each task she embarked on made her miss her family. With her mother and the wives of her brothers, there had always been ample hands completing the necessities a household required. Here, it was just she and Uncle William, but the tasks were the same. It just meant they didn't need as many candles, loaves of bread, casks of cider, cords of wood and the endless other things needed to survive.

She shifted the candle molds sitting upon the table. It may have been foolish, a waste to make so many. Soon this house would be empty. The idea of that, of Reverend Hickman scavenging through the household, made her clench her hands into fists. She couldn't stop him while taking care of Uncle William and Gracie and now John. Her uncle and John would interfere, be imprisoned and probably killed. She spun around to face Richard.

He'd pulled a chair out from the other end of the table and flipped it around to sit upon as one would a saddle. Crossing both arms over the back of the chair, he asked, "Who was the old woman taking care of Grace?"

There was no way for her to know with whom he may have spoken in the village. It could have been any number of people. The tavern was sure to be full of people, namely those who'd recently returned from attending the hangings in Salem Towne. She was certain that was where he'd gone. The tavern. That was the gathering place for all men. It had been that way in Maine, too. He could have met John on the road, but she doubted it, and she knew the young man could have shared far more than anyone else.

Maybe the truth was exactly what he needed to hear. Let him know he'd now put them all in danger. "The Widow Holcomb. She took care of your wife and her parents when they grew ill. They were the first to die and some claimed the widow killed them with her herbs. She disappeared afterward. Because the disease is so contagious, the Westbrook home, your wife's family home, was burned with the bodies still inside. It wasn't until Mrs. Holcomb was arrested that—" Marina had to pause to swallow. The image of Gracie inside the shack built of sticks, covered with old blankets and too weak to lift her head, was still fresh in her mind.

"That you went in search of Grace," Richard said.

He knew. Knew far more than she'd wanted him to. Marina swallowed and licked her lips. "If you already know—"

"I want to know if what I heard is true," he

said. "Did you go in search of Grace when no one else would?"

She held no regrets in rescuing Gracie. "Yes. Anna Pullman told me the widow had pleaded for someone to go get the baby in the woods, but no one would listen or dared to. Anna's sister had been arrested at the same time, her mother a few days later." Empathy once again washed over her. Mrs. Pullman was still imprisoned and must be grieving deeply over Elizabeth's death.

"Why did you?"

"I had given Widow Holcomb milk and eggs and other such things over the past few months, so it was easy for me to believe she'd been feeding a child." Marina shook her head. "Several had been left orphans after the epidemic had played itself out. I had no idea it was Gracie until I found her."

"Where?"

"In a shack in the woods."

"What happened then?"

Marina swallowed and attempted to use the act of moving to the hearth to check the beans to cover up how her hands had started to shake. "Someone was watching the shack," she said. "I know I wasn't followed, yet when I carried Gracie out, they were there and tried to take her from me."

"'They' meaning the reverend," he said. "Who claimed Grace was a witch or a witch's familiar."

"Yes and no," she said, returning the lid to the pot.

"Please explain."

She hung the spoon on its hook before turning around. "Yes, he is who claimed such things about Gracie. He'd tried to make her recite a prayer, but she was too weak. He hadn't been in the woods. Those men forced—took us to Reverend Hickman's home, where he questioned me privately."

"Concerning what?"

The dark storm had returned to his eyes, a sign she'd already learned meant his anger was rising. She'd also witnessed how he was able to control it. Something she had yet to conquer at times. Sighing, in hopes of containing her own temper, she admitted, "My powers."

His lips drew into a tight line as he repeated, "Powers." He said the word as if it disgusted him.

"Yes, powers." She'd been foolish to think he wouldn't learn of her secret when in fact it was no longer a secret. Lifting her chin, she said, "I was deemed an outsider from the moment I arrived. Uncle William had already achieved that status, but only as someone who didn't believe in the Puritan ways. He was accepted, though, because of the goods and supplies he purchased from the villagers. They gladly took his money, and for that fact alone I wasn't sent away upon my arrival."

"Because you had money to spend? William's money."

"Yes." At first she'd thought no one would learn of what had happened in Maine and had sincerely tried to befriend others, to fit in despite the differences between them.

"You didn't mind being an outcast?"

Marina didn't need to contemplate that. "No."

"Most people do."

She let her eyes wander over him. Even sitting down, his bulk filled the room. A man his size, with his confidence and pride, wouldn't know about being an outcast.

"Size and gender have little to do with it. I've been considered an outcast many times," he said.

Marina dropped her gaze to her candle molds once again. Her insides had started to churn. She hadn't cared what the community members thought of her. There was no room for that. She'd been ousted by people far more important to her than the villagers. Back in Maine it had been friends, people she'd known since moving there as an infant, who had turned on her. Blamed her for things beyond her control. It had taken time before she'd accepted that, and even though she finally had, the pain still lingered. Thinking Richard might have experienced that same kind of pain seemed impossible. He was too strong. Too powerful.

"Why didn't you let them take Gracie from you?"

Marina blinked and questioned her hearing. "Why?"

He nodded.

"She's a child. Any decent human being would have wanted to help her."

He didn't so much as blink. "Not if they believed in witchcraft, believed she was possessed—a familiar."

"Hogwash." Nothing would ever allow her to believe any child was cursed. "Children are treasures in God's eyes. They know no evil, except that thrust upon them by misguided adults."

"That doesn't sound like something a witch would say." Eyeing her steadily, he asked, "Yet you admit to being a witch. Threatened to put a hex on the reverend."

Her stomach sank. So did she. Without the will to stop herself, she dropped onto the chair beside her. She hadn't thought Hickman would tell anyone about that. "Yes."

"Why?"

She'd been so full of pain, anger and contempt that day she'd have done whatever was needed to save Grace. Still would. She'd watched a child die before and wouldn't do that again. Holding tears at bay stung the backs of her eyes. "Because I couldn't think of anything else. Grace had been in the woods for over a week, alone. I was afraid she might die in my arms." Her chest was burning as fiercely as her eyes, and air caught in her throat as she breathed it in. Not telling him about what she'd seen in Hickman was growing harder by the minute. Richard was so strong and powerful, she wished he was her ally instead of an obstacle in her path.

He stood and walked around the table, approaching her. Unsure as to why, she wrung her trembling hands together but couldn't seem to pull her eyes from his.

Arriving before her, he knelt down. "I am greatly indebted to you, Marina, beholden for how you saved my daughter from certain death."

Marina was startled by such a heartfelt confession.

A slight smile appeared briefly on his face. "But I don't believe you are a witch. I've known George Hickman for years. The man has a penchant for angering people. And deceiving them."

Realization hit her like the heat of an oven. "But I am a witch," she whispered. "You being here is proof." The curse she'd threatened the reverend with was coming true, whether she wanted it to or not.

"Me?"

She closed her eyes momentarily. "I had nothing to barter for Gracie, so I said I'd take her place if I could heal her first. That wasn't enough for

Hickman. The only other thing I could think of was how Uncle William claimed the man was a farce, so I told him I'd see that his true identity, his past, was revealed to his followers."

Still kneeling before her, a smile filled Richard's eyes. "No wonder he was so startled to see me. If anyone can reveal his sordid past, it's me." He laughed then and squeezed her hand. "This is perfect, Marina. Perfect."

His smile, the way he said her name, touched her in a way she hadn't been touched in a very long time—deep inside where the tiniest flickering of hope had fought to stay lit for so long. "How so?"

"Hickman tried to sully my name as a sea captain years ago. It didn't work, but it's an act I've never forgotten." Richard placed a single finger beneath her chin, making her skin tingle as he forced her to look at him.

Fear overtook her insides, tying a tight and hard knot in her stomach. Marina shook her head. That was why Hickman wanted Gracie. He knew she was Richard's daughter. "I wasn't trying to set a trap. I was trying to save Grace."

"And you did."

Once again she shook her head and had to fight against the tears forming. "No, I haven't. Not yet. She won't truly be safe until she's far from Salem, and she's still too weak to travel." Remorse joined her fear. "You shouldn't have gone to town."

He smiled once more before rising to his feet. His hand slipped off hers as he took a step back. "I don't frighten easy, Marina."

Her heart skipped a beat as his eyes once again turned as turbulent as a storm full of lightning and thunder.

"And don't you fear," he said. "I won't allow you to suffer from the repercussions of my actions. Rest assured of that."

A will not her own overtook her. Marina bounded to her feet and grabbed his arm. "What have you done?" The dread lumping together in her stomach like cold porridge left in a pot overnight told her there were serious repercussions from his visit to the village. There were others besides Gracie. The prison was full of people she had to help. Mothers and daughters, fathers and sons she had to save from certain death.

He patted her hand as one might a child. "Not enough," he said. "Not nearly enough." He turned around and walked to the window, where he glanced out toward the barn. "Your uncle must have told you Hickman used to live in Barbados and then Boston. There wasn't a sea captain who would do business with him. Those who did once never did again. Not after being swindled out of their shipping fees."

Uncle William had said as much. He also claimed the reason the reverend started telling rumors about her was because she was his niece. It wasn't. And they weren't rumors. She was a witch and had known how to stop the spread of smallpox, but no one would listen.

None of that mattered anymore. What did was that her uncle, Gracie and Richard get out of here as soon as possible. The sourness of her stomach increased, and though she feared the question, she still asked, "Why is John here?"

"He's taking your advice." Turning about, he asked, "You did suggest he should leave the village, didn't you?"

"I told him there are other places he could live. He wanted his mother to confess to being a witch so she wouldn't be hanged. She refused because she knew the church would confiscate her property if she did, leaving John with nothing." Marina spun around, pacing the area between the hearth and the table. "I was trying to make him see that the church would end up with their property no matter what. If she confessed, they'd take it and let her rot in jail and cast John out of the community. If she didn't confess, they'd see she hanged and find another way to get the land, possibly by accusing John of witchcraft. That's what they've done to others." Swallowing, she asked, "Is that what happened? They accused him?"

"No," Richard said.

"Then why is he here?"

"He made the decision to leave after Reverend Hickman accused me of being the devil."

Marina felt as if the bottom of the world just collapsed. As she had several times since his arrival, she questioned why she'd sent him a message. She should have waited until Gracie was better and convinced Uncle William to take the child to Boston. He'd already refused, said he'd never leave her here alone, but he'd have to, eventually. They didn't have a wagon, but John did. Mind twirling, she stopped her pacing. "Perhaps Grace is well enough to travel in a wagon. That wouldn't be too tiring and—"

"Gracie isn't going anywhere," he interrupted. "Not yet."

"It's not safe for her to be here. You must see that."

"I won't let any harm come to her."

"You can't stop it," she said. Why couldn't he see that?

"I'm her father. I won't let anyone ever harm her again."

Growing frustrated that his trip to the village had made things far worse, she threw her hands in the air. "Then start acting like her father. Think of her safety first and foremost."

The glare in his eyes told her she may have gone too far.

Chapter Seven

Once again Richard found himself balling his hands into fists in order to contain the anger overtaking his system. Marina had the tongue of a witch. She most likely could cast spells upon people. However, her victims would have to believe in witchcraft in order for her hexes to work—something he did not. He did believe in evil and knew the most evil creatures he'd ever encountered were not witches or beasts. They were men. Men like Hickman. The man might believe her tale of being a witch, of the ability to cast hexes, whereas he knew it was all mere circumstance. Perhaps, fate even. He believed in fate and in Hickman finally getting his due.

"I *am* thinking of Grace," he replied.

The sigh she let out permeated the air with all the frustration swirling inside him. She closed her eyes for a moment, letting her long lashes rest upon her cheeks as if she was hoping to find salvation deep within herself. That too he recognized.

"No, you're not," she then said, lifting her lids to look upon him. "You are thinking of the hatred within yourself."

How did she understand what was happening inside him so precisely? Since the minute he'd seen Hickman in town he'd started to recall the brutality he'd witnessed down in Barbados. The slaves whose backs had been crisscrossed with scabs from whippings. The way they'd flinched every time their master had touched the bullwhip that Hickman always carried on his hip. He wasn't about to tell Marina all that. Or the other things he now recalled. Like how many of those young slave girls had been pregnant—most likely by their master. Hickman's attempt at blackballing him from the Barbados port meant very little in comparison.

Those things had angered him back then but not like they did now that he knew how his daughter had been treated, how close she'd come to being in that man's hands.

Hickman would pay this time.

Marina was still looking up at him with pleading eyes. They were as blue as the ocean near the equator, where a man could get lost looking into the depths of the sea, searching for a bottom that was there, somewhat visible yet unattainable. A person could drop a trinket into those waters, watch it fall and settle upon the ocean bed, but no sailor of this world could dive deep enough to retrieve it. He'd witnessed several attempts and had placed wagers on their failures. He'd place those same stakes on anyone who thought they could defy Marina. There was more to her than a normal eye could ascertain. On the outside she appeared to be a woman like the many others he'd encountered, but inside she held a secret that made her different. It gave her strength, too, considering how she'd stood up for his daughter, and that was the part that intrigued him the most.

As if his silence suggested he needed more of an explanation, she shook her head. "The Puritans are not the kind and loving people others might think them to be. They are righteous and godly, but also suspicious and unforgiving. Not just with outsiders, but with each other. By angering them further, you may ruin your chances of taking Gracie away."

What she had just described was the perfect community for Hickman to easily infiltrate. "Have no fears. No one will stop me from taking my daughter with me when I leave."

"That's my point," she said sadly. "You may become unable to leave."

He was about to say no one would stop him when the door opened.

John paused in the doorway. His weary glance bouncing around the room said he noted the tension in the air. "I—uh—took care of the horse, Captain, and I led the cow into the barn for the night, Marina. Are there any other chores I can perform? Do ye need wood or water or...?"

"No, thank you, John," Marina said, once again moving toward the hearth.

She'd stirred those beans so often they should be soup by now, but Richard refrained from saying that when he caught how she smiled at John. It was so soft and tender it stung one of his internal organs. A vital one. There was compassion in her eyes, and kindness, neither of which she'd bestowed upon him. Such things had never bothered him before. He'd never known a time when he'd wanted compassion or kindness from anyone.

The uneven thud of William's wooden leg echoed against the hallway walls moments before the man said, "Close the door, boy. We have no idea who listens outside the walls of our home. They are everywhere."

Having experienced the oppression in town, Richard now understood William and Marina's fears more. It still surprised him. William was a seaman. He knew the ways of the world and of Hickman. William bowing to the other man's threats made no sense.

"They've been known to peek through windows, looking for spectral evidence to use against the accused," William said when he arrived at the table. With a sigh that could have been the result of walking the distance from the front room to the kitchen or from the topic of discussion, the old man sat upon a chair. "Perhaps we could have a cup of cider, Marina? All of us. I believe the captain needs to hear what has been taking place in the village."

"I believe I know," Richard said. Hickman had known Gracie was his daughter and would have been overjoyed to tell him of her death. Marina had truly saved his daughter's life. Not just from starvation but from the very devil himself.

"You don't know all of it," William said.

Richard's gaze was on Marina's, but hers, tender and full of compassion, was on John.

The young man's chin trembled visibly. "They hanged eight people today," he said. "Eight. And cheered."

"Where are the authorities?" Richard asked. He might need them before this was all over. "Why didn't they put a stop to it?"

"They are the authorities," Marina said softly. "Reverend Hickman and the church elders."

"No, they aren't," Richard argued. "Massachusetts is under English Charter. The people here must abide by the rules set forth by King William."

"King Billy has enough of his own issues," William said. "Sharing his crown with his wife and battling the Whigs and the Tories, the poor fella doesn't have time to be concerned with a religious sect that separated themselves from his country years ago."

Richard had no argument against that. His fleet had close connections to the Royal line of shipping. The reign of William and Mary had served his livelihood well, as had William's victory over James in the Battle of the Boyne. Still, there had to be some order ruling the colonies. "Who is the governor?"

Marina had filled three cups of cider and set them on the table before she'd moved to the hearth to tend her kettle hanging over the smoldering fire again. With a wave from William, John sat down, and both men took long swigs from their mugs before William answered. "A new one arrived a couple of months ago, but little good he'll do. Joshua Matthews went to England and hand-picked the poor bastard."

"The first thing Governor Phillips did was order the creation of a special court to prosecute the trials. That's when they decided to start hanging people," John said.

"They had to figure out something to do," William said. "The jails are overflowing."

Richard swung around the chair he'd occupied

earlier and pulled it up to the table. Sailing was a good life but isolated. Entire wars had been fought during the time he'd been at sea traveling from one port to the other. In some instances he'd been the first to bring news of one country to another; at other times, he was the last to hear of what had taken place during his absence. This was one of those times. He'd never been fully aware of all that was happening in the New World—the area changed daily. He hadn't taken the time to listen to the gossips at the Boston Harbor. Marina's note had greeted him as he'd stepped ashore.

"Being at sea has left me ignorant of many things," he freely admitted. "Perhaps you could start at the beginning and enlighten me."

John nodded, but it was how William looked at Marina that caught Richard's attention. She shook her head negatively. The action was slight, but Richard knew he hadn't imagined it or how William nodded.

"It's a long story," the old sailor said. "John will have to help me with certain details."

Marina made no comment as she walked around the table and entered the hall. Richard dug his heels into the floor to push back his chair to follow, but a hand fell upon his arm.

"Listen up, Captain," William said, "for it is a sordid tale."

Marina entered the room Gracie slept in, and despite his desire to follow her, Richard turned his attention to William. He'd figured out a few things, but his gut told him there was more. Much more, and Marina held a secret that was at the heart of it all. To know what that was burned inside him.

"You know about the epidemic," William started. "It took many lives, but the way I see it, Hickman used it to his own benefit. Most ministers are provided a salary and a place to live, but Hickman demanded more. From the time he arrived, he ordered a large home built and for the villagers to provide him and his family with food and wood and most all other necessities."

"Including my mother's brass candlesticks," John said.

When Richard glanced toward the younger man, John bowed his head.

"There's no shame in speaking your mind in my home," William said. "Tell him what happened, John."

"They'd been my grandmother's, those candlesticks," John said, his voice wavering slightly. "Upon entering our home for the first time, Reverend Hickman took them, declaring my mother needed to provide them as an offering to the church. Mother didn't protest, but she cried after he left."

"Hickman did that to many families," William said. "Flat-out stole from them under the guise of church offerings. I've never been in the village church, but I'd wager those candlesticks of John's mother are in Hickman's home, not the church. He also demanded the deed to the new parsonage and surrounding land."

Richard didn't need to ask why. Greed filled Hickman's very essence. "Why didn't the people protest, put a stop to it?"

"Because from the moment he hit the pulpit, Hickman has spouted about the devil overtaking the villagers. He shouts that they shouldn't covet personal possession and chides families for not producing a baby each year. If a spouse dies, he insists the man or woman remarry immediately. He claimed the pox was brought upon them because their congregation is dwindling. There are no more ships full of Puritans arriving from the old country. He's even blamed the villagers for that. Spouted off about how they've let the devil into their lives. He promises it will all change, but only if the people follow his every order."

William's words had hit Richard's nerves like a hammer. On the one and only visit he'd made to the village years before, Sarah's father had said he could return on one condition—if he impregnated his wife upon each visit. That had galled

him and made what Earl insisted—that he was
nothing more than a stud—too real.

He'd refused those conditions and had done
the one thing he'd never do again. He'd begged.
Begged Sarah to leave her family. She'd refused,
said she couldn't disobey her father. Thus, he'd
never returned. He'd put a glitch in their plan,
though. By sending merchandise regularly, Sarah's family couldn't claim he was dead, and divorces were unheard-of, so Sarah had been unable
to marry again.

"When folks started dying of smallpox, Hickman started claiming their property as that of the
church. He said the loss of members was a financial burden the church couldn't bear. If a husband
died and the woman survived, as in the case with
John, his mother had to either turn over her assets or remarry immediately because women are
not allowed to own property. She refused to do
either, claiming the property had become John's
upon his father's death. It's a good chunk of land
and borders Hickman's. Younger children were
deemed orphans and set out on the road. Taking
one in was akin to inviting the devil to live in
your home." William took another drink of cider.
"When people started to protest, again, like John's
mother, they were accused of witchcraft."

As unbelievable as it might sound to some,
Richard could fully accept all William had said.

"Accused by Hickman," he said aloud. More as confirmation in his own mind than anything else.

"No," John said. "By Hickman's daughter and niece. The very girls responsible for my mother's death."

Richard saw something in John then that he hadn't noted before. Hatred. The young man was at a rebellious age, a time when a man desired his life to be his own. He forged onward, breaking away from any claims that might hold him back. Hatred could be a dangerous weapon for a man at that stage of life.

The other danger, from what he'd witnessed and experienced, was women. For most, this was also a stage in life when a man craved a woman's body in ways he might never again. When that happened, many men also discovered their greatest weakness. Marriage had broken many young men's rebellious streaks.

His gaze went down the hall to the door Marina had entered and not exited from. He had to wonder if hatred was what drove John or if it was Marina. If she was the reason John was still in Salem Village.

"Hickman emerged from the smallpox epidemic unscathed and the wealthiest man in the village, which made him want more," William said. "His daughter, niece and her friends started accusing women of being witches. Of afflicting them with illnesses and uncontrollable fits. The village doctor found nothing wrong with the girls, but their strange behavior and outbursts of gibberish didn't stop."

Richard shook his head. "The entire village believed these girls? Children? Forgive me, but there isn't a community in the entire world that holds the word of children above that of adults."

"Hickman saw to that by proclaiming the girls had been bewitched. They started out by accusing spinsters and widows, those with property no one else could claim, but it's escalated. There are now entire families in prison. Wealthy merchant families from Salem Towne. The very families the church elders have been feuding with for years."

Richard let everything settle in his mind. As an outsider looking in, someone who, like him, had nothing to gain or lose, William saw clearly what had happened. He felt no need to intervene, no desire for recourse. That was where the difference lay. Richard desired recourse. For his daughter. For the injustice placed upon him for falling in love, or simply lust, with a woman he couldn't have. Not wholly. Although he'd accepted that and separated himself from it, this time he wouldn't.

"Hickman's not the only one who has profited from all this," William said. "The church elders have, too. Property and possessions have been bequeathed upon them as payment for their devotion. They have formed a tight sect that no one can penetrate. They are the ones sitting on the newly formed court and they don't want it to end."

"Surely the new governor—" Richard started.

"Was handpicked by a Puritan minister," William interjected. "Matthews may live in Boston, be the president of Harvard University, but he owns farmland near Salem Village. So does his family. His brother-in-law is one of Hickman's closest allies, Abner Hogan. The witch hunt has spread faster and wider than the pox did. There's hardly a community that doesn't have a jail full of accused."

Richard made the connection of how the man in town had claimed Hickman attended Harvard but chose to hold that within. "Of being witches, whereas in truth, there are no witches."

"I didn't say that," William quickly replied. "I've known a few in my lifetime. Real witches. You gotta watch out for them." He leaned closer and whispered, "A real witch would never have allowed themselves to get arrested."

The wink William provided before he picked up his mug sent Richard's nerves ticking again. His gaze also shot once more down the hall that was still empty. When he turned back to the table, both John and William were looking in that direction with smiles on their faces.

The tingling of his spine had him turning toward the hall one more time. His breath caught somewhere between his lungs and his throat. Marina stood there, with Grace in her arms. Surely he'd have seen her leaving the room or walking up the hall moments ago. For that matter, he should have heard her footsteps. But he hadn't. It seemed as if she'd appeared right out of thin air.

"Look who is awake, Captain," she said, carrying his daughter closer.

Though soft, he heard her footsteps and the rustling of her skirt as she moved and had to brace his shoulders to keep them from quivering.

"Your arrival has made a great difference," she said. "Gracie is feeling much better."

He turned his focus on his daughter as Marina set her on the floor. Rather than the oversize nightdress, Grace now wore a blue dress covered with a white pinafore. She also had shoes on her feet, and there was color in her cheeks.

Twisting in his seat, he held his arms out in an invitation for her to come closer.

"That is a lovely dress you have on."

"Thank you," she replied softly. "Marina made it for me." As he scooped Gracie onto his lap, she added, "Blue is her favorite color."

"It is?" he replied. "What is your favorite color?"

She shrugged.

"I'm afraid Grace hasn't been taught her colors

yet, Captain," Marina replied. She was near the large hearth again, stirring that pot.

"Not taught her colors?" That confused him. Colors were everywhere. One didn't need to be taught them, did they? He couldn't recall. Then again, he couldn't recall being taught all five languages he spoke fluently. It was just something he'd learned along the way. Things he needed to know. Questioning all that in his own mind, he asked, "What else hasn't she been taught?"

"That really doesn't matter, does it?" Marina asked. "You'll see to her education going forward, won't you?" There was not only a challenge in her eyes, but a hint of hope.

"Yes." Touching the tip of Grace's nose, he vowed, "I'll see you learn to read and write, to decipher numbers and name all the colors of the rainbow."

"I shall like that," Grace said.

"So shall I," Richard responded, looking at Marina. For some unknown and unfathomable reason, he wanted her to fully understand his daughter would be denied nothing from this day forward.

Her response of a gentle, serene smile struck him in such a way his heart started beating faster. What was it about her that caused such reactions? He wasn't the type of man to save damsels in distress. Had never contemplated one way or another what happened to most people he encountered. It wasn't that he was uncaring, just busy. Keeping the hulls of his ships full and his investments profitable didn't happen without a lot of work and commitment. Yet here he was, determined to see that Hickman got his due. Why? Because of the daughter? She was his responsibility, one he accepted, and he would forever protect her, but would he still be here if it had been the old crone in the woods who'd contacted him to come and get Grace? He doubted it. Just as he doubted Grace's recovery was due to him. It was almost miraculous.

An eerie sensation had him glancing at Marina again.

Her smile was even more serene than before.

"You sure look pretty, Gracie," William said, reaching a gnarled finger across the table to flick the end of Grace's nose. "Maybe I should have Marina sew me a dress like that."

Until this moment, Richard had never known how the giggle of a child could fill the air and affect everyone around.

"You can't wear a dress," Grace told William while still giggling. "That would be silly."

"I think you are the silly one," Richard said, gently tickling her side. "Look at how you're laughing, you little magpie."

"What's a magpie?"

"A bird," Richard said. "A beautiful little bird that chatters and giggles."

"Where do they live?"

"All around the world," he said. "I've seen many kinds of birds, colorful ones. You shall, too. I'll show them to you." He picked her up to jostle her slightly in the air and hear her giggle again. "And monkeys who swing from tree to tree by their tails."

Marina wasn't completely sure what supplied her with the unusual bout of happiness but chose to accept it. Grace was certainly on the mend, and her squeals of delight were the sweetest sounds she may ever have heard. The little girl's eyes were shining and her cheeks pink. It appeared as if the arrival of her father had been pivotal in her healing. Richard looked happy, too, teasing his daughter as he was.

A tightening in her chest forced Marina to turn her attention back to the hearth. Her father had once been the most important person in her world, but she'd lost him. Lost her entire family. She didn't want that to happen to Grace and certainly didn't want the child to experience a setback, but that chance might have to be taken if it meant getting her away from Salem Village sooner than later.

A person knew when evil was about to knock

upon her door, and Marina was sure the pounding would soon start. Whether they were completely healed or not, she had to find a way for all of them sitting around the table to escape safely. A fair amount of sun still filtered in through the windows, but evening would soon fall, bringing darkness in which all sorts of things could hide.

That thought, or maybe the idea of being left here alone, made her hands tremble. The spoon clanked against the wall as she hung it on its hook. "I shall go milk Nellie, and then we'll eat."

Her statement quelled the giggling and teasing that had consumed the room.

"I'll milk for ye," John said.

"No," Marina replied. "It's best if you remain inside the house." Berating herself for speaking so swiftly, for bringing an end to the bout of happiness that none of them had experienced for a long time, she added, "Thank you, though." Glancing her uncle's way, she stated, "I won't be long."

His eyes, even clouded with age, told her what she needed to know. He'd not shared her story with Richard and wouldn't. Relief filled her. It was fleeting, for whether or not Richard knew of her past, her future was still set. All of a sudden, that saddened her deeply. Grabbing the milk bucket, she dashed out the door.

Richard might know she was a witch, but just like Uncle William, he wouldn't approve of what she had to do. Nor would he believe she could accomplish it. Men were like that. Other than her father. He'd believed in her, and she wouldn't disappoint him. Dead or alive.

Nellie was standing contently in her stall. Richard's horse was there, as well, and for a moment, she contemplated being an animal. Having no worries of where your food would come from and no repercussions from past happenings. No families to mourn when separated.

She retrieved her stool and entered Nellie's stall. The simple lives of animals. Humans were the dumb ones, not animals, as so many declared. People were never satisfied, never happy. They carried hate around like bags of luggage.

"It would be an awfully dull existence, don't you think?"

Marina closed her eyes at the sound of Richard's voice. She'd assumed he'd stay inside with Grace, but nothing she'd assumed about him had been correct since his arrival.

"Awfully dull," he repeated.

Sighing, knowing he couldn't just disappear into thin air, she asked, "What would be?"

"Standing in a stall all day, waiting for someone to come along and milk you or feed you or, once in a while, lead you out into the sun."

How he'd known what she had been thinking about made her think of kindred souls, but that couldn't be. Thoughts of animals had simply entered his head when he stepped into the barn, no different than how they'd crossed her mind. "I don't know," she said. "There would be a lot less to worry about."

"It must be like living in a jail cell. Being in a barn all the time. No freedom. No hope. If you ask me, there's a lot to be said between existing and living."

Marina pinched her lips together to ward off the shiver racing up her spine. She hadn't thought much about jail cells but would soon. The only way to save those already imprisoned was to join them, be put before the council. "No one asked you. Nellie certainly didn't. She's not worried about what you think about her barn, either."

"I'd agree with that. Nellie doesn't worry about anything. Unlike you. Tell me. Have you always worried about others?"

Milk had begun to stream into the bucket and she continued a steady rhythm with both hands.

"I've witnessed how you take care of your uncle and Grace, and your worry about John."

She'd witnessed those same things about him but wouldn't admit to that. "I won't deny I care about others," she said. "It's the way I was raised."

"In Maine," he said.

She pinched her lips together. Turning the conversation on her was not her intent. "You'll learn to care about others, too," she said. "Children have a way of making that happen."

"You don't believe I already care about others?"

"I don't know you well enough to know if you do or not."

"But because I didn't give up my life as a sailor to live with my wife and child, you assume so. Isn't that correct?"

It most certainly had been, but he had no way of knowing that. "I'm no one's judge or jury."

"Then you are the only one in this community to think that way," he answered.

"Perhaps," she agreed, switching her hands to begin extracting milk from Nellie's other teats.

"I didn't know much about Puritans before I met Sarah and her family," he said. "I can't say I knew a lot about them afterward, either. I had no intention of getting married when that voyage started, and I'm not proud to admit that I have wished many times it hadn't happened."

Her hands stalled as she turned to look his way, rather shocked a man would admit such a thing. "Then why did you?"

He shrugged. "It just happened."

"Marriage doesn't just happen," she said, turning back to her milking.

"It did in my case," he said. "That's the truth. I'm not a man who lies. I don't like being lied to, either. Nor do I appreciate when someone attempts to pull the wool over my eyes."

The trembling of Marina's hands interrupted her ability to coax milk from Nellie. He may have been speaking of Sarah, but Marina had the distinct sense he was talking about her.

"That happened to me once before," he said. "Sarah and her family, along with several others who boarded my ship, had every intention of arriving in the New World with babies in their bellies."

There wasn't as much anger in his tone as repulsion. Marina let her hands grow idle. "Why?"

"Because the New World was no longer theirs. The utopia they'd created was drawing newcomers of different religions and beliefs far faster than the Puritans could reproduce. I didn't comprehend that at the time, but I do now."

Marina had no difficulty in believing what he said. Puritan girls far younger than her already had two or three children. She also concluded Nellie had given up all the milk she would today. Gathering her bucket, Marina stood and picked up her stool by one leg. Richard stepped aside as she exited the stall.

Once she'd set the stool down in the corner, she turned to face him. Curious, she asked, "Didn't you miss them? Sarah and Grace?"

"It's hard to miss someone you don't know."

"But—"

"Sarah and I barely knew each other when she became pregnant, and I only saw Grace once, when she was a tiny infant. That was when I refused to stay. Sarah's father told me not to return. That I wasn't welcome here—however, they never refused the items I sent."

"What items?"

"Furniture, yard goods, seeds, candles, dishes. Any items I thought they might need. I may have been absent from her life, but I never forgot I was responsible for Grace's livelihood."

Marina wasn't sure how to respond or what to think. Uncle William had never mentioned that Richard had provided for his family from afar. No one had. Not even Anna's mother, who at one time had gossiped about everyone. When Elizabeth had been arrested, Mrs. Pullman vehemently accused others, and soon she was arrested, too. Marina could understand the Goodwife Pullman's behavior. Parents tried to protect their children no matter what. That was how it had been at her house. Right to the death.

The images that formed in her mind had her squeezing her eyes closed.

"Marina?"

She drew in a rattling breath and opened her eyes, hoping to chase aside the memories.

"What is it?" Richard asked.

"Nothing," she said quickly. "Nothing."

He reached out and took the milk bucket in one hand and wrapped the other around her elbow. "Your face is as white as your cap."

Lifting her chin, she swallowed a lump and stepped forward. "I'm fine." It wasn't the past she needed to be frightened of.

Chapter Eight

Marina's gaze slipped past Richard and locked on the open barn door. The dark veil of night was already slipping downward and turning everything a muted gray. She liked having the doors locked and the curtains drawn before night completely fell. Richard's hand remained on her arm, and she made no attempt to pull away. The reassurance she wasn't alone was something she hadn't had in a very long time.

"I've been hoodwinked once, Marina. It will not happen again."

The warning in his voice couldn't be ignored or mistaken. "Who do you believe is attempting to hoodwink you?"

He let out a rather wicked chuckle. "Who other than you, Miss Marina Lindqvist?"

"Me?" Marina stopped in her tracks and, while shaking off his hold, took a step back. "I, Captain Tarr, am not attempting to hoodwink you.

Nor have I done anything that would allow you to assume such a thing. A matter of fact, I've told you exactly what I want, but you didn't listen."

"Ah, yes, for me to leave. That obviously isn't going to happen, so let's forget about that one, shall we?"

No, we shan't, she wanted to shout but bit her tongue instead. The softness that had been in his eyes moments ago completely disappeared.

"Am I supposed to believe you rescued my daughter by proclaiming yourself as a witch, the very thing that others are being hanged for, purely because you care about others?"

Already sorely tempered, Marina let out a tiny growl. Put that way, it did sound a bit improbable. Still, she insisted, "That is the truth."

Richard was tempted to grab her with both hands and give her a good shake. He was tempted to give himself a good kick in the hind end, too. Confessing his regrets about marrying Sarah had not been why he'd followed Marina into the barn. Her uncle may have told him what had been happening around Salem Village, but not a word had been mumbled about Marina or her past. That "bit of a mishap up in Maine" William had mentioned earlier today stuck with him. Richard wanted to know exactly what that mishap had been. Leveling his eyes with ones that still held the shimmer of fear, he asked, "I'm supposed to believe that is the only reason you were willing to sacrifice your own life for that of my child?"

The way her entire frame drooped said he'd hit a nerve. As gallantly as a king's soldier, she once again lifted her chin and squared her shoulders. "No. You're correct, Captain. There is something else I was hoping to gain from you."

Taken aback, for he hadn't expected it to be that easy, it was a moment before he asked, "Which is?"

She gnawed on her bottom lip so hard he could expect to see blood at any moment.

He set the milk pail down. "Money?" He should have thought of that earlier.

"No," she said. "I have no need for money."

That he did believe.

Glancing toward the open door, she said, "The beans need to be stirred down and Gracie fed. After we eat, we'll talk."

Richard shook his head.

"Please," she said despondently. "It will be dark soon."

"And you are afraid of the dark?"

"Everyone here is afraid of the dark."

Her whisper went through him with the swiftness of a pirate's sword. Terror had returned to her eyes, and though it went against his better judgment, he didn't like it. Didn't like knowing she was scared. He didn't like not knowing what she was so frightened of, either.

"I won't let anyone hurt you," he said. "I swear."

She shook her head. "It's not me I'm afraid of getting hurt."

"Then who?"

"Gracie—" she bowed her head "—and you and Uncle William and John."

Lifting her chin, he said, "Look at me, Marina. I assure you, I haven't been hurt in a very long time. You don't have to worry about that. When I vow my protection to someone, I give it. Completely. No one in this household will be hurt as long as I'm here."

The tender smile that appeared on her lips was so endearing his heart almost stopped beating.

"I believe you believe that," she said softly.

The desire to step forward and press his lips against hers hit him like a gale wind. Carnal actions had come close to ruining his life once. He'd learned to control them since then. Or so he thought. Marina had gotten under his skin and was stirring up things that should not be stirred.

"Please," she repeated. "We must go inside."

Frustration rumbled inside him. "As soon as we are done eating, we'll talk?"

She nodded and bolted toward the door. While crossing the threshold, she said, "And the kitchen is cleaned and Gracie is put to bed."

In the moment it took him to close the barn door, Richard surmised he'd just been hood-winked. It was in a small way but significant nonetheless. Catching up with Marina before she reached the house, he said, "I will put Gracie to bed."

Richard had every intention of following through on putting his daughter to bed, but they were still eating when someone started pounding on the front door.

The box Gracie sat upon clattered against the floor as she leaped from her chair onto Marina's lap. Richard also took note of the searing look that crossed between Marina and William.

"I'll see who it is," the old man said.

Richard pushed away from the table. "I'll go with you." His gaze bounced to Marina, who was whispering into Gracie's ear and rubbing the child's trembling shoulders. She didn't say anything, didn't need to. The fear in her eyes said enough.

By the time he'd followed William down the hall and across the room, Richard's frustration was boiling as hot as his anger. The persistent pounding had grown louder and had become con-tinuous by the time William stopped to light a candle on the table beside the door. As soon as the wick flickered and caught the flame, Richard stepped around the man and pulled open the door.

William's shout of "State your business" was lost among louder voices.

"That's him! Restrain that man!"

Richard didn't need the evening light to recognize Hickman. He'd instinctively known who it was when the pounding had started, and the opportunity to release some of his pent-up fury greeted him like a long-lost friend.

"Arrest her, too!"

Richard paused in stepping off the stoop to glance to his side. Sure enough, Marina stood there. How did she show up out of thin air like that?

A man stepping forward, arm out, caught his attention. "Touch her and it's the last person you'll ever touch," Richard warned.

The man slowed his approach until Hickman yelled for arrests again. As the man reached for Marina, Richard bounded off the stoop and grabbed him by the front of his shirt. "I warned you."

Holding the man's shirt with one hand, he planted his other fist directly in the man's face. As the man hit the ground, Richard said, "Get inside, Marina."

Without checking to see if she obeyed or so much as glancing to see if the first man stayed down, he balled his fist again to give a second man coming at him from the right a solid punch. Richard's knuckles burned as that man went down. He ignored the sting and continued a steady pace forward, never taking his eyes off Hickman.

"Get him!" Hickman shouted. "Get him!"

Richard grinned as a third man approached. He wished the men were more like the seashore ruffians he encountered regularly. At the moment, a brawl that would have them all bleeding yet coming back for more was his greatest desire. He wanted Hickman to know he wasn't dealing with a simpleton afraid of hell and brimstone, but a man who wouldn't tolerate his family being wronged.

Richard snapped his fist into the face of the third, a bit disappointed when that man hit the ground without taking a punch at him.

For every step he took forward, Hickman took one back. The fourth man who had accompanied the preacher on his late-night visit was already heading up the road. "You wanted to see me, George?" Richard asked, holding his hands out to his sides. "I'm right here."

"Get up," Hickman shouted at the men. "Arrest this man!"

The men got up but made a wide circle around him as they scurried to follow their other companion up the road.

"Looks like it's just you and me, George,"

Richard said. "Your companions have abandoned you. All four of them. I guess they don't mind as well when you aren't whipping them bloody." Recalling how the man had always taken pride in having a big black man driving him around in Barbados, Richard glanced toward the coach harnessed to a set of horses. "It appears you don't even have a driver. Don't tell me you've learned how to drive a coach?"

"Of course I know how to drive a coach," Hickman spouted, his nostrils flaring as he stomped toward the enclosed carriage. "This isn't over, Tarr. You're the devil, a poison. I won't have you infesting the good people of this village."

There were a dozen responses floating about in Richard's mind, as was the urge to stop Hickman from boarding the carriage, but Richard let the desire fade away. A dark road in the middle of nowhere wasn't the place. He wanted to see the man publicly humiliated. "I'd say this village has already been infested. Contaminated by greed. And you."

"Your lies won't work here," Hickman said, climbing onto the driver's seat.

"Lies? Who have I lied to?"

Hickman's response was to wave a fist in the air as he slapped the reins over the horses.

Richard waited until the man steered the horses around and started up the road before he turned to make his way back to the house. William stood in the doorway, his flickering candle in hand.

"I've never seen that before," John said, peering over William's shoulder.

"What?" Richard asked. "A coward fleeing?"

"No," John answered. "Someone taking arms against a man of the church."

William shook his head. "The Puritans claim they don't believe in violence."

Richard paused long enough for the other two to step inside before he entered and closed the door behind him. "Yet they hang innocent people."

In the silence that followed, Richard regretted his reply. John didn't need a reminder, nor did William. Although he attempted to conceal them, thoughts weighed heavy on the old man, and Richard knew they were directly related to Marina.

"They'll be back," William said as he crossed the room, heading for his chair.

Richard made no reply. He didn't plan on giving Hickman a chance on returning, but the confrontation would take place when and where Richard chose, where his family wouldn't be in jeopardy.

Finding the kitchen empty, Richard turned about.

"Marina took Gracie upstairs," John said. "Do ye want me to get her?"

"No," Richard said, his eyes settling on the meal that had been so crudely interrupted. "But you can clean up the kitchen."

The stairway was dark, as was the upstairs hall. No light shone beneath any of the four doors, but memory, as well as a gentle tune, told him which room held Marina and Gracie. Music was a rare thing on the ocean, other than the sweet songs nature sang, and he may never have heard a more perfect melody than the one currently filtering the air. It made him want to close his eyes and just listen to the blissful notes. A response as that had never created itself inside him before. That thought, in addition to the spellbinding tune, made him almost crack a smile.

Some claimed a witch's call could be disguised as many things and did strange things to a person. He shook his head at how his own mind was trying to convince him Marina was a witch. Then again, maybe it was her working so hard to convince him.

Richard grasped the knob and turned the handle slowly to not interrupt the song. Marina turned his way but never stopped singing. Her gaze returned to Gracie, who was tucked beneath the covers. She too turned to look at him with sleepy eyes and a dreamy smile.

He crossed the room and went to the opposite side of the bed, where he knelt down and placed a gentle hand on his daughter's forehead. "Good night, Grace."

Her smile never faded as she closed her eyes to drift off into dreamland as peacefully as anyone he'd ever seen. Marina continued singing, her voice growing softer and softer until it was little more than a whisper. With the last note still floating on the air, she leaned down and kissed Gracie's forehead.

Neither of them said a word as she picked up the candle and stood. Richard followed her across the room and into the hall, pulling the door closed.

"They are gone, I presume?"

"Did you expect elsewise?"

In the golden glow of the candle flame her features were intensified. The light made her skin shimmer and her lashes longer and darker. The blue of her eyes was deeper, too, drawing him in and leaving no room for him to think of anything other than her beauty. How was it possible for this woman to affect him the ways she did? He encountered women around the world. There had to have been others more beautiful, yet, at this moment, he couldn't remember one. He couldn't remember one who had intrigued him so acutely. It almost was if she had the ability to erase certain parts of his memory, implanting thoughts of her in their places.

A tiny smile tugged at the corners of her lips,

as if she knew his very thoughts, which sent a fiery chill as cold as it was hot shooting through him. He pulled his gaze off her and fought a few other internal reactions.

"I'm not sure what to expect anymore," she said quietly.

Although he could relate to that, Richard made no comment as he reached for the candle to carry as they walked down the hall. She caught his hand with her free one as soon as the light of the flame settled upon his knuckles.

"You're bleeding."

His hand no longer stung and there wasn't enough blood to pay it any attention. He'd had far worse battle wounds and most likely would again. "I may have knocked someone's tooth loose."

"Oh, dear," she said and sighed.

"I'm sure he'll be fine."

"It's not him I'm concerned about," she said heavily while letting go of his hand. "Follow me. I'll put a bandage on that."

She hadn't said it was him she was worried about, but his heart skipped a beat at the idea. "I don't need a bandage." He didn't want her worried about him, but in an odd sense, it warmed his insides like nothing else ever had.

"Possibly not," she said. "But I don't want to have to wash blood out of sheets tomorrow."

She was a witty one and knew exactly what

he'd thought. "I'll wash before I retire," he said, while taking a hold of her elbow. "Right now, you are going to tell me what it is you want from me. Things have gotten too dangerous."

Marina braced herself for the onslaught. Each time he was near or touched her, no matter how briefly, her insides caught fire as if there was a tiny wick inside her and he a flint. It had grown stronger all day, and a moment ago, while staring up at him in the darkened hallway, she'd discovered why. She was full of admiration for this frank and courageous man. He appeared to be a bit untamed and dangerous, and the men who had just left probably thought he was a living relative of the devil himself. She'd witnessed how anger turned his eyes a perilous shade of amber, and she could only imagine in the evening darkness their glow had confirmed the other men's beliefs.

She knew differently. A man could talk for hours, demanding things or singing his own praises, but words meant nothing compared to deeds. The tenderness Richard bestowed upon Gracie, the respect he displayed to Uncle William, and the friendship and protection he'd so readily granted John told her the kind of man he was inside. That was what affected her. She'd missed the strong and powerful men she'd known all of her life. Missed how wonderful it had been to feel safe and protected, and the idea of being shrouded by such comforts was something she couldn't deny she secretly longed to have again.

Knowing Grace and, perhaps, Uncle William would have those comforts was the most she could hope for, and that should be enough, but it wasn't.

Marina shook her head at the thought and told herself he was right—things had gotten too dangerous. Not wanting Uncle William to hear, she turned to open the door across the hall from where Grace slept.

The past few days, she'd sat in this room, sewing clothing for Gracie while being close enough at hand to respond to the child's softest whimpers. Although she'd been extremely worried about the little girl, she'd relished each minute. The days caring for Gracie would be the closest she'd ever have to being a mother, and as much as she knew they had to, she didn't want them to end.

Another trait of being a witch. Selfishness.

Marina sucked in a breath against how badly her heart ached, knowing there wasn't anything she could do about it. As Richard followed her into the room, she held out a hand. "May I?"

He handed her the candle. She used it to light several others that sat upon the long table she'd used to lay out material and cut it into pieces before sitting in the nearby chair to stitch the sections together. The remnants of that work, as well as another partially sewn dress, still covered the table.

"For Grace?" Richard asked.

"Yes." Marina made no effort to explain the condition of Gracie's clothes when she had brought her home. There was no need. He was an intelligent man and had already comprehended such things.

"Where did you get the material?"

"Uncle William has a large supply of yard goods," she told him. "From his sailing days, along with other items I used to take to the marketplace to exchange for things we needed."

"Used to?"

"Before I had the opportunity to plant our own garden and buy a cow. I purchased Nellie, as well as the chickens, from John's family." Recalling the bare cupboards upon her arrival, a smile overtook her lips. "I honestly don't know what Uncle William ate before my arrival."

"Sailors are a hearty lot," he said. "They can survive on most anything."

"I discovered that. He had a large barrel of salted fish when I arrived, which I fed to the birds and hoped it didn't kill them."

His chuckle lightened her heart at the same time it increased the ache. She wished she could laugh again, freely, happily, if even for a short time.

Envy. Another trait.

"How did you come to live with William?"

Marina swallowed. She'd recalled the event often enough that pain no longer seared her throat, but it would forever remain inside her. Dissecting how the devastation of her village came about helped. Perhaps because when she did that, she didn't have to take responsibility. That too, blaming others, had to be the witch inside her.

"The fur trade in Maine was prosperous for many, including my family. My father and brothers had several fishing boats and did a great deal of trading fish for furs with the Iroquois League." Her knees began to wobble at the memory of the home that had been so full of love and laughter, and she lowered herself onto a chair before continuing, "There are several bands within the league, some friendlier than others. My brother Ole married a Mohawk woman, Nessa."

The tightening of her chest stole her breath and pulled her brows into a tight knot at the thought of little Gunther, Ole and Nessa's baby. He'd been only three, but so smart Ole had already started taking him on the fishing boats. If only they'd been fishing that night, but the storm had kept them off the water.

"What happened?"

Attempting to remove herself from the explanation, she said, "The battle between the French and the English for control of the fur trade. At least, that was the basis." She took a breath to disguise the pain. "A band of marauding Indians aligned with whichever side had promised them the most attacked our village."

"Your family?"

"Were all killed," she answered. "Everyone."

"Except you."

That part of her story was not open for discussion. "A short time later, a ship captained by a friend of Uncle William and my father arrived in the bay and brought me here." Captain Farleigh had done more than that; he'd saved her life. Was that why she found herself liking Richard more each hour? All the sea captains she'd known had been likable. Honorable, too, and caring.

He'd taken a seat in the adjacent chair and the wood creaked as he shifted his weight. She kept her gaze from meeting his and forced her breathing to remain even. Whether she liked him or not didn't matter, but the fact he was honorable and caring did.

"And that brings me to what I need from you, Captain."

The room remained silent, even after he stated, "Richard."

Why he was so insistent upon being called "Richard" instead of "Captain" was of little concern, other than that she'd prefer to call him "Captain." It seemed to provide her an inner barrier. One she needed.

Suddenly realizing her lungs were on fire, she emptied them. "Richard," she repeated for his benefit only. "My uncle's health is failing and I'd like you to take him with you when you leave."

"Your uncle is old."

"I know his age," she said, "but he's grown breathless lately and forgetful. I understand such things happen when people grow older, but I also know he's not happy here. He does little except sit in the chair, longing for the sea. A sailor yourself, surely you can understand that."

A certain level of compassion was included in his single nod. It was the doubt she also noted in his eyes that concerned her. He was a smart man and she had to be just as wise in order for him not to see other things. The care he bestowed upon others could include her, too. If things were different, if she was different, she'd cherish that. Any woman would. They'd cherish his handsomeness, too, and his strength and protection, and—

"Why haven't you contacted one of his sailing friends? He has several. I can assure you of that."

Pulling her mind back in line, she said, "I've suggested that, but he feels responsible for me and claims there is no place for a woman at sea. He also refuses to leave me alone."

"What makes you think he'll leave with me?"

She released the air out of her lungs as slowly as possible, using the time to form an answer. Unfortunately, that didn't happen. "I don't," she answered honestly. "But I do trust that you could convince him. Make him believe you need his assistance on your ship."

"Why would I do that?"

Marina ignored how the candlelight softened his features, making him look nothing like the man who'd scared the wits from her mind when she'd opened the door this morning, and she used the only leverage she had. "Because I rescued your daughter, I'd like the same in return. For you to rescue my uncle. Save his life. For he will die if he remains here."

He frowned. "You expect me to believe you saved Gracie because you were looking for a way to get William back on the water?"

The urge to swallow burned, but she refused even her throat muscles to move as she kept her stare locked with his. Skepticism was evident in his expression. The only hope she had was to stand her ground. That grew harder as her throat started to lock up, trapping air in her lungs.

When Richard was the first to look away, she almost coughed at how swiftly the air rushed out of her lungs. His eyes were back on her instantly, and the makings of a grin sitting on the edges of his lips made her cheeks burn.

He stood. "I've admitted I'm indebted to you." Once again he touched the dress on the table. "And, no doubt, your uncle, as well."

She stood and bowed her head. "Thank you, Richard."

The heat of the finger touching the underside of her chin sent shivers down her neck. With slight pressure, he lifted her chin. She had no idea why. Their conversation was over.

"I didn't say yes, Marina."

In that instant she understood an intimacy unbeknownst in her life so far. The way he said her name reminded her of how Ole had said "Nessa," how Hans had said Rachel's name and how her father had said her mother's name. Her mouth had gone dry and she licked her lips. At one time she'd imagined she'd hear a man say her name like that, with a whisper that left her ears ringing. A man who would love her and protect her and provide her with children to love. The fact none of that could ever be made her throat burn all over again.

"But I will think about it."

It took her a moment to comprehend what he'd said. "Think about it? You just—"

"Said I'd think about it."

The way his finger slid back toward her throat and then down her neck, stopping just above her collar, made responding impossible. He leaned forward and she started to tremble on the inside, having no idea what he was about to do.

When his chin was near her ear, he said, "I suggest you think about something, too."

He was too close for her to think about anything except the way her heart thudded.

"Next time," he said softly, "I suggest you tell me the truth."

Chapter Nine

Richard left Marina standing where she was and walked out the door before he let the air escape from his lungs. He should be mad, furious that she continued to withhold the truth from him, but excitement hummed through his veins. She was one beautiful woman.

Sitting in the dark, with the candlelight glistening on her golden curls, had stolen his ability to think, at least with a clear head. His thoughts had been floating in more directions than a ship without a sail. That had never happened before. He must be under some sort of spell.

Richard shook his head to gather his senses. Or knock loose other thoughts. Those of kissing her.

He huffed out a breath.

Indian attacks were not unusual. The war over the fur trade had cost many lives and created many enemies, but there was more to her story than she'd shared. He'd have to be a simpleton to believe the only reason she'd rescued Gracie was so William could sail again. He was thankful for what she'd done and would repay her, but he still wanted to know why she'd done it.

"Richard."

He twisted and watched the single flame coming down the hallway. A footstep before she was at his side, and then he said, "I won't have the wool pulled over my eyes again. It would benefit you to remember that."

He may not have noticed her slight stumble if the candle flame hadn't flickered. He also fought a grin at how she pretended it hadn't happened and took another step to brush past him. She also pinched her lips together and lifted her chin into the defiant little tilt he admired so much.

Without a word, she marched down the steps.

The darkness would hide a grin, so he released it.

John was in the front room, and he bounded from one of the chairs. "William turned in for the night."

With all the curtains pulled there wasn't so much as a sliver of moonlight to assist the beeswax candles in lighting the room. The torches on the ships provided light for men to play cards or games or, as he himself liked to do on quiet evenings, read. "It's too dark for anything else," Richard stated, although he was far from tired.

A soft clatter echoed from down the hallway. "I cleaned the kitchen," John said. "Like ye asked."

"I've no doubt you did," he answered. "Marina's probably getting things laid out for tomorrow." She certainly wasn't an idle woman, or like any other woman he'd met, in several ways, including her stubbornness. He admired that about her yet had a strong inclination that it could be her downfall. "I'm going to take a stroll outside before turning in."

"I'll join ye," John said.

Richard understood why. He'd never met a man who appreciated a chamber pot. They exited through the front door. Although clouds floated in front of the large, yellow full moon, it was far brighter outside than indoors. While John walked around the house to where the outhouse sat beyond the barn near the edge of the brush, Richard went in the other direction, where trees lined the road. He spent several minutes examining the road for places one of Hickman's men could have hidden. That was doubtful. He imagined they hadn't stopped running until reaching the village, but there was satisfaction in checking to make sure.

Night sounds on land were far different from those on the sea, and he gave himself time to listen long enough to recognize the swish of the wind rustling the leaves, the hushed clatter of nighttime critters scurrying about and the silence itself before he turned around to make his way back into the yard to check for stalkers.

From the corner of the house, he watched John enter the back door and heard Marina's soft voice greet him. Something inside him froze. Was that why she wanted him to leave so badly and take William with him—so she could marry John? Had William forbade the union?

A thud behind the barn pulled his attention off the door. Instincts told him it wasn't an animal—not one with four legs, anyway. Cautious, he slowly made his way in that direction, but his thoughts were still on Marina. John was too young to handle a woman like her. She was too willful, too stubborn.

The snap of a twig coming from the side of the barn had him easing his way to the corner. Staying well within the shadows, he peered around the edge.

A dark figure wearing a caped overcoat was stealthily making its way to the outhouse. The long but cautious strides said the intruder was a man, and his black clothing said he was up to no good. Richard took a step, ready to call the man out, when the stranger lifted a hand and knocked on the side of the outhouse.

"John-boy, ye still in there?" The man's whisper was raspy and rushed. "It's Oscar Pullman. I've come for ye, boy."

Richard stepped around the barn. "Why?"

Terror flashed across the man's face before he ran for the woods.

Richard took chase, entering the tree line on the man's heels. Not wanting to lose the stranger in the wooded area, he doubled his speed. The man was just out of reach, and determined to stop him, Richard dived forward, grabbing the man's cloak as they both fell to the ground.

The heel of a boot jammed into his chest, knocking the air out of him. That angered him more than it pained him. Wheezing to get air into his lungs, Richard pushed himself off the ground and grabbed the man by his shoulders, flipping him onto his back.

Guarding his face with both hands, the man pleaded, "Please, I have no grievance with ye, sir."

"Who sent you?" Richard demanded, although he had a good idea.

"No one, Captain," the man muttered, keeping his voice low. "I swear. No one knows I'm here."

"Then why are you here?"

"F-for John. He and I have a deed to do. Ask him."

He would, and he'd ask Marina if this man was the reason she wanted to get rid of her uncle. Richard pulled the man off the ground. The long coat made him look larger. In reality he was as scrawny as a pigeon. "What deed?"

The man shook his head.

In no mood for patience, Richard dug his fingers into the man's lapels and dragged him to the edge of the woods, where the moonlight wasn't filtered by the trees. It would do the stranger good to see his face, to know he was as serious as a shark smelling blood.

"Please, Captain. I can't be seen. Please."

Near the edge of the trees, Richard paused to ask, "By whom?"

"Anyone."

Moonlight shone on the stranger's face, and Richard established this man was too old for Marina. "What deed?" he asked one more time. "Tell me."

"To retrieve the bodies of our dead." The man's head fell forward until his chin nearly hit his chest. "My eldest daughter. They hanged her in Salem Towne today. Along with John's mother."

Richard released his hold and took a step back. "Retrieve the bodies?"

"Aye, Captain. John heard me tell me other daughter I would bring our Elizabeth home and asked if he could come with me. To get his mama." The man wheezed heavily and swallowed hard. "Please, I can't stand the thought of my sweet baby being pushed over the edge of that hill, down onto the rocks."

* * *

An unfamiliar sound, or at least one she didn't expect, met Marina as she entered her bedroom. She'd shown John to a room down the hall but knew the voice she heard wasn't his. It was too deep. On her toes, she crossed the room to the open window.

The soft murmurs came from two voices. Richard's tall form stood just inside the trees beyond the outhouse, but the barn hid whoever was conversing with him.

Fear rippled her shoulders and she scanned the entire yard, looking for others. There were none that she could see.

The men slipped into the brush and Marina wasted no time in rushing across the room and grabbing her black wool cloak from the hook on the wall. Richard hadn't been struggling, but the other person could have a weapon.

In the kitchen, she grabbed the poker leaning against the hearth. Quickly but quietly she left the house, flipping up her hood as soon as she'd closed the door behind her.

There was no way to know who else might be lurking about, so she pretended to be making her way to the outhouse, but upon entering the shadow cast by the barn, she scurried toward the woods.

Once among the trees, she grasped a hold of a branch and paused to listen. The pounding of her heart was loud, but beyond that, nothing but silence.

There wasn't a trail on this side of the property. Not like the one on the other side that led to a few of the other farms outlining Salem Village, but instinct said the men had continued this way. Zigzagging around trees, branches and fallen logs rotting on the ground, she kept pausing to catch her bearings and to listen. Why wasn't Richard fighting like he had earlier? He wouldn't willingly go along with one of Hickman's henchmen. Unless he wanted to get arrested. That made no sense. He cared too much about Gracie to put himself in danger. Unless he didn't believe he was in danger. He certainly acted fearless, but that didn't make him immortal. No one was immortal. Not even witches.

The fears inside her doubled. Holding the poker out, she increased her speed.

As she entered the swamp left from when the spring rains had flooded the river, muck squished beneath her feet. The trees became spindly and sparse, leaving her more exposed if anyone was watching, yet she continued forward, even as the muck made lifting her feet close to impossible.

A splash caught her attention. The reeds were

almost as tall as she. Trudging forward, she eventually arrived at a large rock. Climbing upon it with wet soles proved difficult and she felt a sense of accomplishment when she finally managed to scale the top. There, on her hands and knees, afraid she'd fall if she attempted to stand, she stretched her neck to see over the reeds.

A man sat in a small boat. One man. Clearly not Richard. This man wore a caped cloak and could be any one of the men from the village.

Stretching as far upward as she dared, Marina scanned the area. The scream that bubbled in her throat was stopped by the hand that slapped over her mouth at the same time a solid arm wrapped around her waist, pulling her off the rock.

"What do you think you're doing?" Richard whispered.

Thankful in more ways than one, Marina slumped against him for a brief moment. Until ire filled her. Grabbing his hand, she pulled it off her mouth. "What are you doing out here? Who are you with?"

He set her down and picked up the poker—which she hadn't realized she'd dropped—from where it was stuck in the muck near his feet. "I asked first." He grabbed her arm and spun her around. "Come on."

"Where are we going?"

"Home."

She tried to follow, but her feet wouldn't budge. "Who is that man?"

Richard didn't answer but did notice she was stuck. With great ease, he lifted her out of the muck. The mud had released her, but he didn't. He carried her all the way to solid ground. If her heart hadn't leaped into her throat, she might have told him to put her down. Then again, maybe not. She almost grinned at that thought. For once, a witch's way of thinking wasn't so bad.

Once he set her down, it took her a moment to get her heart and thinking in order before she could ask again, "Who's that man in the boat?"

"Who is watching Grace?" he asked. "Did you lock the door behind you? Or did you leave the house open for anyone to enter?"

Marina flinched. In her rush she hadn't considered that.

"John is exhausted and probably sound asleep," Richard said, propelling her forward through the trees. "And William is half-deaf. Anyone could enter the house."

Her heart started racing all over again, this time with genuine fear. She increased her speed, pushing aside brush and ducking beneath branches.

"Slow down before you fall and break your neck."

"We must hurry," she said. "I left so fast I didn't think about leaving the house unlocked."

"Why'd you follow me?"

Focused on moving forward, she answered, "I thought they were arresting you."

"And you thought you'd rescue me with a fireplace poker?"

The trek back seemed much shorter, for her next step led her out of the woods behind the barn. Rushing around it, she let out a sigh of relief to see the house dark and quiet and the back door shut. That wasn't proof no one had entered, but it was a welcome sign, hopefully indicating nothing had happened during her absence.

Richard took a hold of her arm again and led the way across the yard. "You are just brave enough to be dangerous. Do you know that?"

Marina clenched her teeth to keep from responding.

"Or foolish enough."

"I thought you were in danger," she pointed out.

"Even if I was, I wouldn't want you coming to my rescue."

"You'd rather die?"

He wrenched open the door and thrust her over the threshold. "I'd rather take care of myself than worry about you."

"There was no reason to worry about me," she said, spinning around and grabbing the poker from his hand.

"You were perched on that rock like a mermaid."

"I was trying to see who you were with."

"While being wide-open for anyone else to see."

"I'm dressed in black," she pointed out needlessly.

"Your hood had fallen down and your hair shone brighter than the moon on water."

Marina crossed the room to replace the poker. Arguing with him was worse than arguing with her brothers. Truly not worth the breath it took. "What were you doing out there?"

"That is no business of yours," he said, turning back to the door. "Lock this behind me and don't leave this house again."

"You can't—"

"I'll make sure she doesn't leave."

Marina spun toward Uncle William's voice coming from the hallway.

"Me, too," John said, poking his head around William's shoulder.

She should be happy both of them were awake and would have heard any intruders, but that didn't excuse her carelessness in the first place.

Richard pulled open the door. "I'll be back shortly," he said, looking directly at her. "Lock the door and then go to bed."

The darkness swallowed him up before the door closed, and she turned to her uncle and

John, waiting for one of them to ask where he was going. Neither man spoke as William crossed the room and locked the door.

"You heard the captain," he said. "Go to bed."

Marina sat down on the closest chair. "I need to remove my boots," she said. "They are covered in mud."

John pulled another chair away from the table and carried it to the door. "I'll stay here until Richard returns."

It was clear neither of them were going to speculate where Richard had gone, but they were set on preventing her from following again, which irritated her more. Unless, of course, they already knew. "Where is he going?" she asked, while unfastening her boots.

Neither man answered.

"Do either of you know?" When silence was her only answer, she asked, "Don't you want to know? What if—"

"If he'd wanted us to know, he would have told us," Uncle William said. "He knows what he's doing. Rest assured of that, child."

She wouldn't rest assured of anything. "What if he's arrested?"

"It'll take bolder men than those living in either Salem Village or Towne to arrest him," Uncle William said. "Now do as he said. Off to bed with you."

Fully aware she'd get nowhere in questioning her uncle, Marina set her wet shoes near the kitchen fireplace and hung her cloak on the spoon hook for the bottom to dry. Before going upstairs, she poured a glass of milk for Grace to drink if she awoke during the night. In truth, she was waiting, hoping…for what? She had no idea. But she was worried about Richard. He may be big and strong, but her brothers had been, too.

"Good night, Marina," her uncle said.

She nodded his way and at John and left the room.

In her room she undressed and donned a nightgown, but rather than crawl between the covers next to Gracie, she went to the chair in the corner. Where could he have gone? He didn't seem frightened, but he was in a hurry. She squeezed her eyes shut. Where were her visions when she needed them?

Pictures formed, and they made her heart race, but they were of Richard laughing, teasing Gracie and kneeling before her and whispering her name.

She wrenched open her eyes and rubbed at her temples before trying to force a different vision of where he'd gone and why. It was to no avail, and she finally gave up.

Feeling deflated, she recited a nighttime prayer embedded from her childhood, which gave thanks for the day and asked for blessings upon the morrow. Witch or not, there were parts of her old life she couldn't relinquish. Call it stubbornness, call it hope, it made no difference.

She was tempted to once again ask why she'd been inflicted with such a curse. Why her. She'd already done that numerous times in the past and now understood her mission, but she wanted to know why she'd been turned into a witch.

If others knew the turmoil of truly being a witch, there'd be no fear. Witches had no power to inflict ill will upon others. The curses were all on the witches themselves and, unfortunately, those closest to them.

She'd already lost everything—her family, her home—and now would again. That was why she wanted answers. Why did she have to be so cursed? Why did she have to lose those she'd come to love a second time? Uncle William needed her. So did Gracie.

A heavy sigh pressed upon her lungs. No, they didn't need her. They had Richard now, and he would take care of both of them. John, too. He hadn't said he would, but he would. He was too honorable not to, and as much as it shouldn't, that saddened her.

That had to be the witch in her again. No one should feel sad knowing their loved ones would be well taken care of.

Anger began to rise over her sadness. Nothing

had prepared her for such an existence. No yellow bird had sat upon her shoulder. No red cats had appeared in her barnyard and no black man had forced her to sign a book. Yet from the moment she'd awakened in Arlyce Hanson's home, she'd felt different inside. Cold. Dead.

She'd been shocked and confused when people first claimed she was a witch but couldn't deny their claims that she'd been dead. She had died, along with her entire family. She'd wanted to be dead again at that time, which very well would have happened if Arlyce hadn't taken her back to her parents' house and if Captain Farleigh hadn't arrived shortly afterward, insistent upon bringing her here, to Uncle William.

Marina pressed her fingertips against her eyes to ease the burning. Leaving the only home she'd ever known had been hard, but being persecuted by people she'd known her entire life had been beyond frightening. The few who'd survived the Indian attack were certain the savages would return to kill her a second time and were willing to save the Indians the trip.

Uncle William hadn't heard about the massacre before she'd arrived. Her letter to him didn't arrive until months later, but Captain Farleigh heard about it as soon as his ship docked, and he'd wasted no time in collecting her and setting sail south. He didn't believe she was a witch, and neither did Uncle William. He proclaimed she'd triumphed over evil and would do so again.

Those were the words that made her deeply examine what had happened to her, and that led her to scrutinize rather than simply read the scriptures that had become her salvation. More and more dreams came true after that. Little ones at first, like forgotten recipes or where Uncle William had left something, but then smallpox entered the village and the dreams told her the epidemic would be widespread. She'd tried to warn people. Told them to stay home to stop the epidemic from spreading, but they'd claimed she was trying to stop them from going to church, something good Puritans never missed, no matter how ill they were.

Turning in the direction of the open window, fury arose inside her. She was a witch all right and wished she had the ability to cast spells. She'd set one upon Richard. The changes inside her had gotten stronger since he'd arrived, and her thoughts were no longer her own. Too many of them had been focused on him today. Rightfully so. He'd opposed her from the moment he'd arrived. Why, then, was she so worried about him?

She leaned her head back and stared up at the ceiling. When she'd woken up in Maine, her fate had been sealed, her very life no longer hers, and perhaps if she hadn't been so stubborn in accepting it, things would be different now. There was nothing she could do about that. Until she'd rescued Gracie, held that tiny body in her arms, the possibilities of what she could do hadn't been clear. The desire to carry out what had been asked of her hadn't filled her until she'd seen the evil in Hickman's eyes. That was when it all became clear. She'd gladly be put before the council, just as the scriptures proclaimed, and the words would come to her, just as God promised.

He'd used her to reunite Richard and Gracie and, in that action, assured an escape for Uncle William and now John. He would not forsake her now.

Marina's gaze returned to Gracie, and a smile formed. Neither would Richard. He'd let no harm come to his daughter ever again, and that filled her heart.

Her eyelids grew heavy, and for the first time in a very, very long time, she didn't fight sleep. The contentment filling her said there would be no violent and repulsive dreams tonight.

When she opened her lids, the hazy light of dawn breaking danced upon the ceiling. Marina sighed at the sight before she slowly turned her head.

Peaceful and serene, Gracie slept beside her.

Tenderness filled Marina, until she remembered falling to sleep in the chair. She'd dreamed about being lifted out of the chair and laid upon the bed. She hadn't struggled or fought, perhaps because she'd known the arms holding her had been too strong for her to overcome. In the next moment, Marina recalled the phantom in her dream. The arms that had carried her to the bed had been the same ones that had carried her out of the swamp.

She pressed a hand to her chest, where her heart had started to pound. Needing to know if Richard truly had returned unscathed had her climbing out of the bed.

Quiet and quick, she dressed and left the room. The early-morning light hadn't completely lifted the cloak of darkness and the house was completely silent. Not even the floorboards beneath her feet creaked as she made her way downstairs. However, she didn't need light or sound to perceive the presence of another, and the quickening of her heart told her exactly who was in the kitchen.

He turned from where he stood near the fireplace as she entered the room. As angry as she'd been at him last night, she shouldn't be excited to see him this morning. But she was. Very excited. Which made sense. The reason she'd gone after him last night was to keep him from being arrested or worse. Realizing she was justifying things to herself, she huffed out a breath and moved forward.

"Good morning," he said.

She might be happy to see him, but she still wanted to know where he'd gone. However, she knew him well enough to know asking wouldn't achieve any more success now than it had last night. "Good morning."

He waved toward the hearth. "I scraped the mud off your shoes."

She chose not to point out they'd gotten muddy because of him. "Thank you. That was kind of you."

"I am a kind person."

She huffed.

He laughed.

Withholding a grin, she sat down to put on her shoes. "Are you always this cheerful in the morning?"

He walked to the window. "Of course. It's a new day with new possibilities. Watching the sun rise is one of my favorite things." Holding aside the curtain, he shook his head. "But that's impossible to do here with all the trees."

She couldn't stop how her heart skipped a beat. "In Maine the sun came up over the ocean. My father and I would stand on the front porch and watch it together."

"You must miss that."

"I do," she admitted. "And him. Fathers are special people."

"I wouldn't know about that," he said, turning from the window. "I never knew my father."

A pang crossed her chest for his loss. "Nonetheless, you soon will know," she said. "You are a father, and Grace loves you dearly."

"She barely knows me."

Marina grinned. "That is the wonderful thing about families. You don't need to know them in order to love them. I didn't know Uncle William, hardly remembered him before coming to live here, but I love him dearly now."

He stared at her thoughtfully for several long minutes before a grin overtook his face. "I see you are no worse for wear after spending half the night in the chair."

Her heart practically beat itself right out of her chest and continued thumping wildly as he walked around the table. Marina spun in order to keep an eye on him. "Nor you for spending half the night in the swamp."

"I've spent nights in worse places." He picked up the milk bucket and opened the door. "I'll see to the morning chores."

Marina jumped to her feet and was out the door before he had a chance to close it. "Where did you go last night?"

"There was a task that needed to be done."

"Only tasks of no good are completed in the dark of night," she said to his back.

"That's true." He stopped near the well. "I'll bring in the milk and eggs when I've finished."

No one had ever irritated her as deeply as he did. Shooting him a glare, she dropped the water bucket into the well. "I'm perfectly capable of completing the chores." When the bucket splashed into the water, she grasped the rope to pull it up. "What I need from you is the truth. Where did you go last night and with whom?"

His grin was as mocking as storm clouds that never produced rain. If the water bucket had been already in her hands, she may have dumped it on him.

"It's frustrating, isn't it?" He grasped the rope beneath her hold and hoisted up the water bucket. "When you want someone to tell you the truth and they don't."

"I told you the truth." Once he'd emptied the bucket into the one on the ground, she picked it up. "And I can do the chores myself."

The idea of tossing the water in his smug face crossed her mind again. He winked as he started for the barn. Her heart went wild again. Oh, he thought he was so smart, but she was, too. There was more than one way to cook a chicken, and she'd been cooking for years.

Marina saw to Nellie while Richard completed

several other chores and neither spoke a word. It didn't bother her. She'd played the silent game with her brothers while growing up and had won. Men always gave in first.

Chapter Ten

All the while he saw to the chores, Richard kept one eye on Marina. Women couldn't keep quiet if you paid them. She'd soon start asking questions again. Pirates could cut off his fingers one at a time and he still wouldn't tell her or anyone else all the details about helping Oscar Pullman last night. It had been a gruesome deed, but he agreed with the man. Those who'd perished deserved to be buried properly. Leaving the other six hanging there had been hard, but he'd agreed with Oscar on that aspect, too. Taking two bodies was dangerous enough.

He'd helped Pullman bury his daughter on the back side of his property, and together they'd buried John's mother on her property. He'd yet to tell the young man but would have to this morning. Word was sure to spread quickly.

The night had been interesting. Trekking through swamps, cutting down bodies and burying them, listening to Oscar Pullman. The man knew plenty about the chaos taking place and plenty about Marina. There was no man she was interested in, and that provided him with more joy than he'd been prepared for, and the other things Oscar had said put things in a different light. She'd had a tough time back in Maine. Far more than the trivial incident, as her uncle had suggested. Not having a family other than Earl and then Sarah and now Gracie left him pondering Marina harder and perhaps differently. She'd told him about the marauding Indians, and he now considered it remarkable that she'd lived through it. Learning others had ridiculed her for surviving had angered him, until he realized their loss had been his gain. If she hadn't moved in with William, Gracie would have died.

There was still more, though. She was still hiding something from him.

She'd stopped milking but pretended to remain engrossed in the task. He could be a patient man when the need arose and showed it by taking his time brushing down the horse. The sneaking peeks she kept casting his way had him biting his lips together. What he'd told her last night was true. She was brave enough to be dangerous. Then again, she was already dangerous.

To him, anyway.

No woman had ever taken up residency in his mind the way she had.

Her blond hair was a literal mass of wild curls. Long ringlets hung down her back, twisting among themselves. Once again the idea she fit the image of an angel more than that of a witch flitted through his thoughts.

Chasing aside either notion, he left the stall and walked over to stand beside her. "Are you waiting for me to carry the milk?"

He saw her shoulders quiver slightly. "No."

"Then what are you waiting for?" he asked. "You finished milking some time ago."

She spun around and stood all in one swift movement; however, one foot caught on a stool leg and she stumbled.

Richard grabbed for her, snagging an arm with one hand and her waist with the other. He was instantly reminded of carrying her last night, both out of the swamp and then to bed. It was the latter time that had stuck with him. She'd been wearing nothing but a thin gown, and he'd felt her curves and the smoothness of her skin. She was pure perfection. Like a sea vessel built for sailing, Marina had been built for pleasure. A man's pleasure, and he wanted to be that man.

Understanding the dangers of that, he pulled her upright and, until their eyes met, had every intention of letting her loose. The stool that had been tottering beneath her skirt tumbled onto his foot, but not even the sting of that deflected his thoughts. Those sea-blue eyes of hers had captured his full attention, and the honeysuckle scent that had filled his nose last night was there again, making waves in his already flooding bloodstream.

The desire to kiss her hit so hard and fast there was no time to contemplate not doing so. Never taking his eyes off hers until their faces were so close his vision blurred, he captured her lips beneath his.

In a faraway recess of her mind, Marina questioned what was happening, but most of her didn't. It was exactly what she desired. The fascinating touch of his mouth pressed against hers. She'd watched her brothers kissing their wives and had asked Nessa about it while imagining what it would be like. Her sister-in-law had said she'd like it, that it would light up her insides like the sun during the day and the moon at night.

That was exactly what was happening. Her very soul was being lit up in ways she didn't understand. It was enchanting and mystical and peaceful. So wonderfully peaceful. When his hands grasped her cheeks, making the connection stronger, more powerful, her hands found their way to his arms, where she held on tightly while being swept into a magical place full of rainbows and stars. There was no other way to describe it.

When it all ended abruptly—the colors, the enchantment, the kiss—her head was spinning.

Reaching for something to hold on to, her hands found Richard's. The moment his fingers grasped hers, the spinning stopped, but the light inside her didn't fade.

"Marina?"

She shook her head, trying to remember where she was, who she was. As that all became clear, she asked, "Why did you do that? Why did you kiss me?"

"I don't know," he said, dropping her hands. "I shouldn't have. Forgive me."

Marina closed her eyes briefly, still trying to make sense of what had happened—not the kiss or his apology, but the change inside her. Everything about her was warm and bright.

"It's you," he said roughly. "You've put some sort of spell on me."

Her reaction was to grin and say, "I can't put spells on people. I don't know how."

He frowned and shook his head as if she was telling a tall tale.

"Honestly," she said. "If I could cast spells, I'd have put a hole in that boat last night."

Not only did he grin, but he also stepped forward and cupped her cheeks again. However, his eyes then turned serious. "You are not a witch."

"Yes, I am," she insisted. "You just said so yourself." She'd accepted being a witch, but until this very moment, she might not have completely believed it. The kiss had done it. No God-fearing woman would have let that happen, but a witch would have. And would still be rejoicing in it.

"I didn't mean it."

"Yes, you did. You just don't want to believe it. I didn't at first, either." She stepped back, out of his hold, and moved closer to Nellie in order to clear her thinking. A deep and sudden urge wanted her to tell him everything, to make him believe, but another part of her still knew he'd try to stop her. "I just don't have any powers. Or maybe I haven't learned how to use them yet." She hadn't meant to say that. Her tongue was flapping on its own. Like a fish out of water. "I haven't been a witch that long."

He picked up the milk bucket and carried it out of the stall. "You don't have any powers because there are no such things as witches."

Marina leaned against an empty stall. It was all so strange, how disconnected her words were from her brain and…and how disconnected she was from her past. The memories were still there, but the pain wasn't. It didn't hurt to admit she was a witch. As if dipping a toe in to test the water before entering it, she said, "When the Indians attacked our village, they killed me, too."

"That's impossible."

"Not for a witch."

"Marina—"

"I died that night," she said with more calmness than she'd ever known. "Along with all the other members of my family. But later, when the survivors—there weren't too many of them—were burying the dead, I woke up. Right there on Mrs. Hanson's kitchen table, where she was washing my body."

"What?"

"Shocking, isn't it? Imagine how it was for Arlyce Hanson." Marina had never made light of the situation, but the warmth encompassing her gave her permission.

"You hadn't died," he said. "Just been knocked out."

She shook her head. "No, I'd died." Meeting his gaze, she added, "A person knows when they die."

"How?"

There was disbelief in his eyes but also a hint of anger. Marina waited for her fears to appear. The deep-down ones that up until he'd kissed her had never gone away. There was no tightening of her stomach, no quickening of her heart, no heavy dread. She glanced around the barn, catching the sunlight streaming in the door full of dust motes dancing like dreamland fairies. Turning back to Richard, she said, "Because I remember it. We'd all gone to bed, and it was storming. Thundering and lightning, which was unusual so late in the year. I thought the wind had blown the door open, but it was Indians, running in all directions."

She drew a deep breath as the visions entered her head. It was strange, but this time it was as if she wasn't connected to the story, simply a bystander repeating what she'd seen. It had finally happened. She'd been completely transformed into a witch.

"They killed my parents in their bed, and my brothers and their wives. My nephew, Gunther, and I were in the loft, and I tried to keep him quiet so the Indians wouldn't find us, but he started to cry."

Tears fell from her eyes, but here too she felt separated from them. "That's when I died. One second I was fighting them off. The next second I was floating away." She closed her eyes. "My parents were, too, and my brothers, their wives, and when Gunther joined us, we all started moving together. As one. Floating, not walking. We were all happy and peaceful. It was warm and sunny." She'd come to the part that tore at her heart in the past and opened her eyes in order to press on. "We came to a bridge, and they all walked across it, but I couldn't. I shouted for them to wait for me, but they all shook their heads. My father said that bridge wasn't for me. That I had to go back. I didn't want to go back and told him that, but they kept moving farther away. My father said I couldn't go with them, not right then. He said there were others and that I had to show them the way. The next thing I remember is feeling a hand on my forehead and waking up on Arlyce Hanson's kitchen table."

Richard had stepped forward, and when he wrapped his arms around her shoulders, she laid her head upon his chest without thought.

"It was all just a bad dream," he whispered.

"No, it wasn't," she answered. "I remembered everything, even things I couldn't have known. I knew which families had been attacked, who'd already been buried, who'd survived."

"You could have heard people talking about all that," he said. "While you were unconscious."

Marina lifted her head and leaned back to look at him. Deep inside his eyes she saw his confidence was slipping as he tried not to believe her. With a pang of remorse, she stepped out of his arms. "I thought about that, but I knew things, know things, that no one had mentioned."

"Like what?"

She shook her head. That was not something she wanted to think about, to remember, not now or ever. "At first people were nice, caring, but then word spread and everyone grew afraid of me. They feared I'd bring more evil upon them. By the time Captain Farleigh arrived, I hadn't slept in days and knew it was only a matter of time…" Walking toward the sunlight streaming into the barn, she said, "I came to live with Uncle William, hoping I could leave it all behind me, but that wasn't to be."

"What happened?"

"Nothing at first," she admitted. "But then I started having dreams about people growing ill. Whole families dying. I tried to warn them. Told them to be cautious of what they ate and drank and to stay home."

Stopping in the barn doorway, Marina scanned the roadway. There was no traffic, but there soon would be. "After the epidemic, Reverend Hickman came to the house and wanted to know how I knew about the illnesses before they'd started. I didn't say anything and neither did Uncle William. We didn't need to. He'd learned what had happened in Maine." What returned couldn't be called pain—it was darker than that, more menacing. "The only reason I wasn't accused is because he knows I'm a real witch."

Richard couldn't remember a time when he didn't know what to think. As preposterous as her story was, she believed it, and that was the part that twisted his good senses. "Why didn't you and William leave? He has the finances."

She turned to look up the road in the direction of Salem Towne and the gruesome sight he'd witnessed again last night. "I can't. I brought the evilness with me, to the people here, and I have to stop it."

His jaw tightened at exactly who had filled her head with such nonsense. "No, you didn't. Hickman did, and he was evil long before he met you."

"I know that, just as I know what I have to do."

A shiver tickled his spine. "What?"

"What my father told me to do. Show the others the way."

The shiver raced all the way to his toes. "What others?"

"Those falsely imprisoned."

The thunder of hooves interrupted Richard's response. Two horses, with riders whipping the reins over their flanks, galloped past the house.

"Oh, dear heavens," she whispered as they disappeared. "That was Oscar Pullman in that boat last night. You went with him to steal Elizabeth's body, didn't you?" Her eyes fell to his boots, where dried mud still crusted the toes. "And buried her on his property."

The shiver that shot up and down Richard's spine had both his head and toes quivering. Then anger settled. She had to have followed him. "I told you to stay home."

She merely stared at him.

Enough was enough. He grabbed her arms. "You are not a witch. You've simply been sneaking around at night and reading propaganda." He'd glanced through the stack of papers on the desk full of tales of witches that had been distributed by the church. "Those leaflets are all lies."

"Some of it, yes. But only a real witch would know what parts."

A growl rumbled in his throat. "You—"

"Yes, I am."

"Because of a bad dream?" he barked. "Because of—"

"It's far more than dreams," she insisted. "It's written in the scriptures—"

"Scriptures?" Holding his temper took all he had. "People have been misquoting the Bible since it was written. That's what Hickman's doing. You said so. You didn't die, and—"

"I'd been examined and pronounced dead."

He bit his lip in order to form an intelligent response.

"Arlyce Hanson heard me gasp right before I opened my eyes and swore I hadn't been breathing before then."

"That's not proof."

"You want proof?" she whispered. "I watched

the Indians kill my nephew and then chop his hands off at the wrists to take back as evidence of their accomplishments."

Richard froze and his anger dissolved. He'd never seen pain as raw as what was reflected in her eyes.

"He was smaller than Grace, and there wasn't a thing I could do. They'd already shoved me off the loft. I saw my body, crumpled and lifeless on the floor." She took a single step closer, her eyes locked on his. "Gunther was buried before I returned to life, along with the other children. Every child that had been murdered had their hands chopped off. Those who saw it never mentioned it, and others didn't know, until I told them."

The hair on his arms was standing on end. "And that's when they proclaimed you were a witch."

"Yes." She spun around and marched toward the house.

Richard couldn't will his body to do anything but watch. If she'd been crying, he'd have stopped her, comforted her, but the woman who'd just walked away hadn't wanted that.

Chapter Eleven

When Richard entered the house later, Marina, busy cooking, acted as if nothing had transpired between them, which left him both relieved and wary. He'd heard tales of savages doing just what she'd described, but the conviction, the belief with which she'd spoken, was what alarmed him. Furthermore, both John and William insisted she hadn't left the house a second time last night. There was no way she could know what he'd done with Oscar, yet she did.

He couldn't find an answer of how. Not one that made sense. They were in the midst of eating a breakfast of boiled eggs and porridge when the clatter of horses and wagons had Richard rising from his chair. "Wait here." His gaze included everyone at the table.

He arrived on the front stoop before the visitors had dismounted. "Don't bother getting down," Richard shouted. "You aren't welcome here."

"This is official business," Hickman said, rolling out of the driver's seat of his carriage. "Where's the Griggs lad?"

The person who opened and closed the door behind him wasn't John. Richard reached back and took Marina's elbow, bringing her forward to stand at his side.

Hickman eyed the action with a lecherous interest that rubbed salt in an open wound.

Richard leveled a glare on the other man that he usually held for dock ruffians up to no good. Hickman was far more wicked than any ragtag thug. It had been impossible to abide the man years ago, and at this moment he wanted to squash him beneath his boot like a bug that had crept upon his ship. Just like insects, Hickman damaged everything he encountered. "What do you want with John?"

"We are here to arrest him," Hickman said. "For theft. His mother's body was stolen last night."

Richard refrained from pulling his lips into a tight smile. He'd relish telling the man the truth, but considering what Hickman and others believed about Marina, the opposite would serve his purpose better. "John never left this house last night. Marina can attest to that."

Curling his nose, Hickman sneered, "Her word means nothing."

Hickman's men were on the road and made no

effort to move closer, not even when Richard took a step toward their leader. "It should," he said. "It means a lot to me."

Hickman puffed out his chest. "Which also means nothing." Narrowing his beady eyes, he snapped, "Where is that boy? He's under arrest."

"Do you have his mother's body?" Richard asked. "Proof that John took it?"

"Of course not. It was stolen. No one else would have taken it."

Holding Marina's elbow as she stepped off the stoop beside him, Richard allowed a smile to prevail. "Perhaps it wasn't stolen. Perhaps she awoke, cut herself down and, at this very moment, is hiding in the woods, waiting for the opportunity to repay you for your actions against her."

The man's jowls jiggled as Hickman opened and closed his mouth.

He'd clearly hit a nerve, and blood surged through Richard's veins. He relished taking a stance against opposing forces and planted his heels more heavily into the ground, as he would on the ship to counter the rolling deck against heavy sea swells. The strength of his smile increased, too. "Do you really believe a mere hanging can kill a witch? A real witch?"

Cold and bitter rage filled Richard as Hickman's eyes darted toward Marina. Prepared to defend her as he would his ship upon a pirate attack, Richard let loose her elbow in order to drape an arm around her shoulders.

The glow of satisfaction on the other man's face momentarily confused Richard, until a scuffle sounded. His heart stopped as two men dragged John across the ground. A third carried a kicking and squirming Grace.

The roar in Richard's ears, louder than cannon fire, left him deaf. As the rage inside him broke loose, he pulled the blade from the scabbard inside his boot and advanced on Hickman, fully prepared to let fate decree the outcome.

"You bloody bastard," he seethed between clenched teeth. He had a handful of Hickman's hair in one hand; the other he used to hold his blade against the man's throat. "Order their release or you'll die right here, right now."

Hickman gurgled and coughed.

"Now! For God is my witness, I will end your bloody life."

"Let them go," Hickman squawked.

"But Your Highness—" one of the men said.

"You release them," Richard yelled, "or right after I slit his throat, I'll slit yours." He spun, taking Hickman with him, to address the others still near the roadway. "You'll all find yourselves in the hereafter."

"Release them," Hickman said again. "The fool will do as he says."

Richard waited until Marina had Gracie in her arms and was kneeling beside John, who'd been unceremoniously dropped to the ground, before Richard gave Hickman's head a hard wrench backward. Pressing his blade deep enough against Hickman's throat to indent the skin, he growled, "I'm no fool. You, of all men, know that."

"They released them," the coward squealed.

The desire to end it all filled him, but, aware that Marina and Gracie watched, Richard withdrew his blade and, out of spite, gave the man a hard shove.

Hickman stumbled and fell to his knees. "The governor will hear of this," he shouted, crawling toward the road.

"Bloody right, the governor will hear about this," Richard responded. "So will King William."

Once on his feet, aided by two of his cronies, Hickman waved a fist in the air. "You have no authority here, Tarr. I'll see you imprisoned along with that she-devil!"

Despite all that had transpired, the air around him, inside him, was dead calm, much like the aftermath of a storm. He'd defied the odds of vicious storms many times and had no doubt of his abilities to do so again. "I'll see you dead first," Richard promised coldly.

The horses that galloped past must have been from the three men who'd sneaked in the back of the house and captured John and Grace. As soon as the rest of the troop, including Hickman, followed in their wake, Richard returned his blade to his boot and quickly crossed the yard.

Bloody, his face already swelling, John groaned. "William," he whispered. "They knocked him over the head."

Marina's gasp had Richard looking up. "Go," he told her. "I'll bring John inside."

He ended up carrying John, through the front door and down the hall into the kitchen, where William sat at the table with Marina pressing a cloth to the back of his head.

"Bastards," the old man growled. "Hit me atop the head afore I could get out my chair."

Grace sat in another chair, her little head hanging down and her entire body quivering. Rage once again filled Richard. This was no place for a child. No place for anyone. He set John in one of the other chairs and stepped aside as Marina, who'd left her uncle holding the rag on the back of his head, knelt down to start washing the blood from John's face.

"We're leaving today," Richard said.

William was the only one to respond. His thick gray brows were drawn down, his frown more prominent by the deep wrinkles surrounding his eyes. "Aye, Captain. It is no longer safe here."

Richard had to question if it had ever been

safe. He'd never been a man to fuel himself with guilt, but if possible, he'd whip himself for allowing his child to experience the life she had recently. If he'd known five years ago the terror Grace would live through, he'd have taken her with him back then. There was no salvation in the fact he couldn't have known.

"You'll need a wagon," Marina whispered softly. "None of them is up to walking that far."

"Then I shall acquire a wagon." He was in the front room before his feet stalled and an iota of sense penetrated the anger and frustration surging inside him. Leaving the house unattended right now would be insane.

Damn it. He was a man of action, but not having the resources, the men who usually stood at his side, stifled his abilities. That was foreign to him, and infuriating.

He spun around and all but stumbled into Marina. Her blue eyes, so full of sorrow and pain, inflicted yet another bout of incompetency. He'd never lacked the skill or power to protect what was his, to overpower the enemy, yet at this moment in time he felt as if he stood on a gangplank with his hands tied behind his back.

"John has a wagon at their farm, if the church hasn't already seized it," she said softly.

"I can't leave you unprotected," he said. "Not

right now. Hickman's sure to be watching and will see me leave."

"We can lock the doors and—"

"It's gone beyond locked doors and windows, Marina." He didn't stand a chance, outnumbered as he was, not with two injured men, a small child and a woman who thought she had more power than she did. Digging into the crevices of his mind, he searched for ideas, for past experiences that might help. A tale he'd once heard from a shipmate came forward. The sailor had claimed to have been surrounded by natives on an island near Africa and barely escaped with his life. "I'll have to wait for the cover of night," he acknowledged aloud. "And set traps around the house, to prevent anyone from getting close during my absence."

"What sort of traps?"

A tingle raced up his neck, and a hint of elation crossed his mind. A woman who not only thought she was a witch but one who everyone else thought was a witch was precisely the weapon he needed. One that could prove more powerful than cannons or guns. Enticed, he reached out and took her hands. "Witch traps."

Her fingers folded around his, soft and warm, yet she shook her head as if confused. "Witch traps?"

He nodded. "The people here are petrified of

witches." Her frown was so deep he chuckled slightly and acted upon an overwhelming desire. Planting a tiny kiss upon one drawn brow, he whispered, "Go see to the others. I have some planning to do."

Marina desperately tried to gather her thoughts, but the touch of Richard's lips against her forehead made it impossible. His dark eyes, which moments ago had been black with rage, were now a glistening brown and twinkling with mischief. That only increased her utter confusion. "I've never heard of witch traps," she told him.

His smile was as conniving as it was genuine. "Neither have I. Go now." He released her hands. "I'll let you know the supplies I'll need shortly."

"What sort of supplies?"

"I'll let you know as soon as I know." He moved to the desk where Uncle William kept old logbooks and worn-flat quills.

She was still shaken by all that had happened but, as unfathomable as it seemed, wasn't full of fear or dread. There was anger because of John and Uncle William being injured and raw fury for Gracie being frightened so terribly, yet a wholesome belief Richard would save and protect them whatever might come overrode all of that. She used to feel that way, years ago. Protected. Safe. When her father and brothers had been alive and always at hand. Not even telling herself that in the end they hadn't been able to protect their family lessened the strong confidence Richard had somehow instilled.

She hadn't meant to tell him about Gunther earlier. It had just happened and, considering what he'd told Hickman, must have convinced him she was indeed a witch.

All of that left more questions in her mind than she could tolerate right now. Pushing them aside, she walked to where Richard sat. "Did you steal John's mother's body along with Elizabeth Pullman's?"

He leaned back and looked up at her thoughtfully. "What do you think?"

She nodded, having already known the answer. "That was a very dangerous thing to do."

"Perhaps, but I understood Oscar's desire to see his daughter laid to rest."

"Why?" she asked. "You don't even know him."

He shrugged. "You yourself said you don't need to know someone to care about them."

"I was speaking of family."

"Then perhaps I'm speaking of justice," he said. "A person knows right from wrong. What's happening around here is wrong. I want to see it righted."

Marina couldn't say it was kinship she harbored toward Richard right then, but it was something that arose from her very soul. Not certain she had the wherewithal to explore what that meant, she nodded. "I'll go check on the others."

The changes that had happened inside her since Richard's arrival were profound and unsettling.

"Where's Richard?" Uncle William asked as she entered the kitchen. "John needs to lie down."

She didn't have time to respond before Richard appeared and helped John down the hallway to William's room. "I'll make a poultice for his eyes," she told Uncle William. "And one for you."

He grumbled, saying he'd be in the front room with Richard, while she unfastened clumps of dried herbs she kept hanging from an overhead beam near the fireplace.

Gracie climbed off her chair and started carrying the breakfast dishes to the cupboard that held the washing tub. That action made Marina smile.

"Thank you, Gracie," she said. "You are such a wonderful helper."

While the herbs steeped, she filled the dish tub for Gracie and carried a chair to the cupboard for the child to stand upon. Once she'd wrapped the herbs in cotton batting, she said, "I'll be right back, Gracie."

First she attended to John, whose eyes were swollen terribly, and then she prepared another poultice for her uncle.

"They got the jump on you," Richard was saying to William as she entered the front room. "Nothing you could have done."

"Those bloody buggers," her uncle replied. "Knocking a man over the head from behind is just cowardly. Cowardly, I say."

"Aye," Richard answered. "They are a bunch of cowards. Hiding behind tales of witches and lies of children. But…"

He'd leaned back in his chair and Marina bit her bottom lip at the seriousness of his gaze. Her heart started thumping harder when his eyes met hers.

"Cowards are usually desperate, and desperate men are dangerous men."

"Aye," Uncle William said.

Marina tugged her eyes off him to focus on placing the poultice on Uncle William's injury. "You sit tight," she said. "I'll be back to check on you shortly."

"I won't move a muscle," he said. "My head hurts too bad."

"I'll brew some tea to help with the pain," she said, patting his shoulder.

"That would be a blessing, darling."

Her heart skipped a beat as her uncle closed his eyes. In all the time she'd known him, he'd never admitted to being in pain. She'd seen the signs, watched him grimace and wince when under the weather, and had made him slow down when he was winded. Her insides sank at how much peril she'd put his life in by moving here. He could have been killed today. She lifted her gaze and once again found Richard watching her.

"I'll keep an eye on him."

She acknowledged his offer with a nod before leaving the room. Back in the kitchen, Gracie's wary eyes twisted her heart all over again. She'd put the child's life in danger by bringing her here, too. Planting a smile upon her face, she said, "Goodness, but you are a good girl. The best dishwasher I've ever seen."

Gracie smiled.

Marina tapped the tip of Gracie's tiny nose. "I used to help my mother in the kitchen all the time."

"You did?"

"Yes, I did." Although her heart tumbled, Marina kept a smile on her face. Her mother used to tell her that someday she'd do such things with her own daughter. Who would have ever thought being a witch could be so painful. Keeping the pain hidden, she said, "And we used to sing."

"I like when you sing."

"I'll teach you the words so you can sing with me," she offered.

Gracie shook her head. "I can't. It's evil to sing."

Marina bit her bottom lip for a brief moment.

It wasn't her place to impose beliefs upon anyone, especially a child who was not her own, but in this case, she chose to ignore that. To her way of thinking, the Puritans' idea that singing was evil was as wrong as many of their other beliefs. Besides, Richard wasn't a Puritan and wouldn't raise Grace as one. "No, it's not," she answered. "God loves to hear us singing, especially little children."

"He can hear us?"

"Oh, yes, all the way up to heaven, he can hear us, and he rejoices in the sound. It makes him so happy the sun shines brighter."

"I shall like that," Gracie said.

Marina grinned. "I shall, too. While you're washing, I'll brew Uncle William some tea."

"What about singing?"

Marina grinned. "We shall sing the entire time we work."

She started out with a song she sang to the child at night, but upon realizing most of the words were in Swedish, ones Grace wouldn't understand, she switched, making up words as they went along. The tune, about a tiny bluebird flying through the clouds, soon took shape, and Gracie picked up on the words and tune immediately.

The child's voice filled the room like sunshine and lifted Marina's spirits considerably. They giggled as they sang and sang as they giggled, and all in all, it put a skip in Marina's step she hadn't experienced in ages. It was still there when she carried William's tea into the front room.

"Did a flock of magpies take over the kitchen?" Richard asked.

The smile on his face allowed hers to remain intact. "I don't believe so, but perhaps there is a happy little wren washing dishes."

"I've always loved the sound of singing," Uncle William said without opening his eyes. "It cheers a man's soul."

"That it does," Richard agreed.

Once again, Marina's heart skipped a beat. "Here is your tea." She set it on the table. "Let me check your head."

Uncle William leaned forward for her to remove the poultice. The bump was almost gone, providing her much relief.

"It still hurts," he said.

"I'm sure it does," she supplied. "The tea will help."

William took a hold of her hand and squeezed it firmly. "I don't know what I'd do without you, girl. You've saved this old man's life again."

Marina bent down and kissed his forehead, but as she turned to leave, his hold on her hand increased.

"Did you know, Richard, that the court of

Oyer and Terminer won't imprison a woman with child? It's called 'reprieve for the belly.'"

Richard's gaze held enough heat that her insides blazed, right below her heart where she knew babies were conceived and grew. That also sent heat into her cheeks.

"No, I didn't," he answered.

"It's true," William said. "Rosemary Washington was one of the first accused, after she'd caught those young girls splattering her laundry with mud. When the court found out she was with child, she was sent home immediately. Fully pardoned."

"I believe it,' Richard said. "Reproducing takes precedence to the Puritans."

"Aye, Captain. Even over witches," William said.

Her discomfort, the heat swirling inside her, left her at a disadvantage. Marina pulled her hand out of William's. "I must see to John," she said, taking off as if being chased by true witch hunters. Those who would see to her demise swiftly and without conviction. Thinking of such things, of infants growing beneath her breasts, was useless and would leave her with nothing but sorrow. Yet she couldn't stop those thoughts. That of a child with dark hair and eyes, much like Gracie. A child of her own.

If either Richard or her uncle knew what

she knew, neither would have glanced her way. Witches couldn't have babies. They were infertile. That was why they stole other people's children.

Reverend Hickman claimed that was why she refused to turn over Gracie, and she'd agreed. Out of spite, she'd thought, but now she had no choice but to agree. She'd wanted to care for Gracie. Still did.

Swallowing against the burning of her throat, Marina hurried into the kitchen.

Gracie, still playing in the dishwater, started singing again, loudly. Marina managed to pull up a smile and sang a few notes while pouring a cup of tea for John. "I'll be right back," she then told Gracie.

The sound of the child's singing followed her into William's bedroom, where John lay on the bed.

"All that singing sure sounds pretty," he said. "It's like sunshine."

"That it is." She set the tea on the table in order to remove the cool compresses. The swelling near his mouth had slowed, but both eyes were swollen almost shut, and what she could see between the tiny slits showed the whites were bloodshot.

"I'm sure it looks worse than it is," he said.

Empathy welled as she helped him sit up. "And I'm sure your face hurts terribly."

Using his elbows to brace himself, he admitted, "It does."

Marina gathered the cup and lifted it to his lips. "Here, this will help with the pain."

He drank several swallows before falling back upon the pillow with a stifled groan. "Do ye think it true, Marina?" he asked.

"What?"

"My mother. That she arose from the dead."

Her heart dropped clear to her toes, yet she couldn't lie to him. Nor could she reveal the truth behind the night's exploits. "No, John," she whispered. "I don't."

"Then what happened to her? To her body? Who would steal her?"

Marina settled the poultices over his eyes again. "No one stole your mother, John."

"Oscar Pullman said he was going to get Elizabeth and bury her at their place. Do ye think he took Mother, too? I'd asked him if I could go with him, but I forgot about it last night."

Relieved, Marina patted his hand. "I believe that is exactly what happened. Rest assured your mother is buried on her property. But know that is just her body. Her soul is in heaven with the Almighty."

"Do ye really believe that?"

"I do," she answered. "With all my heart, I do."

"I want to believe that, too. I truly do."

Marina gathered one of his hands between hers and recited a prayer softly, then offered one of thanks for providing John's mother the ultimate salvation. She laid his hand back upon the bed and gathered the cup to leave.

"I don't understand, Marina," he said quietly. "How ye can be so close to the Lord, yet claim to be a witch. It doesn't hold true."

John had been the one to tell her that others were talking about what had happened to her in Maine. That had been right before his mother had been arrested. Up until then, she'd remained a silent bystander against the accusations, not wanting to bring more attention to her or Uncle William. However, her warnings about the illness prior to that had already set things in motion. "There is plenty in this world that doesn't hold true," she answered. "I surmise life is like a cobblestone pathway. It's not always smooth to walk upon. The best we can do is hold faith that we don't trip and hope our path will once again become smooth."

"I can't imagine what that would be like. A smooth path."

She couldn't, either, but tried to assure him. "Oh, you'll like when it happens. Your life will be full of promises and sunshine."

"Was yer life that way once? Full of promises and sunshine?"

"Yes, it was," she said. "A long time ago."

"I hope it's that way for ye again, Marina."

The surge of pain that rushed through her was impossible to breathe through. She held the air in her lungs until the hurt diminished enough to speak. "You rest now. Sleep if you can."

Turning toward the door, she stumbled slightly when she saw Richard standing there.

Marina held no delusions that he hadn't heard her and John talking, and she refused to let the consequences of that affect her. There was no room for any more regrets.

Richard waited until she pulled the door closed behind her before asking, "He's not well enough to travel, is he?"

She shook her head. "His eyes are swollen almost shut. The whites, what I can see of them, are bloodshot. It may be a couple of days before he can see enough to move around."

Richard rubbed his head with both hands. Then, smoothing back the hair he'd mussed, he said, "I've seen men lose their sight from eye injuries. It's not a trifle thing."

"No, it's not," she agreed, attempting to remain detached. It was false, of course. She was greatly concerned about John and Uncle William. And Grace and even Richard. In fact, her worries far outnumbered all else.

Until Richard reached out and took a hold of

her shoulders. That created a selfishness in her that surpassed everything. Her heart started racing and warmth once more pooled beneath her stomach. Visions of kissing him again flashed before her eyes. The thought hadn't been far from her mind, even with everything else. Then, out of nowhere, the sweet whimper of an infant echoed in her ears.

She twisted to look into the kitchen, where Gracie still splashed in the tub of water, but she knew the sound had come from inside her, created by the witch within to taunt her already aching heart.

"Looks like she's having fun," Richard said.

Taking solace in what she could, Marina said, "It's good to see her up and about."

"Yes, it is. John will be up and about soon, too. Grace is proof you're an excellent healer."

Marina couldn't take credit for Grace's health; nor could she for John's—whether he fully recovered or not. Looking for something to alter the course of her thoughts, which appeared to want to inflict pain upon her, she asked, "How is your plan coming along?"

He grinned, which almost was her downfall. His chiseled features softened when he smiled and turned him into the kind of man that maidens, giggling and blushing, whispered about after they walked past. She'd seen that in the past. Girls had simpered and fawned over her brothers, and she'd teased them about it afterward. They'd teased her, too, when Adam Wolfstellar had asked to call. That had been the day before the Indian attack. His family had all been killed, too.

"Do you?"

Blinking to clear her mind, Marina asked, "Do I what?"

"Have any black cloth?" Richard frowned and he rubbed her shoulders. "Are you all right?"

"Yes. I just didn't hear you the first time," she supplied. "There are several yards of black fabric in a crate upstairs. I will get it for you. It's in—"

"Your sewing room?" he asked. "I can get it."

She'd been about to call the room that, and she grinned. "Yes. There are several bolts of cloth in the crates along the wall. I'm not sure which one holds the black."

"From William's sailing days?"

"Yes, but some I believe were left by the previous owner."

His eyes narrowed slightly. "Have you met Wiggins Adams?"

"No," she answered. "But Uncle William said Captain Adams left a few items behind."

"More than a few would be my guess," Richard offered. "He's a privateer. Whatever the king doesn't want, he claims as his own, which is perfectly legal. He also makes great profits selling cargo back to the very country he confiscated it from."

"Do you do that?"

He shook his head. "Not only did I have no desire to do so, I had no need. Earl had established a long line of regular customers, merchants around the world for whom I continue to transport goods to and from."

Marina hadn't missed the beginning of his subtle answer. "But you were asked to."

"Many ships and captains were provided the opportunity to obtain a letter of marque. Earl chose not to, and I do, too. Connected to no specific country or cause, I'm no threat to anyone." He nodded toward the kitchen behind her. "Grace may need a change of clothing."

Marina spun around. The water spraying into the air made her laugh. "It appears she truly is your daughter—she loves water."

"Did you have any doubts?"

Chapter Twelve

Richard discovered he was holding his breath, waiting for her to answer, even as her head spun around to look at him again.

"No," she replied. "I didn't. I don't."

He tried to settle a mask of indifference upon his face but found it virtually impossible with the way her curls bounced, settling back into place. It dawned on him then that she wasn't wearing her white cap today. Hadn't been since she'd gotten up. No wonder his desires had grown abundant, his admiration painfully merciless. With her golden curls covered and the cap shadowing her features, Marina's beauty hadn't been allowed to fully shine. Now, unrestrained, it shone with an exquisiteness he'd never encountered. Not in any part of the world. Her eyes looked more polished than gemstones and her cheeks, flushed rosy and shimmering, enhanced her pink lips. The idea of tasting them again evoked a strong tightness in his groin.

"Do you like the water?" Not waiting for her to answer, he said, "Your name, Marina, means 'of the sea.'"

Her lids fluttered shut and desire raced through him. He'd sworn to never be shackled again, never be hoodwinked by a pretty face or the slender curves of a woman's body. He knew the pleasures of such bodies but had long ago learned a wife wasn't necessary for that.

"How do you know that?"

How did he know what her name meant? "See to Grace," he said, turning about. "I'll get the material I need."

Richard lost no haste in his trek to the second floor. His breathing was quick and uneven by the time he entered the sewing room, and not from climbing the single flight of stairs. Taking a moment to calm his breathing, he willed his good senses to return. He must have heard or read the meaning of her name somewhere, but that meant nothing. No matter how lovely she was, how caring and gentle, how charming her voice, he had no expectations beyond seeing all of them out of their current situation.

Once in Boston, he'd find a sailing vessel to take on William. He'd already been jostling names of captains who'd welcome the old sailor aboard their ships. They'd welcome Marina, too, and John. He had considered, while drawing up the traps he intended to set, taking John upon his own ship. The names he'd tossed about now settled heavy in his mind. They were good men, but what would they do with Marina once William was gone? It might be a few years, but she'd have no place to go. Not unless she married and—

Letting out an explicit oath, Richard crossed the room to where the line of trunks sat. Some were simple, with leather straps and tin latches. Others were far more elaborate, with solid gold hinges and locks. The contents of those would be far more sophisticated, too. Silks from the Orient or the sheer, delicate materials the Spaniards coveted. They often had gold strands woven through them and brought extremely high prices.

He opened one of the simpler crates, hoping it would contain the black cloth he sought. After rifling through it, he moved on to the next and the next. These were clearly remnants left behind by Adams. Besides bolts of various fabrics—everything from fine silk to heavy wools and brocades—there were furs and leather. None of it black.

"Did you find it?"

Richard closed his eyes briefly. There was no escaping her and wouldn't be until John could travel. Bracing himself, he replied, "Not yet."

"Once I've changed Grace, I'll help you look."

"There's no need. I'm sure I'll find it."

"And leave a mess in your wake," she replied.

The trunks he'd already searched had their lids askew and material draped over the edges. "I'll see to them."

Her giggle sounded too far away. He spun around and, seeing the door empty, got to his feet. Across the hall, Grace sat on the bed as Marina unfastened the back of the girl's dress.

"Here, now," she said. "Arms up."

Richard returned to the trunks and his search with renewed determination. The singing coming from across the hall interrupted his concentration, and he found himself searching through things a second time, to make sure he hadn't missed any black cloth. He found what he was looking for in the very last trunk. Rising to his feet, he gathered the long length of cloth, wrapping it around his arm several times as the bolt seemed never ending.

"Papa, what are you doing?"

Hearing Gracie call him that shattered something inside him he hadn't known was breakable or even there. He turned and grinned. "Well, look at you. Another new dress."

She twirled about, causing the ruffled green material to fly around her legs. "Yes. It's beautiful."

The change in her since his arrival yesterday

was nothing shy of miraculous and put a lump in his throat. "It is."

Skipping across the room, Grace asked, "Do you need Marina to sew you new clothes like she did me?"

Richard allowed his eyes to linger on Grace a bit longer, half-afraid what might break inside him if he looked into Marina's blue eyes one more time. Women had never frightened him, not ever, but he'd already admitted Marina was not an average woman. There couldn't be another one like her if he sailed around the earth, north, south, east, west and back again. She was one of a kind. A part of him couldn't understand why that scared him, since he relished acquiring one-of-a-kind things. The other part of him, however, recognized he only acquired those things to resell them.

Tired of arguing with himself, Richard lifted his gaze to Marina.

Only to be thwarted.

She was smiling, showing pearl-white teeth. "Did you need me to sew something?"

Richard swallowed. She'd been right all along. She was a witch. One as potent as the sea herself.

Tilting her head sideways, she frowned slightly. "Richard?"

Knowing something and acting upon it were two different things. "I need several things stitched out of this material," he said. "By tonight, if possible."

"Certainly." She stepped forward, arms out. "What do you need?"

"Let's go downstairs," he said. "You can check on William and John, and I'll get my sketches to show you."

"Well, give me one end of that bolt before you have it wrinkled beyond repair."

Richard had never lost coordination in his arms, or any other part of his body, but unwinding that black material from his arm grew impossible. With a giggle, Marina was before him, untwisting the cloth from his arm.

Once done, she handed him two corners. "Hold this."

He did as instructed and sighed with relief when she stepped away. Gathering the other two ends, she stretched the material clear across the room and then started walking toward him again.

"Meet me in the middle," she said.

Richard had folded sails and knew this was the easiest way, but the simple little action stirred up a lot of trouble inside him. In the center of the room, he took her corners and walked backward as she gathered the folded section and pulled it tight.

They repeated the action several times, meeting in the center of the room and walking away from each other. By the time the material was in a neat stack, he was ready to run for the door. Folding sails had never done that to him. Then again, most of the men he sailed with had breath that would make a dog's eyes water.

Marina didn't. And the want to kiss her was eating at him like a rat gnawing at a fish barrel.

"I'll carry that," she said. "If you don't mind carrying Gracie."

"Not at all." Richard handed over the material and scooped up his daughter. "You are so light you could fly down the steps," he told Grace.

"People can't fly," she said between giggles.

"You can," he said. "Like this." Holding her flat in his arms, he headed for the door. "See, you're flying."

She held her arms out at her sides. "I am, Papa. I am!"

He flew Grace all the way down the stairs and across the front room.

"Look, Uncle William, I'm flying," she squealed.

"Have you turned into a bird?" William asked. "I thought I heard a bunch of twittering."

"No, I'm still a girl."

Richard flipped her upright and then set her feet on the floor. Kneeling in front of her, he flicked her nose. "A girl who can fly."

She nodded and, to his utter surprise and delight, flung her arms around his neck.

"I sure am glad you came," she said next to his ear. "I sure am."

"So am I," he answered, hugging her close. "So am I." Richard glanced up in time to watch Marina swipe a hand across her cheeks before she turned to walk down the hallway.

He patted Grace's tiny back before letting her go.

"Come here, Gracie," William said, patting his knee. "I have a story itching to be told."

She skipped across the room. "I like stories."

Richard grabbed his sketches and headed down the hall. In the kitchen, he set the old ledger on the table. "Here're the drawings," he said. "There are a few things I need from the barn."

"Do you think—"

"It's safe?" he interrupted. "I think Hickman has men watching the place, but as long as they know I'm around, they aren't going to approach the house." At the door, he spun around. "Don't even consider stepping outside."

"I won't."

Though he couldn't see them, Richard felt eyes on him as soon as he stepped out of the door. He made a show of carrying water and wood into the house and performed a few other outdoor chores, all the while peering deep into the woods to spot onlookers.

There was only one, across the road, settled

behind a thick hedge. Concluding that, he went into the barn. He kept the door open after leading the horse and cow out to graze, generally using the time to get his wits back in order and mainly to get Marina out of his mind, which wasn't easy, even as he tried to focus on his plan. It was a good one, and the trickery that went along with it was enough to make him smile as he thought about Hickman's men encountering the witches. The tree branches hanging over the house and road would make rigging the dummies as easy as stringing up sails to catch a prevailing wind. There were still a few things to figure out and plenty of work to be done.

His gaze went out the door to the house. It would take longer than he had first thought to make sure he got everyone away unscathed. Marina would be going with them. She had to see that now. No matter how strong her beliefs were, a single woman armed with nothing more than a Bible was no opponent for Hickman.

Grabbing a basket, he filled it with straw and then left the barn for the garden. The sentry across the road couldn't see him from here, and he needed to get a solid layout of the land in order to sneak around after dark.

With the location of each tree solid in his mind, he glanced around. He'd never stepped foot in a garden and had no idea if anything was ready to pick. Recognizing carrot greens, he pulled out a handful. The orange roots were stubby and scrawny, but it was just for show. He drew a deep breath then, bracing himself to face Marina. That woman was under his skin like no other.

Of course, she was like no other. She was a witch.

Grinning at his own humor, he headed for the house.

"What are you doing?" Marina asked as Richard opened the door and carried in her harvest basket. Plucking a baby carrot lying atop a bunch of straw, she explained, "These aren't ready to pick."

"I figured that out," Richard said. "But we need the straw."

"What for?"

"Didn't you look at my sketches?"

"Yes." Other than crude human shapes, she hadn't been able to decipher much else. Not wanting to insult his abilities, she pointed toward the hearth. "I had to put some salt pork on to cook." Gathering the rest of the carrots from the basket, she added, "I'll cook these with it. Thank you."

He set the basket on the table and picked up the old ledger. "I had to draw over some of William's old captain logs, with his permission, and the ink is thick, so they are somewhat hard to make out, but ultimately, we need to make dummies for me to rig into the trees."

She moved closer to look over his arm at the sketches. "Dummies?"

"Yes. Large dolls."

"What for?"

"So I can rig them in the trees."

The smile on his face said there was far more to his plan; she just didn't fathom what. "You said that."

He set the ledger on the table and used a finger to point at specifics. "This is the house, and these are the trees. I'll rig ropes to hold the dummies out of sight until someone trips them. Then they'll drop down, scaring whoever is sneaking about."

Still trying to understand, she said, "The Puritans don't believe in dolls—they don't believe in any playthings—but I don't believe they'll be frightened of them."

"They will be of these," he said. "They'll be covered in black cloth and look like witches when they come sailing out of the tree branches."

It all came together in her mind, forming an image that included Hickman's men tripping over their own feet in their haste to retreat. Marina pressed a hand to her mouth to contain a laugh. "Oh, my," she said behind her palm. "That's almost evil."

The glimmer in Richard's eyes was full of mirth. "I know," he said. "And fun."

A giddiness she hadn't experienced in a long time bubbled inside her. "I've been making rag dolls since I was little. But I'll need something sturdy for these." Her mind was tumbling so fast the words just kept flowing. "Oh, Uncle William has several old walking sticks in the room John slept in last night. Those will work. There are crates in that room, too, full of ropes and cording, and old sails. I can use that for the body. Oh, and the furs—those will work for hair. And there are gold buttons in one of the trunks. Large shiny ones that will glow in the moonlight. They'll work perfectly for eyes."

"We'll need the straw to stuff their heads."

Marina shook her head. The dolls had already taken shape in her mind. "No, we can use the material upstairs. There is plenty and it's just rotting away. I attempted to sell some when I first arrived. Although some admired it, the colors are too bold and the fabrics too fine to be useful to anyone in the village." She'd rather use the material for trifles than have Hickman scavenge it. "You start gathering items upstairs. I'll get the noon meal done. Once everyone's eaten, I'll start sewing."

Richard agreed, and as soon as he exited, Marina went to work, making plenty so her sewing wouldn't be interrupted when it was time to eat again this evening. She questioned the gaiety filling her, for their plan was full of trickery and deceit, until she later discovered, besides his eyes being fully swollen shut, John's ankle was twice the size it should be. Then she welcomed the excitement that filled her, as any witch would. Hickman and his henchmen deserved more than trickery.

After they'd eaten, she joined Richard in the front room, where he'd gathered their supplies. Uncle William was full of advice, and upon remembering some pieces of bamboo he'd stored away, he took to whittling. He insisted that when he was done, and his creations hung, they'd howl when the wind passed through them.

Gracie helped, too, stuffing the heads and bodies and holding things still when Marina was ready to tie them shut. They needed three dolls, and sewing the stiff canvas made her fingers hurt, but that was easily ignored.

Richard was busy measuring and tying lengths of rope together, and running upstairs to search for something else he'd think of or she'd suddenly remember. A sense of cheerfulness filled the room and Marina was reminded of when her family all gathered to work on various tasks together. There had always been laughter and teasing. Today was even better. Her heart had never felt so full. Each time she and Richard met eye to eye, happiness made her smile.

Their conversations covered many subjects besides the witch traps. Richard talked about sailing with Captain Earl Burrows, and about the sailor from whom he'd gotten the idea for the dolls, and how the man had escaped an island far away. He spoke of other places, too, and things she had no idea existed. Uncle William corroborated his tales and shared his own. Her uncle had never been so full of life, either, and Marina almost wished the day would never end.

Before it grew dark, they set everything aside to complete the evening tasks. She insisted upon joining Richard, stating two hands would accomplish things faster. He'd accompanied each of them outside when needed, to the outhouse. That had been when she noted the man in the hedge across the road. His position allowed him to watch the front and back doors at the same time, and Richard assured her that was the only man watching the house.

"There's a different man there now," she said to Richard as they carried water to the barn.

"How do you know?"

"The one earlier today had on a gray shirt. This one has on a white one. If there are no clouds tonight, we'll easily be able to keep track of him in the moonlight."

"You're right," Richard answered. "How much black material is left?"

"Plenty," she said, setting aside the bucket she'd emptied into Nellie's trough. "Why?"

"I'll need a black cloak so I'm not seen while putting the riggings in the trees."

"I'll sew it right after we eat." She gathered her stool and sat down beside the cow. That part of his plan concerned her. Climbing through the tree branches at night was going to be dangerous. He could easily fall and break several bones or worse. Pulling her mind off that, she said, "I saw a horseman go past earlier."

He'd led the horse in and was securing it in its stall. "I did, too."

Horses, the ones men rode, were rare in the community. Most farms had plow horses for farming or pulling wagons, but very few rode horses. Other than those who carried out deeds for Hickman.

"I'm assuming it was a rider sent to Boston, to the governor," Richard said.

"That's what I'm assuming, too." He'd shared the rest of his plan. Tonight he'd hang the witch traps, and tomorrow night, he'd sneak into town to get the wagon from John's farm. When he returned with it, she was to have everything packed for the trip to Boston. She would, for everyone but herself. Even though she'd already told Richard she wouldn't be leaving, he seemed to have forgotten that part. She hadn't. Despite how it tore at her heart, she had to stay behind. Whether he believed she was a witch or not, she had to stop the evil she'd set upon the community. She was the only one who could. A vision of arguing with him, of her refusing to leave, flickered nonstop in the back of her mind. That could very well be the hardest thing she'd ever have to do. Not leave with him and the others.

She turned, found him looking at her and, at that moment, wished above all else that she was not a witch. That was a terrible thought. Those in jail needed her to fulfill her duty. She had no choice.

"Marina."

Grabbing the milk bucket, she headed for the door. "It'll soon be dark."

After they'd supped on leftovers from the noon meal, she put the finishing touches on all three dolls—strips of fur for hair and gold buttons for eyes on the thick canvas faces. Up close they looked crude and rather comical, but once they were flying through the air, she imagined they'd look just like the witches they were meant to resemble.

"I'm laughing inside already," Uncle William said as she laid the final doll on the floor near the others. "Those men are going to have wet britches while running back to the village. I can't wait to see Adams and tell him how we put his goods to use."

While Richard and William conversed about meeting up with their shared acquaintance, Marina took note of Gracie rubbing her eyes.

"Come on, little one," she said, picking up the girl. "It's time for bed."

"Will you sing to me?" Gracie asked, snuggling in close.

"Of course," Marina answered.

In the bedroom she dressed the girl in a nightgown, saw she used the chamber pot and then tucked her into bed. After helping Gracie recite a prayer, Marina kissed the top of her dark hair and started singing softly. She was going to miss this so much. Miss everything about taking care of the child.

Grace was asleep before the song ended, but Marina sang to the end before she eased off the bed and tiptoed across the room. The dark shadow in the doorway didn't surprise her. "She's sleeping."

Richard nodded and stepped aside for her to exit. Upon closing the door, he said, "The watchman changed."

"Is there still just one?"

"Yes, across the road like before." He held up the material draped over one arm. "I'll need that cape now, but they might see what we're doing with the candles lit."

She gestured toward the room across the hall. "They won't be able to see up here. I'll fashion it here and sew it down by the hearth."

The moon was bright and filled the room. Along with the candles, Marina had plenty of light. "You'll need to remove your shirt," she said. "The white will be seen even covered with the black."

She took the material from him and used her arms to measure a length that would suffice. After she'd cut two such lengths, as well as large holes in the very center of each, she turned around.

The air stalled in her chest and whatever she'd been about to say died a slow death in her throat. Richard had indeed removed his shirt, revealing a span of bare skin, rippled with muscles and shimmering in a bronze color that had been created by the sun and wind. Her home had been small, and she'd grown up with two older brothers, who often worked outside during the warm weather without their shirts on, but not even that could have prepared her for this vision. His skin looked smooth and hard and had fascinating ripples and indentions from his breastbone and ribs. There was also a thick mat of hair, as silky looking as the furs she'd used on the dolls, swirling downward until it disappeared into his breeches.

Her ears started ringing and her mouth went unusually dry. She closed her eyes, too, but snapped them open as the image of her pressed against his bare chest formed.

"Marina?"

Spinning about, she grabbed one of the lengths of cloth and tossed it his way. "Slip that over your head." Snipping a narrow length off the bolt, she tossed that to him, too. "Tie it around your waist with this."

A few very brief moments later, he asked, "Like this?"

She willed herself not to react, not to see beyond the tunic, before she turned. He'd done as she told him, and the black cloth molded him in a way his white shirt never had. Perhaps because it merely covered his chest, leaving the skin at his sides showing. Her mouth was still too dry to swallow. "Yes."

"Now what?" he asked. "My arms—"

"I know," she snapped. The bronze skin of his arms still glistened in the moonlight, too, doing unusual things to her insides. Her stomach was full of warmth and her breasts felt heavy, as if they were swelling as John's ankle had. Grabbing the other length she'd cut, she handed it to him. "Put this one over your head, but the opposite way of the first. So the length covers your arms."

"Ingenious."

"Hardly," she muttered. Once he'd put on the material, she had no choice but to step closer to note where she needed to stitch the sleeves. "Hold your arms out."

He did so and she quickly marked the width and length with a couple of pins before telling him to take it off. "I'll sew the sleeves and attach a hood downstairs."

She couldn't pull her eyes away as he tugged the material over his head, his muscles stretching beneath his skin as he did so. Near her breaking point, Marina drew in a breath. She wanted to be kissed by him again so badly her entire being burned. Needing to escape, she spun, but he caught her elbow.

Chapter Thirteen

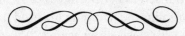

Richard knew what would happen the moment he touched her, yet he couldn't stop it. With deliberate slowness, he turned her around and took a hold of her other arm. She trembled beneath his touch. It wasn't fear. A sensitive, physical chord had been struck and continued to play between them all day. Each time he'd looked at her, met her gaze, his pulse had quickened and his thoughts had gone beyond mere attraction.

Light reflected in her jeweled eyes as they settled upon him and her teeth sank into her bottom lip. In that moment he was as petrified as he was excited. That had never happened before—him being petrified. He wasn't scared, just stiff. Time stopped ticking as they stood there, not moving, barely breathing.

She lowered her lids slowly, and when they opened, a new glint shone in her eyes. "Are you going to kiss me again?" she asked softly.

"I'm thinking about it," he said. "Seriously thinking about it."

Her smile was soft and tender, as was her whisper. "How long before you make up your mind?"

She was bold and beautiful, and the idea of burying himself in her warmth, her softness, was driving him insane. Dipping his head until their lips were very close, he answered, "I've decided."

She sighed, a mere puff of breath that softly floated over his chin, before asking, "And?"

"I am going to kiss you."

Her chin came up slightly and she leaned closer. "I was hoping that was your decision."

A combination of elation and raw passion rushed through his veins. It had been a long time since he'd wanted a woman. Not one to just provide relief, but one to share heat and passion as men and women were meant to do. In truth, he may never have wanted one this badly, this completely, for he certainly had never known the restraint he experienced right now. He wanted her slowly, softly, and lifted his hands to the top of her head, running his palms over her hair until holding the sides of her face firmly.

He tilted her head slightly, and their lips met at such a perfect angle his mouth fully covered hers. She came to him, a slight step forward while her hands slid beneath the makeshift tunic tied around his waist. Her touch was as potent as a thunderstorm at sea, where lightning charged the air with snaps and crackles one had to experience to understand.

Kissing her exceeded all his expectations, and he gave her the lead, simply enjoying the experience. There was no crushing of lips, no hard, fast movements and gasps like the seashore wenches provided. Marina's soft, slow and deliberate explorations were like none other and caused him to want her more than a pirate wanted gold.

When he parted his lips, curious as to how she'd react, he had to plant his heels firmly against the floor to maintain his footholds. She nibbled his bottom lip and the top one, before her tongue glided over his lips, past his teeth.

As slick as silk, her tongue slid across his, teasing and playful. Her taste was sweeter than sugar from Barbados and more potent than Scottish whiskey, and Richard stuck it out as long as he could. Then, unleashing his tongue, he twisted it with hers, swept it deep into her mouth and back out again.

They kissed until they were both breathless, parted long enough to draw in air and met again with a passion that was unsurpassable. His hands had gone as wild as his tongue, caressing her sides, her neck, her back. There were so many places he wanted to touch, to feel, but he had lost control of his hands—they roamed where they chose. He held no disappointment; there wasn't room for that. Not with his body throbbing, pounding in places with a need so feral he might never walk straight again.

He reached down and grasped Marina by the waist, lifting her up until her body was flush with his. If he was hoping for salvation, a touch of relief, he got the opposite. His loins were on fire, his blood boiling, and he'd never known such contentment in his life. A contradiction, if there ever was one. Just like Marina, his angel witch.

Her arms were locked around his neck, and when her lips left his and she sagged against him, he tightened his hold.

"Oh, goodness," she gasped. "My head is spinning."

He nuzzled her neck as she dropped her head onto his shoulder. "Just your head?" he mumbled against her skin. His entire bloodstream was swirling out of control.

She giggled and sighed.

Richard held her until their breathing slowed and then lowered her to the floor and held her a bit longer. He was greedy enough to want more but smart enough to know that couldn't happen. Not right now. "We probably should go back downstairs."

She nodded.

He waited until she made the first move, a slight step back, before releasing her. Then he picked up the material he'd dropped on the floor earlier. Marina moved farther back and he reached out, catching her arm as she stumbled slightly.

"Give yourself time to catch your sea legs."

She tossed her head back slightly. "I've never needed sea legs before." Bringing her gaze back to meet his, she asked, "What do we do now?"

He could think of several things, none of which he could act on but would surely like to. "We go downstairs, where you sew and I finish my rope riggings."

She nodded and turned to gather another section of the black material. "Of course."

Richard waited until she'd blown out the extra candles and then took the lit one. He questioned if he'd completely lost his sea legs when they started for the door, but it didn't last and he led her down the stairs as if nothing out of the ordinary had just transpired between them.

"Do you need any help?" he asked her at the bottom of the stairs.

"No. This won't take me long."

She carried the material down the hall and he crossed the front room to where William had angled his chair to peer out the edge of the curtain.

"No one has come or gone," the old man said.

Richard set down the candle to gather up the

varying lengths of rope he'd tied and coiled. "I'll need some sort of diversion to get all this outside."

"We could make several trips to the outhouse again, all of us," William said. "So many trips, the sentry won't know who is outside and who's not."

"That could work," Richard answered, hoping a more solid plan would form.

"Of course it will work," William answered. "I've pulled a sly one off myself a time or two."

"I'm sure you have," Richard agreed honestly, but trips to the outhouse wouldn't get him in the other directions he needed to go.

Close to an hour later, they had a plan and put it into play. Marina had done an excellent job sewing up the sleeves and attaching a hood to the second tunic, just as she'd done sewing all of the dummies. She'd also been the one to come up with their plan, suggesting they use the window in William's bedroom. It was on the side of the house that couldn't be seen from the road. The window was large enough for him to climb in and out. Richard surmised the only reason he hadn't thought about that was because he wasn't focused. At least not on what he should be focused on.

After insisting the activities in the house needed to continue, he carried John to the chair

next to William. With the curtain drawn aside
and the window open, the two men pretended
they were playing the card games that had become the rage in England.

It was a ruse. John couldn't see a thing, but
William could, and he would keep a constant eye
on the hedge across the road. A whittled flute
rested on his lap, ready for him to sound if the
man made the slightest move.

Marina helped carry everything into William's
bedroom and then handed it out to Richard. "Be
careful," she whispered, sticking her head out the
window.

The opportunity was too great to ignore.
Richard cupped her cheeks and kissed her lips
firmly. "I will. You make sure William doesn't
fall asleep."

"He won't. He's having too much fun."

Richard flipped up his hood and gathered the
first few items he'd need. He'd examined the trees
he'd use from the house windows several times
during the day but still knew traversing them in
the dark wouldn't be easy. Once again, he found
himself wishing he had one of his shipmates at
his side.

There was no chance of that, so he sent up
gratefulness for the luck he did have. The night
sky was on their side. The moon that had shone so

brightly earlier was now hidden by a thick layer of clouds. The rather miraculous cloud formation left one beam of light to shine down—directly on the hedge.

Marina waited until the darkness swallowed Richard before she let out a deep sigh. Contentment was not easy to accept when it had been absent so long. It was also not something she should be experiencing right now. What they were doing may seem fun, but, in fact, it was dangerous. Seriously so.

Still, she didn't harbor fear. It just didn't want to form inside her. Nothing could penetrate the swift and encompassing excitement of Richard's kisses. If she'd ever questioned being a witch, it had ended. No mere human would allow kissing someone to forsake their livelihood or those of others. Yet she was. When the thought of kissing Richard entered her mind, everything else was forgotten. When she was in his arms, there was no coldness inside her, no darkness.

Marina pushed off the window. Her fate was sealed, and there was no sense wishing otherwise. After checking on William and John, she peeked in on Gracie and then went into the last bedroom, the one Richard had slept in last night. The window faced the tree he was to set the first trap in.

There was nothing visible through the glass, and she swung it open.

Silent except for insects and the ruffling of leaves, there was no sign of anyone. Being idle had never been her way, so she hurried back downstairs.

"Richard needs my help." Knowing Uncle William would protest, she added, "It's extremely quiet out there. You two need to make noise. Not so loud it wakes Grace, but talk loud enough for your voices to carry out the window." She pointed at the cups of cider she'd already set on the table. "Ask me to get you more cider or something."

"Now, girl—"

"Laugh and carry on about the cards." She waved a hand. "Now."

John, eyes still swollen shut, took her at her word. "I think ye beat me again, William."

Her uncle eyed her coldly but answered loudly, "Aye, I did. One more game, lad, and Marina, get us some cider."

"Tell me thank you, too," she said, while hurrying down the hall to gather her cloak from the kitchen. She tied the hood beneath her chin and made sure her hair was tucked behind her ears. It was then she realized she hadn't put on her cap this morning. She'd never worn one at home but hadn't been allowed to enter the Salem Village without one, and so she had tried to make a habit of donning one each morning.

Another sign of her true being. Witches never abided by society rules or laws. She grinned as she entered Uncle William's room. Witches didn't mind very well, and that part was a bit exciting.

Marina climbed out the window, and once on the ground, she gathered up one of the three dummies still lying there. Staying low to the ground, she made her way across the yard. The tree Richard had chosen had long dangling branches covered with leaves that stretched clear to the ground.

Her heart was pounding and echoing in her ears by the time she crawled beneath the branches. She was cautious to make sure they didn't shake or quiver. Near the base of the tree, she set down the doll, which was far heavier than it looked, and listened for any movement.

The faint sounds of Uncle William's and John's voices floated in the air, but nothing more. She looked upward and kept staring until her eyes adjusted, at which point she made out a foreign shape high in the branches.

A moment later, Richard dropped down, dangling on a rope that was twisted around one hand and one foot. "What are you doing here?" he whispered.

"Helping. I brought a dummy."

"Mar—"

"Hush."

Silence surrounded them for several long moments before William and John could be heard again. She then smiled up at Richard.

He shook his head. "I'll drop a rope for you to tie the dummy on, but if you hear someone coming—"

"They won't."

Richard refrained from saying anything more, though she figured he wanted to. He scampered back up the rope and she watched his dark shape move from branch to branch with the ease and confidence of a squirrel gathering winter food. A short time later, a long rope dropped to the ground. She quickly attached the doll and gave the rope a single tug. Excitement grew as the doll silently slipped up into the branches and then disappeared, but shortly afterward, waiting beneath the tree became worse than it had been in the house. She sat still and watched, but couldn't see anything.

When the long branches on the other side of the tree fluttered slightly, she held her breath, praying it was a breeze.

It wasn't, but she let the air out of her lungs as Richard appeared. "How?"

He crawled closer. "I climbed to the next tree to attach the other end. Why are William and John being so loud?"

"I told them to make noise so you wouldn't be heard."

His kiss upon her cheek was swift but sweet. "Good thinking. Come on."

They crawled out of the branches and remained on their hands and knees until the house hid them. When he took her hand to help her stand, she whispered, "I'm not going back inside, so don't ask."

"I won't. I'll need you to get the other dummies in the trees."

She grinned.

So did he.

The next trees were near the outhouse. The trunks weren't hidden by branches, but the base of the first one was wide and branched out in several directions, giving her, along with the dummy, a place to hide. The wind had picked up, which caused her concern for Richard's safety, but the rustling of leaves hid any noises he might make. Marina got the doll ready for when he dropped the rope to pull it up and kept one eye on the hedge across the road. They were far more likely to be seen this time, and that not only heightened her anxiety—it gave her the tiniest thrill.

She'd never been part of such things, sneaking around at night, laying traps. Having Richard as a partner made it all the more exciting. Marina found that as unsettling as his kisses. Her life had changed in many ways when her family died. She'd had to become the one others depended upon instead of the way it had always been. Richard had changed that again, flipped things back to how they used to be, and she found such comfort in that. Or maybe it was relief. Burdens were lighter when shared—more fun, too.

She couldn't help but wonder what her life would have been like if she'd met Richard before the Indian attack, when she'd have been free to pursue happiness, a family of her own.

A rustle had her glancing up, and she reached out to catch the end of the rope as it fell beside her. Quietly and quickly she attached the large doll and gave the rope a tug. As soon as the dummy disappeared among the branches, she stretched to see between the deep V in the base of the tree. There was no movement from the hedge, yet small pieces of the man's white shirt glowed behind the foliage in the same places they had before.

Once again noise had her looking up. Her heart quickened as Richard scampered down the tree, and it thudded wildly when he crouched down beside her. If they had met way back when, she'd have done everything in her power to remain at his side forever.

"Any movement?"

Swallowing the lump in her throat, she shook her head.

He gestured toward the next tree over. "I have to attach the other ends."

Forcing aside thoughts she should never have conjured up, she asked, "Where's the rope?"

He gestured to a tree a distance away. "I tossed it over there."

"You'll be seen."

His hand was on the center of her back, heating her skin right through her cloak and dress, especially when he moved it in a wide circle. It made her want to close her eyes and bask in the pleasures of his touch, his nearness. Images of his strong, powerful body merging with hers flashed inside her head, and they were far more sensual than she'd ever have imagined. The witch in her was certainly wicked.

"No, I won't," he whispered into her ear. "Stay here."

Too lost in her own thoughts to protest, she turned his way. As if it was the most natural thing in the world, their lips met. Marina lost whatever control she may have had. Her arms twisted around his neck and she kissed him, long and repeatedly.

He was the one to pull away, and by the time she opened her eyes, he was gone. Spinning about, she saw him crawling through the tall grass, and a glance toward the hedge said the watchman was none the wiser.

Richard soon scaled the tree and Marina let out the air she'd been holding. Her body was thudding in ways it never had, and her thoughts shifted slightly...to Sarah. Had Richard loved his wife? He'd said the marriage just happened, but he wasn't the kind of man who let things just happen. Men like him made things happen.

She held no disillusions when it came to marriage. Very few people began their lives together loving one another. Her own parents had been bestowed to one another at birth. That was how it was in the old country, her mother had said. Marriages were arranged to unify families or lands or businesses, or at times, countries. Even here, in the New World, arrangements were common. Girls far younger than her were wed to older men in order to strengthen communities and families, and to populate, as was the case in Salem Village.

Richard had clearly shown his disgust of that, yet he'd participated in it. Freely. Whether he'd been younger back then or not, she couldn't imagine him being forced into doing anything he truly didn't want to. Yet if that had been the case, he'd have left the sea for his wife and child, because when he committed to something, he did so wholly.

Marina had to wonder how Sarah had reacted to his leaving. The few times she'd seen the woman, she'd kept her head down, following in her mother's footsteps and dragging little Gracie by the hand. Had that been because Richard had broken her heart by never returning? Would she have gladly sat at home while he went to sea, content to wait for his return?

There was no way to know, but Marina solemnly concluded, if put in that same predicament, she wouldn't have. Whether a marriage was arranged or not, it was a commitment that should not be broken. Nor should the couple be separated. Nessa had been sold to her brother Ole for a cow and its calf, and the two of them barely looked at each other for weeks. Yet by the time little Gunther had been born, they'd grown to love each other very much.

The same was true with Hans. Rachel's first husband had died on the voyage to Maine, and their mother had invited Rachel to live with them when the ship landed, Rachel being ill and all. Being one of the only marriageable women in the area, a line of men had visited the house, begging for Rachel's hand. Hans had put a stop to it by claiming he'd marry her. Marina still remembered how Rachel had cried, but before long, her tears had stopped and Rachel and Hans were barely apart from each other. It hadn't been until after Gunther had been born that Marina learned the reason Rachel had cried so hard had been because her illness had stolen her unborn baby and left her barren—something Marina could now fully relate to. Rachel had cried again when she'd said that was why she hadn't wanted to marry anyone, especially Hans. Because she couldn't give him the babies he deserved. Rachel had smiled afterward, though, ending her story by claiming she'd never have believed a man could love a woman who couldn't have babies and that Hans had to be the only man that wonderful.

"Any movement?"

Marina spun at Richard's voice and shot a glance across the road. "No." She hoped she was telling the truth. Lost in the past, she hadn't been keeping a vigil on the hedge.

"The next one will be easier," Richard whispered. "That's why I saved it for last."

"Where will that be?" When in truth, she wanted to know if he could ever love a barren woman.

"Up the road a piece," he whispered. "Before the curve. The first two are to scare them away from the house. This last one is so they don't follow when we leave."

Marina pinched her lips together and crawled along beside him, moving as slowly as earthworms to keep the tall grass from swaying. The witch part of her seemed to be taking over more and more of her thoughts. Wasn't it enough she'd become one and accepted her fate? Did she really need to be tormented by things that could never be?

Once behind the barn, they stood and hurried around the garden fence, but crawled again from there to the edge of the house, where she was glad to once again stand. She'd knotted her skirt between her legs before crawling to the first tree and her knees were starting to chafe, but she refused to complain.

"If I'd been thinking," Richard said, picking up the final coils of rope, "we'd have taken everything with us the last trip and hid it behind the barn."

"I doubt we'd have been able to haul it all. Not safely."

"I suspect you're right," he said. "We'll go back the same way."

Marina gathered up the doll and followed. Given the choice, she'd follow him around the world. To all the places he talked about full of colorful birds and swinging monkeys.

This time, rather than sneaking behind the barn, they entered the woods and carefully picked a pathway that ended on the road, a fair distance from where the watchman sat behind his hedge.

"I have to figure out which trees to use," Richard said. "They were too far from the house to examine without notice. Keep an eye on the road."

She kept her mind out of the past and off the future while standing near the edge of the woods, watching the hedge and the road. The only time she moved was to fasten the doll to the rope when Richard required it. He made several trips back and forth across the road. Each one strained her nerves, and she almost ran into the woods when he proclaimed they were done.

Chapter Fourteen

Marina may never have been so happy to be inside. Not even in the dead of winter when icicles had clung to her eyelashes and she'd been unable to feel her face. It hadn't been until she'd climbed through the window and stood upon the solid wood floor that she realized her heart had been in her throat the past hour. Moving aside so Richard could enter, she flipped the hood off her head and ran her hands through her hair, chasing away the tingles that had been covering her scalp.

Something bad was going to happen on that road. She could feel it.

"If I ever need a night stalker again, I'll choose you," Richard said, removing his hood.

Although the opportunity would never appear again, she bowed her head. "Thank you. I have the same sentiments."

His hands settled on her hips and he pulled her closer. "Do you?"

The sparks that erupted inside her chased away all thoughts but him. Good heavens, but she had grown wicked practically overnight. She'd been kissed today for the first time and then several additional times, and that was exactly what she wanted again. Along with the excitement came boldness. She reached up and rested her hands on his shoulders. "Yes, I do."

Richard relied on sheer will, which was hard. He wanted to kiss her again, a long leisurely kiss, but William could enter the room at any time. Instead, he pulled Marina close enough for a fast hug and then let her go.

"We need to tell those two they can stop shouting now," he said. She was looking at him with such startled disappointment he couldn't hold back a grin. He also needed an escape. The ability to control his desires was slipping. "I hope they didn't wake Grace."

Worry flashed across her face, and with a single, graceful move, she removed her cape. "I'll go check."

"I'll see to William and John."

Her blond hair floated in her wake as she hurried toward the doorway. Richard watched and bit the inside of his bottom lip in an attempt to deter the desire to run his fingers through the long locks. He wanted to touch far more than her hair.

He thought she'd been disappointed he hadn't kissed her again. So had he, but he found a sweet sense of solace in knowing she'd wanted him to kiss her.

Richard pulled his eyes off the doorway. Why was he tolerating such thoughts? Or even thinking them? Tasting her, touching her made him want more, and that couldn't happen. He wouldn't apologize for already kissing her—he'd never been an apologetic man, and what was done was done. Tomorrow night, once he'd retrieved the wagon from John's farm, they'd head to Boston, where he'd find a ship to plant them all on. He didn't even care where it was headed. Except for Grace. He'd see she was taken care of on his ship until this fiasco was settled, because he would return to Salem and see to the downfall of Hickman.

He could hear Marina talking with William and John in her charming, graceful way, and his heart grew heavy. Grace would be sad—she was as enchanted by Marina as he—but that couldn't be helped. The child would soon forget, as children did. Adults did, too, over time.

If things were different, if William and John were more of a help than a hindrance, he'd send Grace and Marina with them and stay behind, but neither man would be any form of protection if the wagon came upon highwaymen. Both William and John were proud, and neither would surrender, which would cause far more harm than good. Alone, he'd have already brought Hickman to his knees, but he wasn't alone, and therefore getting the woman, child and injured to safety had to be his first and foremost matter of business, and where his thoughts should lie.

Before leaving the room, Richard removed the outer tunic he'd need again tomorrow night. Marina was nowhere to be seen and he approached the men at the table.

"All set?" William asked quietly.

"Except the snare lines. I'll set them tomorrow night," Richard said. The older man's injuries from this morning seemed to have no lasting effects. John, however, looked as if he might slide off his chair at any given moment. Laying a hand on the younger man's shoulder, Richard said, "I'll help you to bed."

"I fear I can't make the stairs."

"I'll make you a pallet right here on the floor."

Richard spun around at the sound of Marina's voice.

"He can take my bed," William offered.

"No," John said. "The floor will be fine."

"He's exhausted," Marina said. "Just give me a moment."

She disappeared down the hall and Richard turned back to John. His stomach coiled at the beating the boy had taken. There could easily be more extensive injuries that none of them knew how to treat. If anyone was responsible for that, it was him. He'd been the one to cut down John's mother and bury her.

Back in no time, Marina used the furs and the material he'd hauled downstairs earlier, and after topping them off with a quilt and pillow, she gestured the pallet was ready. Richard lifted John from the chair and gingerly laid him on the makeshift bed.

"I've never hurt so," John said with a wince. "Never."

"I'll make you some more tea," Marina offered.

Already fading, John said, "No. Sleep. Just sleep."

"I'll stay out here tonight, too," William said. "In case the lad needs anything."

"No," Marina whispered while covering John with another quilt. "I will."

Richard took a moment to level a glare on each of them. "You," he said to Marina, "will sleep upstairs with Grace." Turning to William, he said, "And you in your own bed."

"Now see here," William started.

Richard merely lifted a brow. The old man was wise enough to end his challenge and, with a grumble, headed for the hallway. Marina, on the other hand, didn't move an inch. Nor did she blink an eye. The cool defiance in her eyes made him wonder if she'd ever accepted authority, from her father or anyone else. He doubted it. From the time she'd been a small child she'd most likely defied everyone, doing only what she wanted, when she wanted. He hoped Grace would be like that. Strong. Proud. Self-righteous. Her mother certainly hadn't been. Sarah had been meek and mild and had accepted every order or rule her father laid down with a mind that held no rebelliousness or questions.

That was the main thing he remembered about her. She'd accepted their union so willingly because her father had ordered it. Richard had known that before now, but while meeting the blue eyes narrowed upon him, he wondered why he'd also agreed so readily. He'd always preferred his women seductive and eager and a bit rebellious.

"What will you do if John awakens?" she asked. "If he grows feverish or—"

"I'll awake you," he interrupted smugly. It wasn't the answer she'd expected, and she responded just as he'd surmised. With a soft smile and a gentle nod. She was indeed the perfect woman. Proud, strong, yet gentle and caring.

"Go to bed, Marina," he said. "I'll call if I need you." Regret struck him as soon as the words crossed his lips. Need already had his loins on fire. He stepped away to blow out the candle on the table near the window and scanned the hedge across the road while closing the hinged window. Specks of white were still visible behind the leaves.

"Good night."

Richard didn't turn around. There was no need. She hadn't taken a step. He lowered the curtain to fully cover the glass while wishing her a good night, hoping by the time he turned around she'd be well on her way up the stairs.

She was, and disappointment once again rested upon him. He clamped his jaw against the lure of following her. Instead, he checked the lock on the front door and then moved down the hallway to check the back. Fate had never been his friend upon land. At sea, his destiny was set. Success flowed through him as easily as his vessel crossed the water. Yet it seemed as if every time he set foot on land, he was plagued with one malady after another.

The back door was securely latched, and after checking the window, he walked around the table. The hearth was on the inside wall in order to share the same chimney as the fireplace in the front room, and though the stones were still warm, the ashes were cool. He scooped some into the ash bucket so he'd be sure to have them when needed tomorrow night. The house was shrouded in darkness, but his eyes had adjusted. After a final glance around, he headed back down the hallway. The creaking of the stairway had him folding his arms and waiting until Marina—for there was no doubt it was anyone else—stepped off the last stair.

"What are you doing?" he asked at that precise moment.

Startled, she tripped and he reached out to grab her, to keep her from falling. He ended up with a handful of something soft that wasn't human. Quickly recognizing it as a blanket, he tossed it aside and reached for Marina again. She'd already thudded against the steps and his actions had him falling forward. He stretched out his arms, hoping to break his fall before he landed on her.

At least that worked. His arms were on either side of her shoulders, his knees between hers, trapping her skirt on the floor. The tips of their noses almost touched when his fall ended.

"Why'd you do that?" she asked.

Without a moment of hesitation, he answered, "So I could do this." Her lips were warm, soft and as ready as his.

Richard allowed the kiss to grow, encompassing him completely before checking his senses. Restraint weighed heavy, leaving him feeling like a plank close to snapping. He'd love to go on kissing her, take what she offered, but there within was the problem. Marina didn't know what she was offering.

Even if she did, he couldn't take it. William might not survive too many more years, and Marina would then be alone. She'd still be beautiful and bold, and could easily attract a husband worthy of her. Not a sea captain who'd visit her but once a year. That was what would happen if he acted upon the desires boiling inside him. He'd have to marry her, and that would not happen a second time.

Richard broke the kiss, but his attempt to rise was interrupted. He'd rarely, if ever, met a man who dared stare him down, yet she'd been doing it since his arrival. Her gaze didn't falter this time, either, even as a slow smile graced her lips.

"I brought down a blanket and pillow," she said softly.

"For me?"

"Of course you. Who else?"

He leaned back on his haunches and then bounded to his feet. Reaching down, he took her hands and assisted her to her feet. She made his blood flow like no other, and that alone was treacherous. "I can take care of myself," he said, more sternly than intended. "Have been for a very long time."

"You're a guest in my house. I'm being hospitable."

"Hospitable?"

* * *

Marina nodded. She couldn't pinpoint what it was she wanted from Richard but was well aware of the desires driving her actions. Was it because she knew their time together would soon end? It would, no doubt, and that was breaking away chunks of her heart. She'd never thought it would be whole again, but it was—she was—when his arms were around her. Maybe that was why she wanted him so badly, because it was her last chance to ever feel human again. To experience the pleasures that would never present themselves again.

To feel loved.

Stepping aside, he retrieved the pillow and blanket from the floor. "You've been more than accommodating. Run on up to bed now."

Run on up to bed? Did he truly believe he could dismiss her like a child? He would not get rid of her that easily. "I'll make you a pallet first."

He grasped her arm before she took a step. "No, Marina. Go to bed."

His eyes held a hint of something she'd never seen before. It wasn't the dark anger she'd witnessed yesterday or the whimsical sparkle that had shone so often today. It was more like danger, but not of an outside force. "I'll—"

"You'll go to bed," he said firmly. "Now."

"Don't—" His actions stalled her protest, all except a startled screech.

He'd grabbed her waist and hoisted her into the air high enough to flip her over his shoulder. Her head hung down his back, and he held the backs of her knees tight to his chest. His arms, so solid they were like a band of steel, prevented her from moving a muscle.

"Put me down."

"Shut up before you wake the house." He'd already started up the stairs and, hanging upside down, the movement left her disoriented.

His strides were quick. Pounding her fists against the backs of his thighs didn't slow him down. When he bent forward and pulled, she swiftly catapulted backward. Landing on the bed, she muffled a scream, not wanting to wake Grace. She also lay still for a moment, gathering her senses and listening for signs the girl may have been awakened by the bouncing of the bed.

"Do not leave this room until morning," Richard snapped.

The anger that exploded inside her was shocking, although it shouldn't have been—he was acting like a bully.

"I don't make idle threats, Marina, and I'm not making one now. Leave this room and you'll regret it." He slammed the door then, loud enough that Grace whimpered.

Marina flipped around and found the child in the dark. "Hush," she said softly. "Everything is fine." The thundering of heels marching down the stairs echoed in the house. "It's just the wind," she told the child. "Just the wind."

When Grace was sleeping again, Marina rose. Her first instinct was to march downstairs and tell Richard he was acting like a beast. A miserable, hateful beast. An odd detachment happened then, as if her body and mind were disconnected. Faraway thoughts told her to stay put, to follow Richard's orders. He already had enough to worry about and certainly didn't need her to blame him for the things happening inside her. Things she didn't even understand.

She dressed for bed then, taking her own advice. It wasn't easy or pleasant, for she had plenty of arguments to make against her better judgment. That had to be the witch inside her again. Never before had she squabbled with herself. Others, yes. Herself, no. She'd never experienced such wicked pleasures, either. There was no other way to describe the things that happened when Richard touched her. It was no longer just heat pooling in her stomach or her heart beating faster. Those things still happened, but now a spiraling heat had formed between her legs and in her breasts and everything grew hotter when Richard kissed her.

The most fearful part was that she enjoyed it. Not just his kisses but how they made her body react.

No God-fearing woman would ever respond so immorally. It had to be sinful.

"And therein lies the problem," she whispered. "I'm no longer a God-fearing woman. I was cast out of heaven and sent back to earth as a witch."

Chapter Fifteen

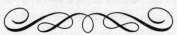

Marina wasn't certain she'd slept, but was ready to crawl out of bed when the sun rose. She dressed quickly, remembering her cap, and, after assuring herself that Gracie slept on, left the room. The house was quiet, and she walked softly, pausing when a board creaked beneath her feet. John was on the pallet, and she knelt down beside him. His forehead was warm but not overly hot. Or at least she hoped that was the case. It was hard to tell— her hands were chilly despite the warmth of the summer month.

Of course they were. Witches were cold-blooded.

Snores still came from Uncle William's room, and though she pretended not to be looking for Richard, she was concerned when he wasn't in the kitchen. The back door was unlatched, and she pulled it open, to see him drawing water from the well.

She closed the door and her eyes briefly, attempting to eliminate or, at least, ignore the re-actions taking place inside her. It was inevitable that she'd eventually become aware of the changes about her. Dreams and visions had been easy compared to the things happening now. She had to wonder what other changes would come about. Other than her sinful regard toward Richard, she felt no evilness, desired no pact with the devil or felt any revulsion for the church.

Or did she? Was her inability to understand the Puritan ways proof? Reverend Hickman stated witches were sinful, immoral and impulsive, yet he never really defined their acts. He claimed once a pact was made, a witch received supernat-ural powers she could then use against all God-trusting souls. This was written in the letters he'd had delivered to all the households in the area, telling everyone to be on the lookout for those demonstrating demonic behavior. Besides other things, the letters described telltale signs such as people hosting unexplainable injuries or suddenly becoming deaf, mute or blind.

None of those things had happened to her, but her heart skipped a beat at the thought of John losing his sight permanently.

The doorknob rattled and she hurried across the room to the hearth. There, she focused on building a fire. She was in enough turmoil with-out looking upon Richard again. The dream she'd had last night was about as sinful and immoral as one could get.

"Good morning."

She replied in kind without looking his way.

"I've brought in water and eggs," he said. "I'll go see to the milking."

"Thank you," she replied, adding a log to the kindling that had already taken a flame.

"Did you sleep well?"

She drew a breath to quell her nerves. It would be much better if he was grumpy and short this morning. Feeling anger toward someone being so courteous was difficult. Especially when her dream wouldn't die.

"Marina?"

"I slept fine," she said, gathering a kettle from the shelf. "I need to make some tea for John."

"He had a restless night."

"There's little I can do for him." Stating that aloud shattered some of her more selfish thoughts. "He needs a physician."

"We'll have him seen by one as soon as we arrive in Boston."

All the will in the world couldn't keep her from reacting to the warmth of the hand on her shoulder. She did, however, stop herself from turning toward him and laying her head upon his chest as the powers inside her suggested she should.

"John's going to be fine," he said.

Although John was still sleeping and she rarely shucked chores onto someone else, she couldn't stand this close to Richard. Stepping aside, she said, "I have to get the tea made. Thank you for milking." She'd much rather accompany him to the barn as she had yesterday morning. With two of them, the chores had been completed in half the time. Of course, that had also been the first time he'd kissed her. Her evil mind had to point out that little detail.

"Would you like me to accompany you to the outhouse first?"

Water slopped over the side of the kettle because of her shaking hands. She told herself not to turn around, not to look at him. And once again she wished he wasn't being so nice. "No, thank you."

"I won't be long. Stay in the house."

She clamped her lips tight and sighed aloud when the door closed behind him. After brewing tea for John, whose eyes were watering, which she didn't know was bad or good, she insisted he remain on the pallet and fixed more cold compresses for his eyes.

There were eggs boiling and a pot of porridge bubbling, and William and Grace were both awake and in the kitchen when Richard returned. They welcomed him as one would the sun after several cloudy days, which had Marina pinching her lips together. She couldn't decipher exactly why she was so upset with him. It wasn't necessarily anger, more like disappointment, and that was directly associated with the longing inside her. The ones made worse by her dream.

All that left her in a sour mood she chose not to remedy. Keeping her distance seemed the best alternative—in several ways. Her silence and briskness brought curious gazes from Richard and William. Ignoring them was her best choice, too. She showered Gracie with the same attention as always, and once breakfast was complete, she had to smile while assuring the child she could again wash dishes.

"We'll need to get things packed today," Richard said, still sitting at the table. "But keep the load light. We'll be traveling swiftly."

"Marina and I can say good riddance to most everything here," William said. "My pouch of gold coins will buy us whatever we need elsewhere."

Marina was aware that Richard's gaze was on her back and fought the compelling urge to turn from where she stood preparing the wash water. A single look into those dark eyes could shatter her resolve. She didn't comment, either. She'd arrived here with little more than a bag of clothes and her Bible. There hadn't been much to bring from Maine. The Indians had destroyed what they hadn't stolen. Not that it mattered. She wasn't leaving with the rest of them tonight and wouldn't need anything where she was going.

While the men discussed the length of the trip, she settled Grace on a chair near the dish tub and then went to see to John. The swelling on his face may have gone down slightly, but his ankle was worse. He was still on the pallet but attempting to fit a boot over the swollen foot.

"You'll make it worse," she said, removing the boot from his hand.

"I have to help Richard."

"I'll help with whatever needs to be done. You need to rest so you are up to the trip tonight."

He slapped the blanket beside him. "I've never felt so useless. Never."

Her own agony increased. She might never learn what would become of John and whether his eyes and leg healed. That was true of Uncle William and Gracie, too. As well as Richard.

"You aren't useless," she told John. "It will be your wagon that hauls everyone out of here."

"I have to show him where it is," he said.

"Oscar Pullman will help me retrieve the wagon."

Marina closed her eyes at the sound of Richard's voice. Her insides quaked and her lips went dry. Nothing had changed. She still had to right her wrong. Still had to go before the council and see that the innocent were released from prison, but the desire to do so wasn't burning as hot as it used to. All the fire inside her was now focused on Richard.

"Oscar knows where everything is," John said. "He's borrowed the wagon several times."

"That's what he told me," Richard answered.

Marina's eyes snapped open. She was about to ask when he'd spoken to Oscar when Richard took a hold of her arm.

"I need your assistance."

She rose but didn't risk glancing his way. She concentrated on her footsteps, too, rather than the heat penetrating the sleeve of her dress from his hand. His touch left more than her skin in turmoil, and breathing through that took determination.

He led her into the kitchen, where Uncle William stood beside Gracie, helping wash the heavier kettles. Richard didn't stop until they were at the back door, upon which he said, "We'll be in shortly."

Marina dug her heels into the floor, but her opposition was no contest for his strength.

"It's safe," he said, once they were on the back stoop and the door firmly closed behind them.

He was referring to Hickman's men, but they were not who she feared at this moment. Neither was he. It was her traitorous self that concerned her. Her insides were flooding with sensations brought on by his closeness. The idea of never seeing him again was tearing her apart. She twisted her arm from his hold and moved forward. "What is it you need?"

He chuckled, then asked, "Still mad I didn't take what you offered last night?"

Pretending she had no idea what he meant, she marched forward. "You took what I offered. A pillow and blanket."

Once they crossed the threshold of the barn, he grasped her elbow and spun her about.

"You offered far more than a pillow and blanket. We both know that." He let her loose then and ran a hand through his dark hair. "Another place, another time, I'd have gladly taken you to bed, and most likely would still be there. Enjoying the pleasures we'd find."

"To bed?" The mortification he knew exactly what she'd wanted blazed through her, heating her cheeks faster than a roaring fire. An attempt at insult launched forward as her defense. "I offered no such thing."

"Didn't you?" He shook his head. "I recall things differently."

"Then you are addlepated."

He laughed and she spun around, marching down the center of the barn. "What was it you needed my assistance for?"

"Nothing," he answered. "Other than to say I'm sorry."

This time she turned around slowly. An apology was not what she'd expected. "For what?"

"For kissing you. For allowing you to think—"

"You have no idea what I think." Frantic at the very idea he might, she continued, "And you should be sorry for kissing me. It was a barbaric way to behave."

"Indeed," he said with a nod and a grin.

The mockery in his eyes was what struck her the hardest. If she knew how to harvest and use her powers, she'd cast a spell to make him disappear into thin air, leaving behind nothing but dust. Her thought flipped at that moment, telling her she wouldn't do that. She loved him. As unbelievable as that was, she cared as much about him as she did for Uncle William and Gracie. More in some ways, different ways. Witches weren't supposed to love anyone but themselves.

Frustrated beyond all else, Marina stomped forward, toward the door. "I have things to see to."

Once again he stopped her by taking her arm. "What I said earlier is imperative. We must travel light. Only the essentials. Oscar will help me retrieve the wagon tonight, but it'll be late. Very late to ensure the village is asleep, and then we'll need to travel fast."

The seriousness of his eyes dulled the rapid beat of her pulse in one way but increased it in another. "When did you speak to Oscar?"

"This morning. He was in the woods behind the garden. The villagers believe the tale of his daughter and John's mother arising from the dead. Panic is overtaking the community. Five more arrests were made yesterday."

"Oh, dear heavens," she whispered. "Who?"

"He didn't say."

Remorse filled her head with pain and she pressed at her temples. "This has to stop."

"It shall," Richard said.

Knowing her role, Marina nodded. "Yes, it shall."

Richard's hand cupped the side of her face, and a tremble encompassed her body. Not just from his touch, but from the vision forming behind her eyes. She saw herself going to him, her lips hot and demanding as they met his. The apparition was more real than others had been and full of emotions. She could feel the joy, the power of justice behind the kiss. It made little sense, for he wouldn't be here when justice was served.

Richard fought the desire to pull her close, to once again feel the heat of her lips, taste the sweetness of her mouth. He'd spent most of the night berating himself for what he'd already done, and he couldn't afford to waste any more energies on things that couldn't be.

Dropping his hand, which instantly felt cold and instilled a bitter loneliness inside him, he said, "Oscar also said Hickman dispatched a rider to Boston yesterday."

"The one we saw."

"I assume so," he said. "The rider was to deliver a message to the governor." He didn't add the message called for his arrest.

There was no surprise in her eyes, just as he hadn't been surprised to hear the news.

"Has he returned yet?"

"No, not according to Oscar." The rider was of little concern. It would take far more than an order from the governor to arrest him. Richard flayed a hand in the general direction of the barn stalls. "I'll create a safe hiding spot for anything you can't take with us tonight but wish to have retrieved at a later date."

"That won't be necessary."

Her tone held a potency he may have pondered if her eyes hadn't looked so forlorn.

"Perhaps you'll find something while packing today that will change your mind."

She shook her head. "The house will be scavenged as soon as everyone's gone. There will be nothing to retrieve."

Chapter Sixteen

The day lingered with impotent slowness even though there was much to be done. William discovered things he wanted hid in the barn, and Richard pried up several boards along the back wall to secure a hiding spot for them. He was a bit taken aback by Marina's willingness to comply with her uncle's wishes. His nerves also grated against one another at her avoidance of him. He'd set his ground rules and had to abide by them. He not only had her future to contend with, but his own and Gracie's.

His life now included a daughter, and that would impede upon his sailing days enough. He'd considered that last night, too. And how Grace was about the same age he'd been when Earl took him to the sea. Leaving her to be raised by an acquaintance at a seaport no longer appealed to him, not like it had upon his summons to retrieve her.

Grace had been little more than a thought then, a problem he needed to solve. Now she was a flesh-and-blood person. His daughter, who had wheedled her way deep inside his heart. Something he did not regret.

The sun was falling behind the trees when he made another trip out to the barn, this time to complete the evening chores. He'd just finished milking the cow, a part of him wondering where he'd get fresh milk for Gracie while sailing, when a knock drew his attention to the side of the barn. Setting the milk bucket aside, he ventured out the back door and around the side.

Oscar Pullman stood near the corner of the building, peering across the road. Turning, the man whispered, "It's gone."

"What's gone?" Richard questioned.

"John's wagon. Along with his team of horses."

Richard cursed beneath his breath. Getting everyone to safety without a wagon was impossible. He'd already considered a boat, but getting John through the swamp would be impossible. William wouldn't be able to trek it, either. Richard had depended upon his strength many times but knew he couldn't carry two men that far.

"The reverend's slaves hitched up the team and loaded the wagon earlier today," Oscar said.

"Slaves?"

Oscar nodded. "A black man and woman the

reverend brought with him when he moved here. I suspect no one else was brave enough to enter the house, not with the rumors of the Goodwife Griggs coming back from the dead."

The way Hickman had treated his slaves in Barbados made Richard wonder why some would still be with him, but it didn't surprise him. The man relished being waited on hand and foot.

"Who else has a wagon?" Richard asked.

"No one we can trust," Oscar said.

"I don't need to trust them. I just need their wagon."

"That's the problem," Oscar said. "The church has confiscated most of them. They are packed full of personal possessions and inside Hickman's barn. He keeps the place locked tight."

"What about the horses?"

"One of the church elders, Thomas Bolton, takes them out to his place. It's several miles from town."

Another idea was taking shape in Richard's mind. "What about Hickman's carriage? His horses?"

"They're at his place, but ye can't be considering…" Oscar's eyes grew wide as his voice trailed away.

"It's the only option. I have to get John to a doctor and the rest of them to the safety of my ship." A chill rippled his spine. "Tonight. Tomorrow may be too late."

The other man nodded. "I'll be in the woods. Waiting to help."

Richard gestured toward the barn. "After we're gone, take the cow and chickens and set my horse loose. It's too slow to be any use, but will find the way back to its stable in Boston." He turned around and made his way back into the barn through the back door. The weapons upon his ship came to mind, guns and cannons, cutlasses and daggers. All he had was the short blade in his boot. It had already come in handy but was hardly what he'd need if taken upon while stealing Hickman's carriage. William had scrounged up what he had. A pair of rusty dueling pistols that weren't worth cleaning.

He cursed everything about their predicament while making his way to the house.

Marina had supper on the table and the meal was a somber event. John was still in the front room, growing weaker by the hour. Even little Gracie seemed to sense the tension hanging in the air and ate with caution filling her eyes. That goaded Richard and increased his determination. As if he'd needed any more reason to want this all over.

"Get a few hours of sleep," he said to no one

in particular while pushing away from the table. "You'll need it."

He retreated to the front room to tie the last set of ropes he'd secure after taking care of the night watchman later.

The house had gone quiet except for a clink or clatter coming from the kitchen. Marina had carried Grace upstairs earlier and he wondered what she was doing now. Against his better judgment, he went to see.

She was sweeping the floor. He leaned a hand against the door frame. "Is that necessary?"

"What?"

"Cleaning? The house will soon be empty."

"I will not have the scavengers believing we lived in a hovel."

He laughed. Perhaps she wasn't that different from other women. Gesturing toward the single bundle near the back door, he asked, "Is that everything you're taking?"

"Yes. Gracie's clothes. Enough until more can be purchased."

"Thank you. I do appreciate all you've done for her."

"Getting John to a doctor and William to the sea will more than repay what I've done for Gracie."

Her tone once again tickled his brain, but they were all on edge, anxious for this night to be over.

Things weren't settled between them, either, but there was no settling to be done. Marina had no future with him. Not the one she deserved.

"You should get some rest. I'll be leaving in a few hours."

Her eyes glowed in the candlelight and held more thoughtfulness than he had the ability to perceive at this moment. His loins were tightening, growing hot with desires and thoughts of what could have been. Fighting them would take energy he'd need later, so he left the room.

He stationed himself in the front room, in William's usual chair, where he could hear any movement outside through the slightly open window. The day had been warm, and the house held that heat long after the sun fell. Sweat beaded upon his brows and increased as Marina entered the room. Without a word, she checked on John and then climbed the stairs.

Richard rested his eyes for a short time, using the quiet to pick apart his plan, making sure he hadn't left out a single detail. When the hour came, time to set things in motion, he stood and, after donning his black tunics, gathered the things he'd need.

Before leaving the house, he awoke William. "I'll be back in an hour. See everyone is ready."

"Aye, Captain," the man answered, rolling to the edge of his bed to secure his wooden leg.

Using William's window again, Richard left the house. He used the same pathway he and Marina had last night, to the garden and then into the woods. There was no amusement filling him, not like last night when Marina's enjoyment of slipping around in the dark had made her face shimmer in the moonlight. He shouldn't miss her companionship, but he did.

Cautious to not make a sound, he made his way through the woods and across the road. He left one rope near the road and picked up a couple of rocks before proceeding toward the sentry. There had been a change in guards shortly after sunset, leaving him to assume this man was alert, listening and watching for anything out of the ordinary.

A smile touched Richard's lips. Things were certainly about to get unordinary.

Surprise was always the best tactic, and he relished the upcoming attack as he sneaked forward. The watchman was on the ground, leaning against a tree. Richard tossed a rock into the hedge and watched as the man stiffened and then straightened to peer toward the bushes.

Richard tossed another rock, and then he opened the pouch hanging from the belt of his tunic to withdraw the tankard full of the ashes he'd mixed with spices from Marina's kitchen. The watchman had climbed to his feet but stood still, as if waiting for the noise to happen again.

With a roar that sounded beastly even to his ears, Richard jumped to his feet and rushed forward.

The watchman spun around. "Who goes there?"

Richard tossed the ashes directly in the man's face. "It is I," he growled. "The devil who has come to reward you for your deeds."

The man stumbled backward, rubbing his eyes with both hands. "Reward?" he screeched. "I have done no wrong."

"Aye," Richard replied. "You have already aligned yourself with Satan."

"No. No. Not me." The man fell to his knees. "My eyes. They are burning. I cannot see."

"Because no one is allowed to see me." Richard tugged out a length of cloth he'd tucked into his belt and used it to gag the man. Then he dropped a bag over the man's head and tied it with a rope around his neck. Next, he pulled the man to his feet and planted him upright against a tree, where he secured him to the trunk with several lengths of rope.

The man's muffled cries had grown into whimpers by the time he was done. Before leaving, he whispered close to the man's ears, "George Hickman made a pact with Satan years ago, and anyone who aligns himself with the man shall rot in hell at his side." He then let out a mocking laugh at the man's increased whimpers before moving on.

It took little time to set all of the snare lines for the dummies and to tie up the final rope, which he left lying across the road. Richard then entered the woods for the trail that led to Oscar's place and on into the village.

From the bedroom window, Marina saw the dark figure enter the woods. As her heart tightened so severely she feared it might strangle her, she sent up a silent prayer, asking God to protect Richard. She wasn't certain that was appropriate, considering he was on his way to steal a wagon. It was John's wagon, she then justified, and he needed a doctor.

Everything was set for Richard's return, so there wasn't much for her to do other than carry the sleeping Grace down to William's bed. They would need Richard's help in getting John out the door, so she left him sleeping in the front room.

"He'll be here shortly," Uncle William said as the two of them stood in the kitchen, not doing anything except moving to glance out the window now and again.

"You have your gold," she said in half question, half statement.

"Yes. No worries, girl. We have plenty to start over."

She blinked at the tears forming. Enough tears

had flowed upstairs, where her heart had filled with such pain it must have finally broken in two, leaving her numb. It was time to tell him. "I'm not leaving."

"Not leaving? Yes, you are. Richard will be here—"

"I can't leave." She lifted her shoulders and let them fall, feeling rather hopeless. "Not when I'm the reason this all started."

Uncle William let out a line of curses that were as much a part of his sailing days as his wooden leg. "I'll hear no such thing," he shouted afterward. "You had no part in it."

"You know that's not true. You know the accusations didn't start until Hickman heard about what happened to me in Maine."

"Only because he was trying to get rid of me. He knew I remembered him from my sailing days."

She shook her head. That had been her uncle's response since the beginning. "There's no sense denying it, Uncle William. I'm a witch. Captain Farleigh sat in this very kitchen and told you what happened."

"You were dropped from the loft onto your noggin."

"There are things I can't explain to you." Tears fell onto her cheeks. "I wish I could, but I can't. I don't even understand them, but I know all those people in jail, all those people being murdered, are because of me. I have to put a stop to it."

He stomped across the room and had her by the shoulders. "Put a stop to it? How? I've told you before I won't let you be arrested. I won't—"

The back door flew open. "Hurry! Into the carriage!" Richard ran through the room and up the hall.

"Grab the bundle by the door," Marina said, running herself. "I'll get Gracie."

With the child in her arms, she paused at the door while Richard rushed past carrying John, and then she followed him. Oscar Pullman was holding the reins of a team of horses, but they weren't hitched to John's wagon.

"You stole Hickman's carriage?" she asked.

Richard set John on one of the seats before turning to take Gracie. "It was all I could find." After handing Gracie to William, he reached for Marina.

She stepped back and shook her head.

He waved a hand. "Climb in."

"I'm not going."

Shock briefly covered his face before his eyes narrowed. "Yes, you are."

He launched forward, but she'd been prepared for that and leaped in the other direction. His hand had brushed her arm, so she spun and ran. Passing the carriage door, she slammed it shut, and then, although it was dangerous, she ducked beneath the harness rails and came out on the other side. She knew he'd never fit between the horses and carriage.

He ran around the front of the horses, while she ran around the back of the carriage. "Bloody hell, woman! Get in the carriage!"

"No! Someone has to make sure you aren't followed."

"Oscar will do that!"

"Captain!" Oscar yelled. "I hear horses!"

They each rounded the carriage again, and Marina's heart stopped. "Go," she said to Richard over the horses. "Please, go. I have to stay. These are the people my father told me to save."

"Bloody hell," Richard cursed. "They are not!"

"Yes, they are!"

"Your father is dead!" he shouted.

Tears rolled down her face, and she sought a way for him to understand. "I know. And so is Earl, yet you sail the seas in his honor."

"I sail because I want to. I must."

"And this is what I must do."

"Captain, they're coming!" Oscar yelled. "Ye must leave. I'll hide Marina."

The storm on Richard's face could have taken out buildings. He cursed loudly but jumped into the driver's seat and grabbed the reins. "I'll be back. I'll be back before sunup."

The carriage jerked forward as the horses took off. Marina's tears fell faster than she could wipe them away. The carriage was a blur and then disappeared around the corner.

"Get in the barn!" Oscar shouted. "Out of sight—and stay there."

Marina swiped aside her tears. "We have to stop them from following."

"The captain set traps," Oscar said.

She'd forgotten about the dummies. Marina ran into the house and grabbed the cloak she'd draped over a chair. As she exited the house again, a thunder of hooves filled the air. Barely making out Oscar Pullman running for the woods, she darted forward but only made it as far as the well before shouts filled the air.

The pandemonium started before she could hide herself. Two men on horseback shot around the house. The first horse tripped, tossing the rider over its head. The second horse reared. That man held on until a strange howl filled the air. It was a moment before Marina recognized the sound of Uncle William's bamboo whistle. The black figure that sailed through the air frightened the already rearing horse. It went wild and the man flew to the ground.

Both men scrambled to their feet and charged nearly as fast as their horses for the road. Marina ran toward the house and peered around the edge.

Two other men were racing for the road, telling her that the other witch doll must have been triggered and fallen from the trees, too.

The running men almost collided with three others coming up the road on horseback. There was much shouting, but the men running toward the village didn't stop. Neither did the ones galloping toward the house.

Hickman's voice was clearly recognizable as he shouted, "Don't stop! After that coach!"

Marina ran in the wake of the horses, crossing the road to cut through the woods to where she'd helped Richard hang the third dummy. Air wouldn't catch in her lungs and she could barely hear the bamboo howl over her heart pounding in her ears, but she neared the edge of the trees in time to watch the black figure fall from the trees and sail before the horses.

The animals went wild, rearing and bucking. The first two men lost their seats and hit the ground as their horses shot onward, leaving the men clouded in dust. Hickman was slower and still on his horse when suddenly, as if hit by a great force, he flew backward. His horse twisted and reared, breaking the hold the man still had on its reins before it followed the trail of the other two, leaving Hickman lying on ground.

The first two men were already on their feet and ran past her as if their heels were on fire.

Hickman was shouting for them to wait for him as he kept tripping himself while attempting to scramble to his feet.

A rather wicked sense of enjoyment filled Marina, and she started to cackle. It was like no other sound she'd ever made. She leaned her head back, letting the noise grow louder and more beastly. The sound split the air, making the men run faster. Except for Hickman, who looked like a rabbit with one foot in a snare, running on all fours as he was.

Marina drew in air and stepped out onto the road as she let out another cackle, not caring if she was seen or not. In truth, there was a part of her that hoped Hickman would look back, just so he'd know what he was dealing with now.

A bona fide witch.

Another man stumbled out of the hedge. He held one hand over his eyes, the other out in front of him, as if feeling his way. Hickman stumbled into him and they both went down. After a tussle, they were both on their feet with the second man holding on to Hickman's coattails, while he ran in zigzags trying to shake the man off.

She watched and cackled until the men had been swallowed up by the darkness. Her throat burned, but she felt a sense of pride in having stopped the chase so completely. Richard would surely make it all the way to Boston now.

Someone else walked out of the hedge and she froze for a moment, until recognizing Oscar.

"Sakes alive, Marina, ye scared ten years off my life with that laugh."

She turned her gaze back to the road. "I hope it did the same to them."

"I'd say it did."

"Where were you?"

"I had to tie up the final rope. The one that knocked Hickman off his horse. Richard had it tied to one tree, but I couldn't fasten it to the other until after he left in the carriage. Then I had to cut loose the watchman he told me about."

"How did you come about helping?" she asked out of curiosity.

"He helped me," Oscar said. "Ye do good to them which do good to ye."

Marina nodded. Her elation was gone, leaving her empty.

They stood silent for a moment, watching the dark and quiet road. She realized then that she was standing exactly where she had when the carriage left. The exact spot she'd known something heartbreaking would happen.

It had.

Oscar was the first to move. "I have to cut those dummies down. Richard doesn't want anyone to know they were fake."

"I'll help."

"Why didn't ye go with him?" Oscar asked as they started to walk up the road.

The witch inside her must have completely taken over because her entire being had grown cold, yet she was still alive. It was just as well. There was no one left for her to care about. No family to love—or lose again. "My work here isn't done." Glancing his way, she added, "An eye for an eye."

Chapter Seventeen

Richard had been mad before, furious, irate, but he'd never been this totally enraged. When he got back to that house he would blister Marina's backside. He'd never raised a hand to a woman, but she should be inside the carriage behind him. Not back there with men hunting her down as if she was a wild animal. That was how it would be once they discovered she was still there.

With renewed fury he whipped the reins over the galloping horses. His greatest desire was to turn the coach around, but he couldn't. He'd always rationalized things, and some evil, righteous voice inside him said saving three lives overrode one. That twisted his guts until they burned hotter than hell. He didn't like it, but was honor-bound by some damnable code instilled within. Marina was instilled within, too, whether he wanted her to be or not. That too played hell inside him. So did the fact he understood her action. Although twisted, she believed this was how she could avenge the cruelty imposed upon her nephew and the deaths of her family. She was too damn stubborn to see what had happened then and what was happening now were not related.

Too damn stubborn to admit a woman armed with a Bible couldn't save anyone.

He drove the horses until he feared they'd drop and then slowed to give them a chance to recoup. From buying and selling cargo, which more than once had been horses, he knew this was a fine pair, and as unusual for a preacher to own as everything else in Hickman's coffers.

The horses continued onward at will, and Richard gave his mind the same freedom. Pullman was a good man, and he'd see to Marina's safety until Richard could return. Oscar had seen enough to believe all Richard had said about Hickman. The man agreed no other preacher had ever made such demands or had shown such greed. Oscar also believed Marina wasn't a witch. That she'd merely been ill in Maine and had become the victim of rumors, just like his daughter and wife.

Minutes ticked by slowly, and the miles grew longer than any he'd ever trekked. Richard's mind went down many roads, and various scenarios formed before he once again lifted the reins, coaxing the horses into a faster pace. Despite what Marina thought, her father hadn't sent her to save those other women. The bridge in her dreams, the one her father said she couldn't cross, was so she could live. Richard would make sure that happened.

By the time the carriage rolled into Boston, the sky was already pink and Richard cursed. He wanted to be on his way back to Salem by now. Driving the last bits from the tired horses, he steered them to the water's edge, not letting them come to a stop until his ship was before his eyes.

A deckhand, one who'd sailed with him for years, Beauregard Abel, ran up to the road, taking a hold of the horses even though they barely had the strength to stand.

"I'll need help," Richard said, leaping to the ground.

Beau let out a whistle, and by the time Richard opened the carriage door, several other hands stood near. Questioning how fast they'd appeared, Richard glanced around.

"The governor's taken over the *Concord*, Captain," Beau said. "Said they're confiscating her."

"The hell you say," Richard growled.

"It's true, my friend."

Richard spun in the other direction. "Wellstead."

Emerson Wellstead nodded. "It's been a while, Richard."

The two of them had sailed side by side for

years, often sharing cargo and ports, until Emerson had accepted a letter of marque a few years ago. Richard's gaze went from the sea captain to the *Concord*. Men stood on deck, but they weren't his men.

He turned back to the carriage, where William was stiffly making his way out. Richard reached in and scooped up Grace. Looking at Emerson, he said, "I need a doctor and a safe place for my friends and daughter."

Emerson turned to a man standing at his side. "You heard him—get a physician. A good one." The captain then said, "They'll be safe on the *Victoria*. This way."

Richard had barely taken a step when his name was shouted.

"You can't run from them," Emerson said. "They are the governor's men." He held out his hands. "Give me your daughter. I'll personally see to her and your friends."

Richard knew it was best to get away from the carriage, to never give the men looking for him the opportunity to see Grace, William or John. "Her name is Grace," he said to Emerson while handing his daughter to the other man. "I won't be long."

"I'll get word to you," Emerson said. "Wherever they take you."

"They won't take me anywhere," Richard insisted, as he started toward his ship.

Those had been optimistic words.

He argued and fought but eventually came to the conclusion he'd soon be in no shape to help Marina. As four bulky men hauled him back up to the road, he demanded an appointment with the governor. After a short trek in an enclosed wagon, where none of them released their hold, they unceremoniously dumped him in a dark and dank brick cell that smelled like piss.

Richard bounded to his feet and rubbed at his knuckles, still stinging from getting a few good punches on the thugs before conceding there were too many of them. The scabs he had from taking down Hickman's men had broken loose, leaving him bleeding again, and he was reminded of Marina not wanting to get blood on her sheets.

"Bloody hell!" He had to get back to Salem. Pounding on the solid wood door, he shouted for a guard.

"They won't come."

He turned, scanning the darkness for where the voice came from. "Show yourself."

"Which one of us?"

Shifting nothing but his eyes toward the other corner, he asked, "How many are here?"

"Three." The dark figure that stepped closer said, "I'm Ben Hart."

"Orin Crompton," said one on the left.

"Frank Bancroft," added the first one who'd spoken. "And you are?"

"Tarr. Captain Richard Tarr."

"Of the *Concord*?"

"Aye," he replied. "Ben, was it?"

"Aye, Captain. I sailed with Earl when you were but a lad."

Richard rubbed his forehead where a lump was forming. "I don't remember you."

"No reason you would. You were his cabin boy. I was just a sailor wanting to get from one shore to another."

"Why are you here?"

"That, Captain, is a long story," Ben replied. "Why are you here?"

As deflated as a windless sail, he slumped against the door behind him. "That too is a long story."

The sun was casting the world with its morning glow when Marina closed the front door of the house for what she knew would be the last time ever. She drew in a deep breath, stepped off the stoop and started across the yard. There wasn't a single sign left of the chaos from the night before. Oscar Pullman had helped cut down the ropes and dummies and hidden everything deep in the woods. He'd also taken home Nellie and the chickens, leaving Marina one less thing to worry about. Richard's horse had been let loose and shooed down the road. Animals were smart. It would eventually find its way back to Boston.

When her steps reached the road, she flipped up her hood. The black cloak fit her image, the one the villagers had of her and the one she had of herself.

By now the others should be in Boston. John would have a physician looking after him. Guilt rolled in her stomach. Richard had been angry, Uncle William hurt, but they were old enough to understand. Gracie wouldn't, and she'd question why Marina wasn't there when she awoke this morning.

The iciness that had settled in her chest remained, but there was pain there, too. It was familiar. That was how a person felt when they lost those they loved. She did love Gracie and Uncle William. John had been a dear friend, and Richard…

Marina shook her head. She'd come to love him most of all, and knowing she'd never see him again hurt terribly. Blinking at the tears, she told herself the important thing—what she must remember—was that they were all safe now. If they had made it to Boston.

"They made it," she said aloud. "I'll not think otherwise."

That quelled the argument inside her, perhaps because of how heavy the weight on her shoulders had become. This wasn't something she'd have chosen, given the choice. She'd have crossed that bridge with the rest of her family, if someone had asked what she wanted. No one had asked, though.

She could also wonder what might have happened if she'd stayed in Maine or never met Richard, but that wouldn't change anything. There were lives she could save, and that would change things. Not for her, but for others. And that was why she was here. She'd read the chapter of Matthew this morning—from where Jesus brought a young girl back to life to where he told his disciples they'd be brought before councils on his behalf—to give her strength.

Holding her Bible in one hand, Marina never slowed her steps or faltered from her destination. Despite the people peering out their windows, she marched straight to the parsonage. Her knock was answered by a black woman. Hickman's slave had been one of the first accused of witchcraft but had been acquitted and released. Having someone in his own home accused and cleared had given the reverend more power, and others looked to him for counsel. Marina had deduced it meant nothing more than that the slave hadn't had anything of value for her master to steal.

"I'm here to see Reverend Hickman," Marina said.

Upon opening the door, the black woman had backed up, her eyes wide. Marina took a step forward, crossing the threshold so the door couldn't be closed. "I'll wait here."

The woman spun and hurried down the hall. Marina took in the surroundings. Fine furniture filled the room and colorful rugs covered the floor. Beyond that, the room reminded her more of a store than a home.

George Hickman appeared in the hallway but didn't come all the way into the front room. "What do you want?"

"I'm turning myself in, as I said I would."

"Why didn't you leave with the rest of them?"

"Because my work here isn't finished." Marina moved toward a table and picked up a candlestick. An identical one sat on another table. "The Goodwife Griggs inherited these from her mother. They were one of her finest possessions."

"Those are my wife's," Hickman said. "Her mother gave them to her."

"Others may believe you, but I do not." She set the candlestick back on the table. "Because you don't frighten me." Swirling so her black cape swished, she leveled her stare upon him. "You, however, were quite frightened by my friends. Tell me, Reverend. Is there gravel in your knees from your escapade last night?"

His face turned red. "Get out of my house!"

"Gladly. I'm just waiting for you to escort me to the jail." The ungoverned courage filling her was potent and a bit shocking. She'd never known such power. Such supremacy. It was rather addictive. Without blinking, she added, "The accused need their leader. Much like your men."

The arrival of two men at the front door started the procedure of her arrest, which, with the loss of the only carriage in town, meant she walked all the way to Salem Towne, followed closely by Hickman and two others. They sat upon horses.

Passing Uncle William's home was surreal, but she kept her gaze on the road ahead. The only time her feet stumbled was when they arrived at Salem jail. It was a dungeon, built of thick timbers near the river. The stench that assaulted her as a guard opened the door made her nose burn.

"Enjoy your new home," Hickman said mockingly.

Marina crossed the threshold of her own accord. A long corridor lay before her. As she walked it, mazes of small cells ran in all directions. The meager light creeping in from above the walls and beneath the eaves diffused the darkness enough for her to make out people chained and tied to the thick timbers and the rats scurrying about. Water squished beneath her feet and a cold dampness penetrated her cloak and clothing and her skin, chilling deep into her very soul.

Nothing could have prepared her for this.

Five days of hell left Richard in a ruthless and nasty mood. If not for his cell mates, he may have gone mad. The only reason he hadn't was because they had looked up to him from the moment he'd arrived. A leader didn't go mad. Not even when word had spread through the jail of two more hangings in Salem Towne. Yesterday and the day before. Six more each day.

He'd prayed to a Lord he hadn't given much credence to most of his life and cursed the devil who seemed to be taunting him. Neither had done a shilling of good.

The jangle of keys sent him across the small cell. If he had one thing, it was hope. Well, that and friends on the outside.

The knob turned and he moved into the space created by the door being pulled open. The light blinded him for a moment, but he'd seen enough for a hint of rejoice.

"Wellstead."

"It took some finagling, but I have an appointment with the governor for you."

Liberation raced through his blood. Stepping

forward, Richard slapped Emerson on the shoulder. "Thank you, my friend."

The guard started to shut the door and Richard spun around, grabbing the wood. "They are coming with me."

"I—"

"Who are they?" Emerson asked, interrupting the guard.

"Men who sailed with Earl."

Taller and broader than most men, his head and face covered with carrot-orange hair, Emerson let out a laugh that echoed against the bricks. "You pick up more baggage than anyone I know. Release them, as well," he told the guard.

As they started up the corridor, walking shoulder to shoulder, Emerson said, "The lad, John, is doing well. His sight is fine, but his broken ankle will take longer to heal. I've hired a nursemaid for your daughter. They are getting along soundly. And I've taken pleasure in getting reacquainted with William Birmingham. I thought the crusty old bugger went down with the *Golden Eagle* years ago."

"I'm deeply indebted to you," Richard said sincerely.

"More than you know," Emerson said. "I now own the *Concord*." Knocking into him with one shoulder, he added, "It's going to take more than a few gold doubloons for you to buy her back."

Richard's stride didn't stumble, but his mind did. "How could you have purchased my ship? I didn't sell her."

"The governor confiscated her. But my letter of marque trumped his authority."

"So you stole her," Richard replied.

"Aye."

For the first time in his life, the *Concord*, or any other ship, wasn't his main concern. "At least I know she's in good hands." He wished he could say the same about Marina. He'd thought of little else but her. "I have to get back to the village."

"Aye. Birmingham has told me all about your blonde witch."

"She's not—"

Emerson's laugh once again filled the corridor. "I'm not the one who needs to be convinced of that, Captain."

Chapter Eighteen

The changes that had come about were for comfort, and Marina took a small amount of satisfaction in knowing that might be the most she could hope for. Her visions of leading others out of the dungeon were waning. She'd read scriptures to the prisoners, tried to make them understand how they'd been wronged, but she worried it fell on deaf ears. Everything about this place left her exhausted, and when she closed her eyes, all her dreams were about Richard. That did her no good other than to wish things were different.

A useless wish.

No great powers had been granted upon her, either. If they had, she'd have made Richard appear and steal her away. Together they'd ride off and live happily ever after. That, however, was nothing more than one of her many dreams. Odd ones for a witch to have, all about love.

Tales of witches flying through the air at Uncle

William's home had spread quickly and had become far more elaborate than the actual event had been. The guards were genuinely afraid of her, and unfortunately, so were most of the other prisoners. Nonetheless, she used what she could. The guards kept their distances but responded immediately to her demands—once they'd been told of the evils that would befall them if they didn't.

Buckets of water and brooms had been supplied. At first it had just been her, but others soon joined in with cleaning out the cells. Chains and ropes were removed, and straw for the feeble to lie upon had been supplied. Drinking water and food, too. After she'd thrown the moldy and weevil-contaminated rye back at the guards.

It was a miracle more than four prisoners hadn't died in the dungeon. Even with the changes she'd made in the past six days, filth abounded and rats still occupied the cells along with the rest of them. Despite all she'd done, the hangings hadn't stopped. Eleven others had been hanged since her arrival, and one stoned. He'd refused to confess so his family wouldn't lose their estate. Others had been tried and acquitted, but unable to pay their bail. They were still in the dungeon, sentenced to remain here until their families could pay the accumulated tab of imprisonment, a six-pence a week for every week they'd served. An atrocity. People could be here for a year and not obtain a sixpence worth of food and hospitality.

"Marina?"

Bringing her broom to a halt, she leaned against the handle. Moments of reprieve were few. It had been appalling how easily these people had accepted their confinement and the filth. Then again, that was the Puritan way. To obey. Shifting slightly, she asked, "Yes, Goodwife Pullman?"

"Are ye frightened?"

The lump in her throat was too large to swallow. "No," she lied. "And you shouldn't be, either."

"They'll find me guilty. I know they will. Just like they did my baby girl."

Marina leaned the broom against the wall in order to fold her arms around Mrs. Pullman's quaking shoulders. Whimpers that first night had led her to the goodwife. Standing upright with her arms spread and her wrists chained to the wall, reduced to little more than skin and bones, Mrs. Pullman had been barely recognizable to Marina.

At noon they'd be taken to the courthouse, she and Mrs. Pullman and four others, to stand trial for their crimes. Not wanting to impress upon the other woman's already strained mind, Marina had withheld from telling Mrs. Pullman about how her husband had assisted Richard and her.

Pulling up a smile, she leaned back to look into

the woman's sunken eyes. "You just need to tell them the truth." That was the only weapon she had, and what she used on the prisoners. Insisting the truth was what would set them free. She pointed out that the people who had been hanged had given in under pressure and admitted guilt. That, she insisted, was what they must not do.

Having grown old and haggard the past months, Mrs. Pullman shook her head. "I don't know what that is anymore."

The knot in Marina's stomach grew bigger and tighter. Did anyone know the truth anymore? What was happening was real. People were dying. Although it was all a lie. With a burning throat, Marina whispered, "Yes, you do. It's inside you. You just have to find it."

Hours later, Marina and others were led out of the dungeon. The daylight caused yellow specks to flash before her eyes, but she kept her head up rather than shield her eyes as those in front of her did. She walked alone. Guards poked and prodded at the others, but they kept their distance from her.

People flowed out of the courthouse and into the street, and others were still arriving. On foot, in wagons and on horseback. Word of her trial had certainly spread. And of her hanging, no doubt. It was already scheduled for eight o'clock tomorrow morning.

At the sight of a large horse, her heartbeat in-

creased but then dulled. The man in the saddle
looked nothing like Richard. She didn't expect to
see him here; nor did she want to. There wasn't
anything he could do. No dolls hanging in the
trees would help her this time. Her dream last
night had been so real. He'd been holding her
and kissing her, and it had been wonderful. Too
wonderful. Especially when she'd awakened to
the stench and chill of the dungeon.

If she'd learned one thing this past week, it was
that, given the choice, she'd have left with Richard. That was, if she'd been her old self, the one
who'd died back in Maine. The girl who'd wanted
a husband, children, and had dreamed of a wonderful future. Being who she was now, a witch,
she knew that choice had never been hers.

The guards guided them around the crowd and
through the back door of the courthouse. Chat-
ter filled the rooms but grew quieter as the other
prisoners entered. It fell completely silent when
she crossed the threshold. Marina didn't let it
daunt her as she moved to stand along the side
wall with the others. They would remain standing
there throughout the proceedings, merely stepping forward when their names were called.

Dressed in black suits with white ruffles
around their necks and wearing flat-brimmed
hats adorned with brass buckles, six men, including Reverend Hickman, sat in high-backed chairs

on a raised platform along the front wall. Other than the small open area between the accused and council, the room overflowed with people.

Hickman's daughter, his niece and another young girl about the same age—little more than ten or so—sat on the platform near the men's feet. They whispered among themselves, pointing at the accused and nodding.

Marina had never attended a trial, but John had told her how the girls produced evidence against his mother. They'd gone into a state of fits, rolling on the floor and barking like dogs when the Goodwife Griggs had been ordered to address the girls. John had also said his mother had been stripped naked in the courtroom and searched for extra teats or markings that familiars had used to nurse from her.

Marina swore that would not happen today, no matter what she had to do. The scriptures told her the words would come to her when the time came, and she glanced up, letting God know the time had come.

The first name called was Abigail Newman. A girl no more than six and ten. In the charges read against her, it was claimed Abigail had been seen in the woods at night, gathering roots she used to make potions.

"What say ye, Mistress Newman?" Abner Hogan, the speaker for the council, questioned.

Head hanging down, with her hands tied behind her back, Abigail shook so hard Marina feared the girl might collapse where she stood.

"Have you gone mute?" Abner questioned loudly.

The movement that caught Marina's attention was the slight nod Hickman made to his daughter. A moment later the girl shot to her feet, screeching. She then spun in several circles before falling to the floor. Landing on her hands and knees, she started barking and howling.

Gasps in the crowd turned into cheers, and soon the building roared, as if all the onlookers were excited about the happenings. As the momentum of the crowd grew, Rebecca Hickman rose to her feet and walked back to her seat. It was the satisfied smirk upon the girl's face that sent Marina forward.

Her hands weren't tied. No one had dared. She used them to catch Abigail before she buckled and held the sobbing girl to her side. "Stop this! Stop this!"

The noise was too loud to be heard over. Marina filled her lungs and shouted again and again. Pausing briefly, she recalled the noise she'd made before. Opening her mouth, she released a cackle as she had the night at Uncle William's house. Her throat and lungs burned, but she took another breath and continued on.

She stopped abruptly, as did the crowd, when a resounding crack filled the room, along with a shatter. The council members were ducking and covering their heads. Marina looked up to the window high above them. The glass was gone, splintered into tiny pieces that rained on the council members.

Marina was as shocked as everyone else in the room, but then she realized her witch's call had provided the silence she needed for the words God would give her. Turning toward the council of men who were still cowering in their seats, she shouted, "Who claims Abigail was in the woods?" Pointing and scowling at Rebecca Hickman, she continued, "That child who is so starved for her father's attention she acts like an utter fool?" Shifting her attention, she then asked, "And what sort of father, Reverend Hickman, are you to allow your daughter to wander through the woods at night? There could be no other way for her to have seen Abigail or anyone else. Your daughter is the one who needs to be punished for her behaviors of late." She then spun toward the crowd. "And you, all of you—have you been so desperate for a leader you've let lies and trickery lead your lives to where you now find joy in torturing and killing innocent people? What have you gained for it? From any of this calamity? Do you not know the Ten Commandments? Thou shall not kill?"

The only movement in the crowd, other than a few heads hanging, was near the door, where people were being shoved aside.

A moment later, when the person shoving his way into the room presented himself, Marina's heart soared and sank at the same time.

"Remove that witch from the court!" Reverend Hickman shouted.

"Now see here, Reverend," Richard shouted in return, still shoving people aside. He'd had no idea if the ball he'd fired from his gun would hit anyone or not. All he'd known was that Marina was inside the building where the crowd was screeching like jungle monkeys. He'd chosen the highest window, just to be sure to not hit her. "Miss Lindqvist has not been tried and found guilty." At least he hoped that hadn't happened. He elbowed through the final line and crossed the small open space to put himself between her and the council.

"She's already admitted to being a witch," Hickman said.

"To whom?" Richard asked. "You? Or your daughter who can have fits on command?" He'd heard Marina's voice while clambering up the steps. Relief hadn't been the only thing that filled him. Pride had, too. "If that child was my daughter," he continued, "I'd turn her over my knee. As would most every father in this courtroom."

"You have no authority in this court," Hickman shouted. "Remove him. Remove that man, I say!"

Marina stepped closer, as if she could hold off the guards. Richard smiled inwardly. He wanted to twist about, grab her and hold her close, just to be sure she was real and not the mere vision of the woman he'd dreamed about every night since leaving the village. He wanted to kiss her, too. Long and hard.

Keeping one eye on the guards who hadn't moved to follow Hickman's orders, he pulled two envelopes from his pocket. "I may not have any say in this court, but the governor does."

"What have you there?"

Richard cast a devilish grin upon the speaker. "Abner Hogan, isn't it?"

The man nodded.

"I have a letter for you. From your brother-in-law, Joshua Matthews. The very man who sailed all the way to England to bring over Governor Phillips to Boston." Richard stepped forward, holding both letters in the air. "Joshua will be out to see you tomorrow, Abner. Although other places have had witch incidents, he's questioning the number of accused in such a small area as this. He's also questioning the confiscation of property happening here." Not handing over either letter, he said, "The letter from the governor is much more eminent, though, and he's sending a copy of it to the king and queen. It states spectral evidence can no longer be used as evidence. For any trial, any crime, the court must use solid facts that can be verified." Shifting his smirk to the preacher, he said, "That should come as a relief to you, Hickman. Your daughter will no longer need to make a spectacle of herself."

Hickman appeared speechless, and Richard grinned.

After handing the letters to Hogan, Richard turned his gaze to Marina. Seeing her clearly for the first time since he'd entered the room, his heart dipped. Her blond curls were limp and snarled, and dark circles marred the skin beneath her eyes. Dirt covered her dress, and the bottom of her skirt was wet almost up to her knees. Anger once again bellowed inside him. Spinning to the crowd, he asked, "Does anyone in this room have irrefutable proof that Marina Lindqvist is a witch?"

There was barely a shifting of feet. He turned, and after letting his scowl settle on the three girls sitting before them for a moment, he lifted his gaze to the council. "Anyone?"

"Your ignorance is showing, Captain Tarr,"

Hickman growled. "That is not how court proceedings take place."

"It is this time," Richard said. "Marina was never officially arrested. Therefore, she is free to leave." Turning back around, he crossed the room and took her arm. "Let's go."

Sorrow filled her face.

His heart rose into his throat.

A tear trickled down her cheek as she shook her head. "I can't leave," she whispered, gesturing to the women lining the wall behind her. "They need me."

Chapter Nineteen

Richard considered flipping her over his shoulder as he had once before, but he couldn't. Not when his mind went to the men who'd shared his jail cell up until yesterday. "I know they do," he whispered.

Still sorrowful, she shrugged, as if unsure what to say.

"Miss Lindqvist owes for her accommodations," Hickman demanded. "She will not be released until the fee is paid in full."

Richard's jaw went hard as he turned about. "How much does she owe?"

"That needs to be calculated."

The preacher's attitude had Richard seeing red all over again. "Start adding."

It was Hogan who stated an amount. Richard didn't blink an eye as he pulled money from his pocket. "And the five others along the wall. How much do they owe?"

"They have not been—"

Interrupting Hickman, Richard asked Hogan, "Do you have any solid evidence against any of those women?"

The man tucked the letters in his pocket. "No, sir." He then stated an amount far less than what Marina's had been.

"Times five?"

"No. Total," Hogan said. "Miss Lindqvist requested an overly large amount of provisions."

Richard had no idea what sort of provisions she could have ordered or received. He'd swear she'd lost ten pounds since he'd last laid eyes upon her. "I'll need a receipt for each of them," he stated as an afterthought.

After Hogan nodded to the council member acting as scribe, Richard crossed the room to Marina. "Gather your friends so we can leave."

"But there are others," she said softly.

"I know. We'll return tomorrow and see what can be done." Despite the crowd watching, he laid a hand upon her cheek. "I want you out of here."

Marina was torn. There was nothing more she wanted than to leave with him, but there were so many others, and her life wasn't hers to do as she pleased and hadn't been for a long time. But his palm was so warm and gentle upon her cheek.

The argument happening inside her caused a tear to fall from her eye.

He brushed it aside. "You'll do more good on the outside than you will on the inside." Glancing over her shoulder, he said, "If you don't leave, they can't."

He was right. The idea of any of them returning to the dungeon was appalling, more so with him touching her.

"Please don't deny my request, Marina. Not again."

The burning of her throat prevented her from refusing, even if she'd wanted to. She shook her head, then nodded, not exactly sure which was correct.

His smile was soft and understanding. "Let's gather your friends," he whispered.

Pride filled her as she walked beside him to the wall. The other women immediately started thanking him and continued to do so as he withdrew the knife from his boot and started cutting away the ropes securing their hands behind their backs. The women rushed to hug her as soon as they were free.

"It's a miracle, Marina," Mrs. Pullman whispered. "Your captain is a miracle."

Marina had never witnessed a miracle before but was in agreement that one was happening right now. They would all be headed for the gallows in the morning if not for Richard.

He squeezed her arm before he turned to the council. "Are those receipts ready?"

"Not quite, sir," the scribe answered, dribbling sand over the paper on his desk with a shaky hand. "But almost."

A short time later, Richard had the receipts in hand, and Marina said to the others, "Come. Stay close, and follow us."

The women took a hold of each other's hands, and when Richard clasped hers, Marina's breath caught at the happiness that erupted inside her. She pinched her lips, but her smile was too strong to contain.

Richard grinned at her briefly before his expression turned stone hard as his gaze went to the council and then to the onlookers. The crowd parted peacefully, leaving a wide-open path to the door. Marina didn't have to think about keeping her chin up. The pride of walking beside Richard filled her too completely.

The sunlight that met them on the steps may have been the brightest, the most spectacular that ever shone upon the earth. Oscar Pullman was the first to greet them when they parted from the crowd.

Stopping directly before them, although his

gaze went past Richard to his wife, the man said, "I owe ye all I have, Captain. All I have."

"No," Richard said, letting go of her hand to pick through the receipts. Pulling one out, he said, "We are now even."

"But Captain—" Oscar started.

"Say no more, my friend," Richard said, patting Oscar's shoulder. "Take your wife home. She's tired."

With tears streaming from his eyes, Oscar quickly skirted around them. The reunion of husband and wife added to the joy filling Marina.

More people gathered close, family members of the other women. Richard passed out receipts, saying no repayment was necessary. All of the reunions were heartfelt, and no one lingered. The women who'd had a hard time walking to the courthouse were now scurrying along beside their families, leaving Salem Towne as if it was on fire.

Richard wasted no time, either. Marina wasn't sure how his horse had appeared before them, but he'd swung into the saddle and hoisted her onto his lap before she had a chance to blink, let alone protest. As if she would. Her dream had come true.

The horse started forward, past people moving away from the courthouse. Both her legs hung over one side, and having nothing else to hang on to, she wrapped her hands around Richard's arm stretching around her to hold the reins.

Cheers greeted them as they passed people on the road. The Pullmans along with others. Her cheeks burned at such show, but understanding how they felt about Richard saving their family members, she waved.

Twisting, she asked, "Where's Gracie? And Uncle William? And John. How is he? How are his eyes and—"

Richard laughed. "You have to stop asking if you want me to answer."

She giggled. "Of course."

"Gracie is fine. She has a nursemaid and—"

Her spine stiffened. "A nursemaid? Who? Are they trustworthy? Do they understand—"

"Mrs. Reynolds is a wonderful woman. I questioned her thoroughly and am very confident in her abilities. In fact, William is very taken with her. They are rather close in age."

"She's as old as Uncle William? She'll never be able to keep up with—"

"Whoa, there," he said. "Although William may have appeared to have one foot in the grave while living here, being on the ocean has brought back his youth. He practically skips across the deck."

"The deck?" she questioned. "So they are on

your ship?" Satisfied knowing that, she asked, "And John? Is he on your ship, too?"

"John is healing nicely. Mrs. Reynolds is seeing to his care, too. His eyes are as good as ever. However, his ankle was broken and will take longer to heal."

"Broken. Oh, goodness. I feared he had broken bones."

"I did, too," he said. "Hold on."

She was already holding on, but her hold on his arm tightened when the horse started trotting. The ride turned smooth a moment later as the animal entered an even and swift gallop. Her skirt started flapping around her ankles. The hem was wet and covered with grime and, to her shame, her hands were almost as filthy. She closed her eyes in an attempt to ignore the filth and focused her thoughts on Gracie, William and John. Her belief that Richard would see to their welfare had never left her, but knowing it had happened renewed her spirit so fully her chest puffed from the happiness.

A great satisfaction overtook her, and she leaned her head against Richard. He was so solid, so powerful, so utterly wonderful. All she'd ever dreamed of.

Marina didn't sleep but did enter a peaceful place so wonderful she could easily have stayed there for a much longer time. The horse had stopped, so she opened her eyes. Uncle William's house stood before her. She'd figured this was where they were going, but was surprised it looked exactly as it had when she'd walked away from him. Hickman hadn't burned it to the ground as she'd assumed.

"Can you stand?"

"Of course," she answered.

"Then down you go," he said, grasping her waist and lifting her off his lap.

Her legs wobbled as her toes touched the ground. She noted it wasn't from pain but the separation from Richard. An odd thing, yet nonetheless real.

He was off the horse a split second later. "Come, it's inside with you."

Marina took a deep breath. "Strange," she said, "but this no longer feels like home."

"Well, it is home for the night," he said.

Exactly what he meant eluded her and she truly didn't have the ability to think that hard. Not right now. They entered through the back door. She took a long look around before determining the house was exactly as she'd left it. Nothing was out of place. Richard had moved from her side, and the sight of him bent over the hearth, placing kindling to be lit, sent her heart tumbling.

Her throat locked up and a knot formed in her stomach. Not an ordinary knot, this one heated her stomach in a way that penetrated her soul. The loneliness that had ached until she hurt from head to toe had disappeared the moment he walked into the courtroom. Her hopelessness had disappeared then, too. Whatever rippled through her wasn't shock. She'd done a fair share of thinking about him during their separation. Continuously. Every decision she'd made, he'd been a part of it. He'd been a part of every regret she'd had, too.

He turned, looking up at her with those dark eyes she'd seen in her dreams. A smile lifted the corners of his mouth. "I'll fetch water for you."

His voice barely penetrated the beats of her heart resounding in her ears. "Water?"

He stood. "Yes. Plenty of it so you can bathe."

Catching herself before her tongue stumbled over itself, she dropped her gaze to her hands, her dress. The once-white cuffs of her blouse were as black as her cape had been. She'd long ago lost her cloak, given it to a nameless woman who'd had nothing but two rags tied across her body.

"I know you're tired," he said, while adding logs to the fire. "But you'll feel better clean. I'll find something for you to eat, too."

A bit of her resolve returned. "I am tired, but I'm not injured. You see to your horse. I'll see to the fire and water and then prepare us something to eat."

He bit his bottom lip as she'd seen him do before when holding back a comment or protest. It was a protest. She was fully aware of that. His gaze slipped off her face and wandered down her dress, all the way to her toes.

When his gaze met hers again, her insides fluttered. "I'll take a bath first," she said softly.

His eyes never left hers as he crossed the room. Stopping directly before her, he placed a single finger beneath her chin, making the skin tingle.

"You are a strong and beautiful woman, Marina Lindqvist. One any man would be proud to stand beside. Clean or dirty."

Heat flushed her cheeks.

Chuckling, he said, "I'll carry in the washtub."

Marina spun about but said nothing as he walked out the door. It would take more than a basin of water to wash away the grime of the dungeon, which meant she would need the washtub.

It wasn't long before she was standing in the washtub, soaking feet that hadn't been dry for the past week. Built beside the river, the dungeon had flooded this spring, and the water still hadn't all seeped away. She'd set her wet shoes near the fire and had carried down the soft slippers Nessa had made for her, along with her other bathing necessities and clean clothes.

The tub wasn't very large, but after scrubbing her feet until they tingled, she managed to sit down. With her legs hanging over the edges, she scrubbed the rest of her body. The stench of the dungeon renewed itself when she dumped water over her hair. She scrubbed and scrubbed until all she could smell was soap and then used fresh water to rinse from head to toe.

Richard had said he'd stay outside until she was finished, but now that water wasn't sloshing, she could hear voices. She stepped out of the tub and quickly dried off. In her haste to get dressed, she fumbled with each garment. The voices weren't harsh or argumentative, but it had to be the council. Who else could it be?

Her scrubbing had left her hair a tangled mass. Lack of time had her twisting it and tucking it inside the white cap she tugged on. Leaving it untied, and forgoing stockings and the soft slippers, she rushed across the room.

She pulled open the door and paused in the threshold. Richard was the only one in the yard.

"Do you feel better?" he asked.

Turning her gaze from the empty road and letting it linger on him for a moment, Marina wasn't sure if she felt more relief or confusion. "Who were you talking to?"

"Which time?" He picked a basket off the ground and another off the edge of the well. "Every family of the women released with you has come and gone."

She stepped back into the kitchen in order for him to enter. "Why?"

Tilting one of the baskets, he said, "With food and cider. They must have cleaned their coffers in order to thank you. I'll carry out the tub and get the rest."

In her haste, the kitchen had been left a mess, and she scurried to gather her discarded clothing, which she promptly carried outside, right behind Richard carting out the tub full of water as if it weighed no more than it did when empty.

She tidied the area while he carried in more baskets. Marina fought her eyes, forcing them to remain on what she was doing. Each time she looked at Richard, a powerful tug happened inside her. It made her heart beat faster, and spirals of heat filled her belly. All her dreams about him were twisting in her head, making it hard to remember what was real and what had been illusions. What could be and what couldn't be.

"Your hair is getting your hat wet."

Marina pulled the cap from her head and used her fingers to untangle the mass as much as possible before picking up the brush she'd brought downstairs earlier. She pulled her hair over one shoulder and started to brush the ends. "I thought the council—"

The weight of his hands on her shoulders was light but made her breath catch and legs tremble.

He turned her around. "They won't come after you again. Ever. I promise."

Her fingers trembled, forcing her to stop brushing her hair. "What if—"

"Ever."

There was such fortitude in his voice the brush slipped from her fingers. He caught it before it fell. Marina understood the risk of meeting his gaze, but had no choice with the way he used a knuckle to lift her chin.

"I can't promise it's over for those still in prison, but you have nothing to fear. That I swear."

Marina closed her eyes. His voice, his gaze, his closeness—it was all too much to fight. It wasn't over. Couldn't be. What would that mean for her?

"Here," he said quietly. "Turn around. I'll brush your hair."

She twisted about and tried, but air wouldn't fill her lungs. No one had brushed her hair for a very long time, and she quickly discovered the dangers of Richard doing so. A warm and powerful wave spread through her insides, making her more aware of specific parts of her body than she'd ever been.

"Amazing what a little water can do, isn't it?" he asked while drawing the brush down her hair. "I sorely needed a good scraping and scrubbing when I was released."

A tingle zipped up her neck. "Released from where?"

"Boston jail. That's why I wasn't here sooner."

Instantly concerned, she spun around. "Boston jail? Why?"

He grinned and laid the brush on the table before saying, "Nothing they had proof of. It took a couple of days to get it squared away." He took her hand. "Don't worry. Grace, William and John all were well cared for by a friend of mine."

A hint of guilt flashed in her stomach for not having thought of the others.

"Your neighbors have provided quite a feast," he said, gesturing toward the baskets on the table. "I'm hungry. I haven't had a decent meal since I left here."

A jolt shot through her. She'd never questioned why he hadn't arrived earlier, because she hadn't expected him to. Yet he had vowed to that night, and she should have known he would. He always did what he said he would.

She slipped her hand out of his and walked to the shelf containing plates and tankards. "How long were you in jail?"

"I got out yesterday and met with the governor last evening, but had to wait until this morning for his official note to the council."

Separated from him, even just a few feet, allowed her to think more clearly. She wanted to tell him he shouldn't have come back, but if not for him, she and the others would be heading to the gallows in the morning. That had been her destiny, and she'd been prepared for it. What would happen now? She may have been released, but the desires inside confirmed she was still a witch.

Richard pulled out a chair and directed her to sit as soon as she set the plates, spoons and tankards on the table. The cravings he was fighting were becoming insurmountable. Brushing Marina's long locks had heightened things to painful peaks. He told himself she was exhausted and needed to eat and sleep, but it did little to quell what he wanted.

The generosity of her neighbors was a blessing, for cooking eluded him and she sincerely needed to eat. Her beauty had been restored by her bath, but she still needed nourishment. He'd felt her trembling while brushing her hair and had fought the desire to hold her close. Just to offer her his strength, if nothing more.

Richard piled her plate with items from the basket. He barely took note of the food, until the smell of roasted meat filled his nose and made his stomach growl. "This is from Oscar. His daughter had prepared it for them to eat upon returning from the trial." He was speaking just to keep his mind off other things. Looking at her defied the abilities he'd once prided himself on. All the things he'd believed about himself no longer lay true.

The sleeping giant that had once occupied his inner being had disappeared but had left something far more powerful in its place. Richard would never have known what that giant had been covering up if not for Marina.

"Anna would have known her father would need sustenance when he returned today," Marina said. "If not for you, Mrs. Pullman would be scheduled to hang tomorrow morning."

Richard took a drink of ale to swallow the food in his mouth before replying, "If not for you, she may have died in the dungeon before today. His wife told Oscar about how you forced the guards to bring straw for them to get off the wet floor, water for them to drink, and how you lifted their spirits enough to believe a miracle could happen."

She shook her head. "I requested straw and water, but never promised a miracle."

"You didn't need to promise one. You were it." When she shook her head again, he simply said, "Eat."

She did, but only a small amount compared to what he devoured. Laying her spoon beside her plate, she asked, "What happens now?"

What he wanted to happen couldn't. Richard emptied his tankard and leaned back in his chair. "I'm not sure," he said honestly. "But I believe

Governor Phillips will put an end to the accusations, the trials. He's arriving tomorrow. We'll know more then."

Her bottom lip quivered slightly. "I thank you for saving those you saved today, but nothing has changed."

"Nothing has changed? Everything has changed. The governor ordered—"

"I'm still a witch, Richard," she interrupted.

The frustration that arose in him dissolved almost as quickly. He couldn't indict a person for what they believed. Especially not one who might be right. It just didn't matter to him. Witch or not, this woman had taught him to love. That was what the giant had been hiding. Smothering his heart with justifications that could have defied happiness for the rest of his life. That conclusion hadn't come easily or quickly. It hadn't truly solidified until last night when he stood on the deck of Emerson's ship, staring across the Boston Harbor. The sea, the one thing he'd thought he loved, had held no lure for him. Not even with the waves glistening in the moonlight and promising vast adventures and riches.

Richard stood and rounded the corner of the table to pull out her chair. Once Marina was standing before him, he took both of her hands and lifted them one at a time to kiss her palms. He questioned what to say, how to tell her all that was inside him. Marina wasn't like other women. No vows of love would sway her. She was too stubborn for that—and righteous. He loved her all the more for it.

"Well," he finally said, "you certainly bewitched me, and it was the best thing that ever happened."

Her startled look was adorable. "What?"

"Only a witch could make me fall in love with her, and that's exactly what you've done. The moment you opened that door telling me to state my business, my world changed. The things I wanted changed. Had Grace been with anyone else, I would have taken her and ridden away, ill or not." Wanting her to know he'd considered long and hard what had happened, he said, "Your father was right for not letting you cross that bridge. There were others you needed to lead, to show the way. Namely me."

Her delicate brows were knit together, and bewilderment filled her eyes. "You?" She shook her head. "That's not what he meant."

"How do you know?"

She opened her mouth and closed it.

He grinned, knowing he was gaining ground. Stubborn, yes, but Marina was also intelligent. "I was about as lost as a man could get. Not navigationally, but in life."

She shook her head slowly. "There's more to it than that. The script—"

"I know." He'd thought about that, too, and understood she'd been so lost and alone that turning to the Bible for answers had been her salvation. "The Bible tells us to be kind and just, and you've fulfilled that, too. Shown others how to love, and that is God's will. For us to love one another."

A frown still covered her face and she closed her eyes as if to think. He chose that moment to do what he'd wanted to do since barging into the courtroom.

Her lips were as soft as he remembered, but sweeter. The sweetest things he'd ever tasted.

All Marina ever thought she knew swirled inside her head like leaves in a fall whirlwind. Except for Richard. He was as strong and masterful as ever. His kisses made her want to melt against him and just be.

It took everything she had to pull away. "You make it impossible to think when you kiss me."

His hands grasped her waist, preventing her from moving. "Good. I don't want you to think. Just feel. Feel my love. My strength. For it is yours, too."

How could he know that was what she felt when he kissed her, held her. "Is that why you kissed me that night we set the traps?" she asked. "So I wouldn't think about what we were doing?"

He chuckled. "No, I kissed you then because I wanted to. Just like I want to now."

It was what she wanted, too. What she'd dreamed about. Could he be right? Could her father have been talking about Richard? Had she been sent back to earth to meet him? To fall in love with him? She did love him. And she loved Gracie. Was he right about the scriptures, too? It was what she'd told the others in prison. That God's will was for people to love one another.

Her stomach sank then and she shook her head. "You can't love me."

"I already do, and I'm going to marry you."

She'd been twisted and torn since awaking after the massacre, but never more than right now. "I'm evil. Or at least it follows me."

"You can't believe that," he whispered. "You are the most kind and caring person I have ever met…ever shall meet."

She didn't want to be evil, never had, and certainly didn't wish ill will upon anyone. What she did want was to be loved by him. Forever and ever. Which was too much to ask. "I'm barren," she whispered.

"How do you know that?"

She shrugged. "I just do. All witches are barren."

He leaned close enough so their noses touched. "So?"

"So? What kind of wife would that make me? I can't provide you with more children."

"More children matter little to me. We have Grace." Leaning back, he grinned. "And your uncle William, and I don't foresee John leaving us anytime soon. Not to mention a couple of old shipmates of Earl's I found in Boston."

In spite of her doubts and fears, a smile tugged at her lips.

"How many more people could you want living with us?" he asked.

The idea of living with him, of sharing their lives, brought a full smile to her lips.

"You've been blessed by God, Marina, and given a wonderful gift. The gift of life a second time. Please allow me to share it with you."

She'd never been able to refuse a request, especially not from a loved one. However, her willful self couldn't give in that easily. "What if it's not what you expect?"

The gentle kiss he placed upon her forehead wafted softness through her system.

"I've sailed rough seas before. I'm not afraid, and you shouldn't be, either. You'll not only have all of my love, you'll have my protection against all men, all evils, and I'm a fierce opponent."

Chapter Twenty

∞

His grin was a bit mocking and self-assured, just like him. She loved them both. Him and his grin. He was right about the trials, that the governor would end them. She could feel it. Perhaps he was right about her, too. He had already fought against evil for her, rescued her when she'd thought it utterly impossible.

A smile rose from her heart to settle on her lips. "You are a fierce opponent—I've witnessed that. And a protector and a provider."

"Well, then?" he asked. "Will you marry me?"

There had been times in her life when she'd felt she had no choice. That was true right now, too, but this time, she didn't want a choice. Didn't need one. "Yes," she answered. "I will."

Richard kissed her and she held nothing back in her response. There were no restraints inside her, no fears or doubts. Her future held no destiny, no promises, and she realized it never had.

Life would be what she made it, what they made it, and that thrilled her.

Kissing, with their mouths open, tasting and teasing each other, heated her flesh. Her insides were simmering, too, like a pot about to boil over. She felt brazen and shameless and more wonderful than a human had a right. It fit, for she wasn't a mere human.

When Richard caught her behind the knees and lifted her into his arms, she wrapped her arms around his neck. She kissed the side of his face and chin as he carried her along the hallway and up the staircase.

He set her down beside her bed, but she never released her hold. Not on his neck or his lips. She stretched on her toes, keeping her body flush with his, relishing how the contact had her sizzling and wanting more.

"I've dreamed of this," Richard said, while his lips traveled over her chin, down her neck.

"So have I."

He leaned back to look at her.

No heat seared her cheeks as it may have another woman, and she was proud of that. "I told you I was a witch," she said. "Witches are full of wicked thoughts."

His husky laugh filled the room. Beyond that, actually, the entire house seemed to ripple with laughter, and she joined in.

"I believe there shall never be a dull moment with you in my life," he said.

"I hope not." Recalling their clandestine escapade of setting the traps, she added, "I like excitement."

He started unbuttoning the front of her waistcoat. "I'm about to show you something else you'll like."

The thrill that shot through her was delightful. "I already like it."

Early-evening sunlight filled the room, and Marina wondered for a moment, when Richard pushed the waistcoat off her arms and it fell to the floor, if she should at least act a bit shy. She'd never had a man undress her before. His fingers were now working the buttons of her blouse. It would soon land on the floor. There was no doubt of that, and there was no doubt of the excitement building inside her—the very thing she'd just admitted to enjoying.

Arrogance filled her, for there was no other way to describe the confidence that allowed her to shrug her shoulder, making the blouse slip away. She'd just told him witches were wicked. For the first time in a very long time she found great pleasure in being who she was.

Marina was soon relieved of all her clothing, barring nothing from Richard's eyes, which had grown dark and intense. There was a vibration in the air that had become steamy and hot merely from their breathing. He stood stock-still, watching her, and for a moment, she wondered if he was testing her, waiting to see if she'd flee or cower.

She smiled and stepped forward, out of the pile of clothes at her feet. Fleeing and cowering were two things she'd never do again, and especially not from him, from what her heart desired most.

A triumphant gust of air escaped her lungs when he grasped her waist and pulled her against him. His kiss was hard and wild, and she loved it as much as all the others. She pulled the hem of his shirt out of his breeches and scraped the hardness of his chest with her fingernails when he tugged the shirt over his head. She kissed his neck, his chest, and ran her hands up and down his side, relishing the feel and taste of his skin.

He surprised her by spinning her around. Holding her shoulders firmly, he whispered, "You are taxing my restraint."

She couldn't think of a response, not with how his hands slipped down her arms and then roamed across her stomach. His chin was resting on her shoulder and his hold pressed her back against his chest.

"We have all night," he said softly. "I want you to enjoy every moment."

She leaned against him, feeling small compared to his size but loving how glorious it was to feel shrouded by him. His hands caressed her stomach and then higher, brushing the undersides of her breasts. She placed her hands over his and arched slightly, offering her breasts as if holding out tokens.

Her breath caught as his hands moved up and a ribbon of heat raced over each breast when his thumbs found her nipples. They were hard and throbbing, and the torment of how he caressed and teased each one was spectacular.

"I am enjoying every moment," she said breathlessly, hoping he'd never stop.

"Good."

He nibbled on her earlobe as one hand moved lower. The other continued to fondle her breast, but her attention was drawn downward, where his other hand traveled past her stomach. His movements were slow and easy but caused such commotion her legs wobbled. The juncture he neared quivered with expectancy that was so hot moisture seeped from her. With one knee, he gently nudged her legs farther apart. The air gave a brief cooling sensation before his hand slipped lower, caressing skin that surely should have burned his fingertips.

She nearly slumped against him and couldn't do anything about the soft moan that rumbled in the back of her throat. He explored her thoroughly, until her very legs were quaking so hard Marina knew only his hold kept her upright.

Then, in a swift, easy movement, he once again hoisted her into his arms. At the edge of the bed, he instructed her to pull back the quilts. She did so, revealing the crisp sheets he lowered her upon. She was ready for him to continue, but disappointment made her cheeks flush when he sat down.

He grinned. "I have to remove my boots."

A thrill shot through her and she sat up. "You most certainly do." Scooting closer, she ran her hands up and down his back. His skin was slick and smooth, and she kneaded the hard muscles of his shoulders before lowering her hands to wrap both arms around him. She ran her palms across the ripples of his rib cage and then across the mass of hair that trailed down into his breeches. "You need to remove these, too."

He grasped her hands, lifted them and kissed each one before he held them aside and rose. "You are a vixen."

Not offended in the least, she lay down on her side, propping her head up with one hand. "And?"

He dropped his breeches and kicked them aside. "I love it."

Laughing, she flipped onto her back and held up both arms. "Then show me."

The bed creaked and bounced as he landed on

it. They both laughed and kissed. Kissed until she was dizzy. Until they were both breathless, their bodies slick and their arms and legs entangled.

Richard rolled onto his back and pulled her on top of him, positioning her legs so she sat on his stomach. He pulled her closer then, so her breasts were directly before his face. "Perfect," he whispered moments before he took one of her nipples into his mouth as a babe might.

The sensation sent her body into an unexplainable frenzy, one that was so amazing she braced her hands on his shoulders so he wouldn't stop. His actions played havoc on other parts of her, too. The commotion between her legs had turned into a fireball.

Just when Marina thought she could take no more, he grasped her waist and lifted her while sliding his body downward at the same time. Her parted legs were above his face when he pulled her hips downward.

Her body shook at the first stroke of his tongue. Overwhelmed, she grabbed the headboard of the bed and held on as he licked and kissed and suckled. If she'd ever needed proof she was a witch, she now had it, for no normal woman would let a man do such things to her. She, however, loved it. An intense and powerful force took over, demanding something that was elusive, yet definite and significant. That much she knew.

He was merciless in the most spectacular way. She rode wave after wave of the pleasure he provided until the force inside her grew so intense she tightened every muscle, straining against whatever it was that still eluded her. Richard continued and held on to her hips, keeping her connected to his mouth until a great shattering overtook her. It was followed by waves of gratification that wafted through her like nothing ever had or might ever again.

Unprepared for such an event, her hold on the headboard could no longer brace her and she slowly fell, melting onto Richard. He eased her body downward, until her parted legs bumped into something hard. Despite what she'd just experienced, a new thrill shot through her.

Marina buried her teeth in her bottom lip, trying not to let the excitement already renewing itself show as she lifted her head.

Richard was smiling, and in yet another swift movement, he flipped them both, until she now lay beneath him. "Now you are ready for that."

Running her hands over his shoulders, down the arms hardened by the muscles he was using to hold himself inches above her, she answered, "I believe you're right."

He laughed. "I didn't think I'd ever hear those words from you."

She contemplated his words for a brief moment,

how she'd never admitted he was right, except to herself, before answering, "Miracles do happen."

"That they do," he said. "I love you."

Her heart had never been so full. "And I love you."

"We'll be married as soon as we arrive in Boston."

She nodded, but said, "What are you waiting for?"

"Nothing." Shifting slightly, he used one hand to guide himself inside her.

She felt herself stretching to accommodate him, and her final bits of doubt, if there had been any, disappeared with his swift thrust. An all-encompassing heat struck her first, then a quick sting that startled a cry from her lips.

"Shh," he whispered gently. "It's over now."

There was no time to dwell on the pain, for it was gone, replaced by being filled so fully and deeply nothing but pleasure once again occupied her mind. "I certainly hope it's not over," she said. "I thought it was just beginning."

Shock flashed across Richard's face before he laughed. He started moving then, in and out, and the friction was so perfect, the heat so divine, Marina grasped his shoulders to hold on for a ride she knew was going to take her to places she'd never been.

A feverish pace soon developed between them,

a taking and giving that filled her with a torrent of pleasure. She knew what to expect this time, and when the encompassing pressure started to build within, she gave it all the room it needed, coaxing it onward by matching Richard's movements. When the peak arrived, she was better prepared and ready for it, but Richard, with fulfilling accuracy, took her beyond the point she'd been before. He forced her to climb higher and higher, until she was lost in nothing but him, the world he carried her to.

He'd grasped her hips, kept the fascinating friction going with powerful thrusts that she savored. It was as if the passion between them channeled into something so powerful and brilliant there was no stopping it. No end to where it could take them.

Marina felt her back arch and her body stiffen. Richard had turned rock hard, too. A moment later, a release so brilliant and bright and satisfying left her body shuddering in the throes of something so beautiful a tear slipped from her eye.

She sank deeper into the mattress, spent and glorious. Richard was still inside her, and she kept her legs wrapped around his hips, keeping him there a bit longer, luxuriating in the throbbing and fulfilling aftermath. Dreams had been nothing compared to this reality.

* * *

He'd relaxed but kept his weight off her by bracing himself on his forearms. "I don't want to crush you," he whispered and then kissed her forehead.

"You won't crush me," she assured him.

He slid out of her and then rolled onto the mattress beside her. She needed no encouragement to snuggle up against him, laying one leg over his.

Richard grasped her knee in order to keep it across his thighs. He'd imagined loving Marina would be unbelievable, but he'd been helpless, unable to hold anything back during their union. He'd never seen anything more beautiful than her cheeks flushed with pleasure, her body fully ravaged with passion. He wanted to drown himself in her right there and then and practically had. All of his hardened edges had completely come unraveled, leaving him as bare as the day he was born.

Just as she'd been given a second chance at life, he was, too, because of her. A rebirth of sort, and this time around, he'd made the right choice. Life with Marina would be far more exciting and challenging and prosperous than sailing had ever been.

Exhausted and happy, he let out a satisfied sigh. "So, where do you want to live?"

She rubbed her cheek against his shoulder before kissing it. "Live?"

"Yes. I'll build you a house twice this big, wherever you want."

Her lids looked heavy as she pulled them open. "Why would I want a house twice as big as this one? That would be a lot of extra cleaning."

He chuckled at her rationality. "I'll hire servants to help you."

A frown formed. "Where will you be?"

"Wherever you want that house built."

The single fingertip she used to twist the hair on his chest was enough to tell him he'd never get enough of her. His heart had barely stopped thundering in his chest and echoing in his ears, yet the desire to satisfy his feverish hunger all over again was already rebuilding.

"When you aren't at sea?" she asked.

He tilted his head enough to rub his nose in the softness of her hair. "I forgot to mention that I'm no longer a sea captain. At least not of the *Concord*." In truth, he hadn't forgotten, simply avoided it. A part of him had been afraid to say the words, wondering how his own ears would react. No regret arose within him, but he was wise enough to know the day might come when he'd miss his ship, miss being her captain.

Marina shifted and propped her head on her hand to look down upon him. "What happened?"

"Governor Phillips confiscated the ship. However, a good friend of mine reclaimed it with his letter of marque."

"A pirate has your ship?"

"A privateer, but he's a friend. He offered to sell her back to me."

"Sell her back?" She pulled her leg off his and sat up. "It's your ship."

"I told him to keep her. My sailing days are over."

"Why?"

"Because I'll be a husband and a father." He took her hand. "Don't worry. We have plenty of money, and other ships that will keep sailing, keep making money for us."

"But you told Gracie you'd take her sailing. Show her colorful birds and monkeys hanging by their tails in the trees. And what about Uncle William?"

Her cheeks were flushed, not from passion but anger. He'd seen it before. "I thought you'd be happy."

"You thought wrong," she snapped.

Examining her face, he saw the truth. "You wanted to see those birds and monkeys, didn't you?"

She sighed heavily. "Yes… As long as I'm not going to be hanged for being a witch, I want to live. I want adventures and fun."

He ran his fingers through the long blond curls

cascading over her shoulders, hiding her pert and perfect breasts. "Is that why you agreed to marry me? To go sailing? Have adventures and fun?"

"No." Her gaze was serious and soft. "I agreed because I love you. And I'll agree to live in any seaside port you choose, and wait for you to return from the sea for as long as I have to. I was just hoping I could convince you to take me with you once in a while."

He pushed the hair over her shoulders, improving his view. "How were you planning on convincing me?"

She shrugged, but as her gaze roamed his chest and lower, her lips formed a sly and teasingly wicked grin. "I figured I would think of something."

Trailing a finger over one breast, he said, "I'm open to some convincing."

Epilogue

⤜⊷⊷⊶⊷⤛

Nebraska, 2015

Ashley Tarr sat at the breakfast bar in her kitchen, clicking through and rereading certain parts of the lengthy document on her computer screen. It had been fascinating, but the beginning was her favorite.

The rumble of the garage door made her smile and her heart skip a beat, which it always did at the thought of her husband. She'd never have guessed how empowering loving the right man could be.

A moment later, Ryan walked through the door connected to the garage. "I got your pickles," he said, holding up the bag he carried.

"Thank you."

Setting the bag on the counter, he added, "And ice cream."

"Ice cream?"

He lifted one dark brow above his ever-glistening brown eyes. "Yes. I thought the two went hand in hand for expecting mothers."

Ashley rubbed the baby bump her jeans no longer fit around. She was going shopping for maternity clothes tomorrow with her mother-in-law and looking forward to it. Even more after reading the document she'd been emailed this morning.

"You need to read this," she told Ryan as he put the ice cream in the freezer.

"Why? What is it?"

"Your family history."

He rounded the counter and wrapped his arms around her from behind. Resting his chin on her shoulder while his hands rubbed her stomach, he sighed. "My mother?"

She nodded and giggled. "But it's your father's family history. Your mom had Aunt Jenny email it to me."

His groan was exaggerated.

"Seriously," she said. "It's fascinating." Using the finger pad, she scrolled to the beginning of the document, where a family tree had been embedded. "See this name? Richard Tarr?"

"Yes."

"He was a sea captain. Owned a whole fleet of ships."

"Aw, that's where I get my love of water."

She laughed. Although they lived in Nebraska,

Ryan owned four boats, all of which he insisted he needed for different purposes. Lake fishing, river fishing, duck hunting and whatever else. "Could be," she said. "See here, where Richard married Marina Lindqvist?"

"Yes."

She clicked on Marina's name. "She was your ninth great-grandmother and was imprisoned as a witch during the Salem witch trials."

"Spooky," he said teasingly. He was also kissing her neck.

She scrunched her shoulder into her cheek to make him stop. "It's not spooky. It's sad, really. Over twenty people were killed. Nineteen hanged and one crushed to death. Others were tortured, withheld food and water, kept in dank dungeons. Some died and some, even after their release, were insane from what they'd been put through." She shook against a shiver that tickled her spine.

Ryan rubbed her shoulders and kissed the top of her head. "But not my however-many-times great-grandmother?"

"Nope."

"Why?"

"Because Richard, your ninth great-grandfather, rescued her."

"How?"

Shrugging, she admitted, "It doesn't say exactly. I looked it up online but didn't learn anything more. The few records still around from that time list her name but not a lot else. Your aunt Jenny has researched it all and put together this family history. It covers all the generations, right back to Richard and Marina."

"Your favorites."

She grinned. He knew her so well. "Yes, they are by far the most interesting. They married shortly after Richard put up the bail to get her out of the Salem jail. Her release happened the same time that the governor of Massachusetts declared that spectral and intangible evidence could no longer be used against the witches and he prohibited any further arrests. Others agreed with him."

Scrolling through the document, Ashley couldn't find the exact page. "Somewhere it says a council member stated that it would be better if ten suspected witches be set free than one more innocent person be condemned, or something along those lines. The governor wrote letters to the king and queen about how the estates and property of the accused had been seized and disposed of without his consent, and requested authority to restore the innocent of their property."

"So it ended then?"

"Not immediately. The trials continued, but the accused were found innocent, probably because no one admitted guilt, not as they had before. It wasn't until the governor's wife was accused, supposedly by a Puritan minister, that a lot of evidence points to as the instigator of the entire debacle, that the trials came to an end."

"A minister was doing the accusing?"

"Yes. He'd been profiting from the trials and was ousted shortly thereafter, but your great-great—" she waved a hand for the rest of the *great*s "—grandparents, after they got married, sailed together for years. All over the world. Marina gave birth to three children on their ships. Before the fourth was born—they had a total of eight—they bought land in Maine and your grandfather started a shipbuilding company."

"How did Aunt Jenny learn that?"

"Mainly from family diaries. Offshoots of the family still live in Maine."

"Probably still building ships while I'm stuck on a Nebraska farm," Ryan said.

Ashley twisted to kiss his cheek, knowing he loved what he did, and she was proud of him. "I hear the winters there are brutal."

He spun her chair around. "So was Marina a witch or wasn't she?"

"That's the interesting part. Some from the past generations say she was. That if she said something would happen, it did."

Ryan laughed. "That's not being a witch. That's just being a woman."

She slapped him playfully on the chest. "Are you saying that all women are witches?"

He shrugged before catching her behind the knees and lifting her off the bar stool. "I'm saying my nine times great-grandfather was a very smart man—most likely where I get my brains from. He must have understood he'd been bewitched by his wife the minute he met her, just like I did. And was willing to do anything to make all her dreams come true."

"Are you attempting to seduce me with sweet talk?" she asked, wrapping her arms around his neck.

"No, I'm going to seduce you with much more than words. I probably got that from good old Richard, too."

More than willing to go along with his plan, Ashley kissed his neck. "You probably got your good looks from him, too."

As cocky as ever, Ryan said, "Wait until I drop my pants. You'll see what else I inherited."

She laughed. "I've seen it before." Leaving out the nine *great*s, she whispered in his ear, "Your grandfather would be proud. Mighty proud."

* * * * *

MILLS & BOON®

& HISTORICAL

AWAKEN THE ROMANCE OF THE PAST

A sneak peek at next month's titles...

In stores from 25th February 2016:

- **The Secrets of Wiscombe Chase** – Christine Merrill
- **Rake Most Likely to Sin** – Bronwyn Scott
- **An Earl in Want of a Wife** – Laura Martin
- **The Highlander's Runaway Bride** – Terri Brisbin
- **Lord Crayle's Secret World** – Lara Temple
- **Wed to the Texas Outlaw** – Carol Arens

Available at WHSmith, Tesco, Asda, Eason, Amazon and Apple

Just can't wait?
Buy our books online a month before they hit the shops!
visit www.millsandboon.co.uk

These books are also available in eBook format!

MILLS & BOON®
The Billionaires Collection!

This fabulous 6 book collection features stories from some of our talented writers. Feel the temperature rise with our ultra-sexy and powerful billionaires. Don't miss this great offer – buy the collection today to get two books free!

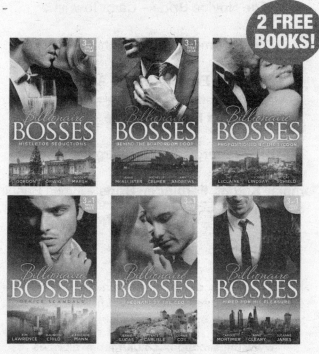

Order yours at
**www.millsandboon.co.uk
/billionaires**

MILLS & BOON®

Let us take you back in time with our Medieval Brides...

The Novice Bride – Carol Townend

The Dumont Bride – Terri Brisbin

The Lord's Forced Bride – Anne Herries

The Warrior's Princess Bride – Meriel Fuller

The Overlord's Bride – Margaret Moore

Templar Knight, Forbidden Bride – Lynna Banning

Order yours at
www.millsandboon.co.uk/medievalbrides